PRAISE FOR KAREN KATCHUR

RIVER BODIES

"Karen Katchur's *River Bodies* has it all: a horrific murder, mysteries resurrected from the past, a storyline packed with tension, and vivid characters to bring it all to life. A riveting thriller that suspense readers will love."

—Mary Kubica, *New York Times* bestselling author of *The Good Girl*

"With a striking sense of place and a foreboding feeling of unease throughout, I was glued to the story. With relationships so complicated and layered that they feel like your own and plot twists that will leave you gasping, *River Bodies* is an unforgettable read."

—Kate Moretti, *New York Times* bestselling author

"Karen Katchur is a master at writing into the dark spaces of our intimate family relationships, and *River Bodies* is her most stunning work to date."

—Mindy Mejia, author of *Everything You Want Me to Be*

"*River Bodies* weaves an engrossing mystery with richly developed characters for an enjoyable, fast-paced read."

—Laura McHugh, award-winning author of *The Weight of Blood*

"Dark secrets of the past flow into the present in this emotionally resonant, deeply insightful tale of family bonds, betrayal, violence, and redemption. Part engrossing love story, part riveting murder mystery, *River Bodies* is a must read."

—A. J. Banner, *USA Today* bestselling author of *The Twilight Wife*

RIVER
BODIES

OTHER TITLES BY KAREN KATCHUR

The Sisters of Blue Mountain
The Secrets of Lake Road

RIVER BODIES

KAREN KATCHUR

THOMAS & MERCER

Published by Thomas & Mercer, Seattle
www.apub.com

Amazon, the Amazon logo, and Thomas & Mercer are trademarks of Amazon.com, Inc., or its affiliates.

ISBN-13: 9781503902398 (hardcover)
ISBN-10: 1503902390 (hardcover)
ISBN-13: 9781503900639 (paperback)
ISBN-10: 1503900630 (paperback)

Cover design by Shasti O'Leary Soudant

Printed in the United States of America

First edition

For Philip, always

CHAPTER ONE

He was watching her.

Becca didn't always have to see him to know that he was there. Sometimes she could just sense him, feel the weight of his stare, aware his eyes were on her as she ran the narrow trail along the river.

He knew her morning routine, timing it right to catch her as she passed by. Under ordinary circumstances, Becca would've found it creepy, if not alarming.

But she knew him. He was family. Although he was older than her by more than fifteen years, he'd been a part of her childhood, her adolescence, someone who had always been in the background of her life, as much a part of the scenery as the mountains and river.

This morning as she stopped to catch her breath, she spied him through the autumn trees. He was standing on the other side of the Delaware River, on what had also once been her side, the Pennsylvania side, where she had grown up in the small town of Portland. Now, she lived on the Jersey side, which on most days felt like a whole other country rather than a mere state away, a simple cast across the river.

She placed both hands on her hips, stared at him. He stood motionless a few feet from the rushing rapids. He didn't attempt to communicate, not even so much as a raised hand. On any other day, she might've glanced in his direction, never slowing her pace, taking the path away from the river, cutting deeper into the woods, forgetting about him altogether. On this particular morning, she couldn't say why she chose to stop and stare.

But she did.

She couldn't look away.

It was as though there were some outside force at work pulling her toward him. She didn't believe in coincidences, but rather she believed all things were tied together for one reason or another. And whether Becca liked it or not, she was tied to him.

She stepped closer, stopping two feet from the edge of the riverbank. Romy, her German shepherd, was alert, ears perked, the tips of her paws nearly touching the icy water. The river roared past, the sound of its raging rapids a constant white noise. Across the river the Blue Ridge Mountains loomed, the trees hemorrhaging red and orange leaves.

Becca took another step closer. Her sneakers sank in the mud. There was something in his hand, something small. She was mistaken. There was something *on* his hand, some kind of glove. He was wearing camouflage shirt and pants, the pants soaked to midthigh from wading in the water. But he didn't fish. She knew this about him. No, he was a hunter. Her heart ricocheted inside her chest.

"I see you," she called, but the river's rapids drowned her voice.

He didn't move. He continued watching her. Then, without warning, he turned and walked up the bank, disappeared behind the trees.

Becca lingered, an uneasy feeling working its way up her spine. It was getting late, and she had another two miles of trail to run before she would be home. She had to hurry if she was going to make her first appointment, with a golden retriever that she suspected had swallowed a large piece of a tennis ball. Still, she hesitated for a few seconds more. When she was certain he was gone, that he wasn't coming back, she patted Romy's head.

"Come on," she said to the dog and took off for the trail once again.

She wound her way over the rocky terrain, careful to watch her step for fear of turning an ankle. She concentrated on her pace, finding rhythm in her legs, matching it with her breathing. The fury of the river's rapids slowed to a hushed whisper. It wasn't until she reached the pedestrian bridge, the one that crossed the Delaware River, that she stopped for a second time.

Out of the corner of her eye, she saw something floating in the water, something with mass. She looked around one of the cement columns, searching the now-calm water, so unlike the white water rapids tumbling over the rocks that made up the riverbed farther up the trail. She didn't see anything, but something had been there. The uneasy feeling returned. If she walked out on the bridge, she was sure she could find out what it was. But Becca couldn't bring herself to set one foot on the cement walk, nor could she place a single hand on the green metal rail. The thought of crossing over sent her pulse racing.

Whatever she thought she had seen made her anxious and uncomfortable. She talked herself down, telling herself she was being paranoid. It could've been a floating log, a thick, hefty branch. Maybe it was nothing more than a shadow playing tricks on her.

The sun was climbing higher in the sky. It was going to be a beautiful autumn day. She stretched her legs and raced toward home, Romy at her side. With each step, she told herself to forget all about it.

She had other concerns waiting for her.

❧

Becca's muscles loosened on the last mile home, and the displaced feeling, the disquiet she'd experienced, all but evaporated when she saw Matt's sedan parked in the driveway. He was home. And wherever he had been the night before didn't matter, or so she kept telling herself. His business often kept him in New York City long after the sun went down. Matt was a patent attorney, a litigator, a job that required more than a forty-hour workweek, and nagging him about the long hours he kept only pushed him further away.

She stepped through the door of their condo and kicked off her muddy sneakers. Romy darted for her water dish. The shower was running in the master bathroom.

Matt's cat, Lucky, greeted her from the top of the kitchen counter. "You're not supposed to be up here," Becca said and scooped the cat into her arms, kissing the top of its furry head. Romy glanced at the two of them, then returned to drinking, too thirsty to compete for Becca's attention.

Lucky was a tabby cat, and Becca guessed she was about five years old. She didn't know for sure since Lucky had been a stray. Matt had inadvertently struck the cat with his car. He'd been driving to work, crossing an intersection, when the cat had darted into the street. Becca had been in her last year of veterinary school, the job in Columbia, New Jersey, already offered to her upon graduation, when Matt had rushed through the doors with the kitten.

He was panicked, his blue eyes glassy. He cradled the small tabby in the crook of his arm where his bicep bulged underneath his white oxford shirt.

"I think I hit her with my car," he said to Becca, who happened to be at the front desk filling out a chart.

"Okay, bring her in here." She led Matt and the kitten into one of the examination rooms.

He carefully laid the kitten on top of the examination table, and Becca was struck by his tenderness with the small creature. She listened to the kitten's heartbeat. It was faint, but it was there. There were no visible injuries.

"Is she yours?" she asked and looked at the kitten's eyes with a penlight to make sure the pupils were dilating properly.

Matt shook his head. He was too choked up to talk. After a few seconds he said, "She ran into the street. I was pretty sure I missed her. But when I looked in the rearview mirror, I saw her lying on the side of the road." He put his hands on his head, looked at the ceiling. "God, what if I hit some poor kid's pet?"

"I think she's a stray." The cat wasn't wearing a collar, and she was bone thin. Her fur had a stray look about it—not necessarily dirty but not necessarily clean either. There were hundreds of strays in Columbia. Becca guessed this one was only a few months old. As a public service, the clinic spayed and neutered what strays they could to manage the population, but they couldn't catch them all, and besides, when you were dealing with nature and procreation, well, nature always found a way.

"I'm going to take her to x-ray," she said after feeling around the kitten's head and neck, pressing her fingers to its abdomen. "Thanks for bringing her in."

She dismissed him, letting him off the hook. He was a guy who had hit a cat with his car, and he'd felt guilty about it. But judging from her experience, and the fact that this guy was gorgeous and impeccably groomed down to his manicured fingernails and polished shoes, his actions only meant he had a conscience. What he really wanted was for someone to release him of his burden. She didn't believe a guy like him—good looks, that body, those strong arms and broad shoulders (she noticed them too)—could be the whole package: gorgeous, smart, and kind. Maybe he was stupid. In fact, she thought as she made her way to x-ray, she was surprised he'd even stopped for the kitten at all, figuring someone like him would've driven away without a second thought to what lay on the side of the road.

An hour later when she returned to the front desk, the kitten bruised but with no life-threatening injuries, she was surprised to find the guy in the waiting room.

"How is she?" he asked.

"She's going to be fine," Becca said, unable to stop her brow from furrowing as she tried to figure out his true motive.

"Oh, thank God," he said and reached for her hand. "Thank you." He searched her white lab coat for her name.

"Becca Kingsley," she said—a bit snootily, she thought later that evening when she was settling down to study for exams.

"Can I take her home?" he asked.

"You want to take her home?"

He smiled. "Is that a problem? I mean, you said she was a stray."

"No, it's not a problem. I guess. Wait here." She went behind the counter and grabbed the paperwork he would need to fill out if he was claiming the kitten as his. She handed him the clipboard. "We'll keep her overnight for observation."

"Good. Great. I'll pay for whatever she needs."

When he handed the clipboard back with the paperwork completed, she couldn't help but glance at his name, Matt Goode.

"Thank you, Becca," he said and left.

"Who was that?" Vicky, one of the surgical techs, whistled after Matt had walked out the door.

"That was the owner of one very lucky kitten," she said.

Matt returned the next day for the kitten, later naming her Lucky, and asked Becca to dinner.

She turned him down, claimed she wasn't hungry, not trusting his sincerity. She couldn't imagine what they had in common anyway. But he showed up at the clinic again two days later, and again he asked her out, this time for coffee, to discuss her thoughts on catnip. She laughed, couldn't think of an excuse to say no.

❦

Becca put Lucky down on the floor. The shower stopped, and she made her way to the master bedroom. She sat on the edge of the bed. Romy jumped up next to her. Becca began checking the dog for ticks, busying herself while she waited. Whenever she spent any time in the woods or near the river, she checked herself and the dog for pests. There was a large deer population that carried the parasite. Although Romy was given flea and tick treatments regularly, one could never be too careful.

Matt stepped out of the bathroom wearing nothing but a towel around his waist. She concentrated hard on not looking at him. Romy kept her head in Becca's lap. The dog knew something was up.

"Don't be mad," Matt said.

When she didn't reply, he said, "Please."

She'd waited up all night for him to come home, checking her phone for messages, worried something horrible had happened, worried nothing had happened. Any other woman might've yelled, fought, clawed, demanded an explanation. But not Becca. Compliant Becca stayed silent, playing her part so well it had become instinctive.

Matt sat next to her, close but not touching. His skin smelled clean and shower fresh. It took everything she had not to give herself over to him, to tell him she wasn't mad. She was *glad* he was okay and nothing terrible, awful, had happened to him. But on some level, she also understood it was her distance, her ability to turn him away, that kept him coming back.

Although at times, like now, it was a struggle to keep a part of her separate, aloof, when all she wanted was to succumb to his every desire. He was so beautiful, his jet-black hair and ice-blue eyes, his sculpted body and lean waist. Maybe she was selfish to want to keep him for herself, locked inside their condominium and away from the temptations that seemed to be waiting around every corner whenever he walked out the door.

"I lost track of time. You know how it can be after a big win. We took our clients out to celebrate." He hesitated. "It really was a big win."

He was quiet, waiting for her to congratulate him, tell him she forgave him. But she wouldn't let him off that easy.

He added, "I know I should've called. I'm sorry. I promise it won't happen again."

At the very least you could've texted, she thought but didn't say. She didn't want to sound needy. Instead, she gave a terse nod. It wasn't the first time he'd stayed out all night without phoning or the first time she'd given him the cold shoulder the morning after. It wasn't the first time he'd showered off the scent of another woman.

CHAPTER TWO

John Jackson looked at the body on the ground, the .30-06 rifle warm in his calloused hand. There'd been a second, a slight hesitation before he'd pulled the trigger, when a small voice in the back of his mind had told him not to do it. He'd never survive inside the walls of a six-by-eight-foot cell. The stale air alone would kill him if something or someone else didn't. He was a man who lived his life outdoors, his home an old farmhouse near the woods at the base of the Blue Ridge Mountains not far from the Delaware River.

As he stood over the body, he tried to sort his feelings, wondered if he felt anything at all. What was done was done. And the hesitation, well, it was something only he would know about, something that would claw at his conscience for the rest of his days.

He leaned the rifle against a nearby tree. His other rifle, a .22 caliber and a decoy on this occasion, he propped against a different tree, one he would pass on his way toward home. It was still October, and deer season was another month away, but it wasn't unheard of for hunters to be in the woods, tracking their prey, building their deer stands with hopes of scoring a trophy buck. If John happened to pass one of these fellows who dreamed of a twelve-point deer mount hanging in his man cave, well, he wanted to make sure he was armed.

The sun started its ascent on the mountain, casting long shadows on the ground amid the blood and autumn leaves. He was running out of time.

He tossed his camouflage jacket and the leather cut he wore underneath to the side and rolled up his sleeves. After pulling on a pair of nitrile gloves, he crouched between the animal's legs, because that was how he chose to see the man—as an animal, a deer, a young buck—the one with a bullet hole in his chest, a barbed wire tattoo around his bicep, a piercing above his left eyebrow. He tried not to think about how young this buck was.

He stripped the body of its clothes, his mind tricking him into believing it was just another skinning. It wasn't, of course, and he felt the truth of it deep inside his bones. But he wasn't willing to let the guys in the club down. He'd given them his word. He'd do what they'd asked of him, what they *needed* from him, a brutality even they had feared.

More and more lately, John was finding it harder and harder to live up to this false younger version of himself. Age had a way of softening him. The things he'd been interested in at one time, macho things like motorcycles, barroom fights, and strippers, now seemed like nothing but a waste of time. He'd even lost interest in much of the club's business. They'd been dealing in arms for so long, at least two decades, it had become routine, hiding weapons in haylofts and underground root cellars on the farms in and around Portland. Besides, the younger club members ran most of the shipments nowadays. And just recently, John had entertained the idea of going nomad, not being tied to one club but a member free to come and go at will.

Until the animal in front of him had done the one thing John couldn't forgive, the one thing that had cost the young buck his life.

It should've put his mind at ease, securing his commitment to the club and its members, pushing away any doubts he was having about his place, his chosen way of life. But it didn't. Maybe he really was too old for this shit. He pulled the hunting knife from its sheath.

He hesitated again. *Dammit.* It was just another field dressing. He'd done a hundred of them on deer and rabbits and, once in Montana, elk and moose. Maybe he'd take another trip out West, take his motorcycle on the open road, visit old friends in the Montana chapter. A few weeks of hunting, a change of scenery, was just the thing he needed. He'd spent his whole life in this small town, secure in his ways. His problem was that he was *too* comfortable here. And a comfortable man let his guard down, making him vulnerable, making him weak.

He stuck the tip of the blade near the genitals, slicing through the skin and making his way upward toward the sternum, careful not to puncture the gut sack, the smell of which would be really bad. Only once had he punctured the gut sack of a deer, and that had been when he was a young boy. Russell, his old man, had told him to finish the job, although the meat had been spoiled not only from the fluids but also from John's vomit. It had been a lesson well learned. A mistake he'd never made again. Russell had had no patience for mistakes and no tolerance for the cowardly.

John held the stomach away from the ribs, cutting the diaphragm from the rib cage wall until the guts flopped out. Then he severed the windpipe and ran the blade along the thin membrane around the heart and lungs, removing the organs along with the liver before tossing the whole mess aside.

"Something for the wolves," he told his old man, talking to him as though he were still by his side, walking the earth.

When he finished, he stuffed the clothes into a sack, all of which would be burned later. He stood, his knees protesting, and picked up the rifle, slung it over his shoulder. Then he grabbed hold of the animal's ankles. It was a short walk downhill to the river, the twigs and dry leaves crackling as he dragged the body behind him. The sound was much too loud for the silence in the woods, the dead quiet that had fallen soon after the first and only shot had rung out. But the closer he got to the river, the more the sound of the rushing rapids drowned all other noise.

He entered the water, the cold rushing to his thighs, soaking his pants, prickling his skin like icicles. He released his burden, letting the rapids take it where they may. There was no point in weighing the body down. The club wanted it found. They were sending a message.

He tossed the hunting knife and rifle into the river. He was about to turn around and head up the bank when he saw her. If he thought about it, which he would later, he would say she was right on time, running the trail on the other side of the river. He couldn't have planned it any better, although he was convinced he hadn't planned it all, at least not consciously.

He stood and watched her as he'd done on other occasions from this same spot over the last few years. He was certain she knew he was watching her, although she'd always pretended she hadn't. He was okay with this. It was how it had to be. She was Clint's daughter. Clint had once been the chief of police of Portland, retired now, and he was also a stepbrother to John's old man, Russell. John had no claim on her outside of being distant family. But he'd watched her grow up and at one time had seen her as something akin to a younger sister. He didn't have any other siblings, nor did he have any children of his own. His late wife, Beth, had been barren, her ovaries giving birth to nothing but cancerous tumors.

He expected her to continue on the trail like all the other times before, only glancing in his direction while making the turn that would lead her farther into the woods and out of his line of view. But this morning she stopped unexpectedly and stared back at him. To say he was surprised was to downplay the hammering inside his chest. He couldn't move. His only thought was how fitting it was for her to be here with him. Like it or not, they were connected. He had no other explanation for it.

She hollered something. The river was loud, and he couldn't make out what she'd said. He waited for her to speak again, staying rooted to his spot, staring back at her. Suddenly, he became aware of time slipping by, the danger they were both now in. He couldn't wait any longer for her to repeat whatever it was she'd wanted to say. He turned and headed back toward the woods, believing her presence wasn't a threat to him.

He hoped he wasn't wrong.

He peeled off the nitrile gloves and stuffed them into the sack with the clothes. Then he slipped on his cut, the patches with the motorcycle club's name scrawled across his shoulder blades, and reached for the camouflage jacket to cover his identity. He grabbed the sack and the .22 and left the small clearing where the animal had gone down and where the guts lay.

With the rising sun on his back and the rifle in his hand, he made his way out of the woods, walking as though he were just another woodsman returning from a morning of tracking. Hap, the oldest member in the club and his old man's best friend, joined up with him about fifty yards from where he'd chased the young buck in the direction of John's deer stand. Of course, he used the word *chased* loosely since Hap was seventy years old, although a spry seventy.

"Didn't take long," Hap said, searching John's face, looking for him to meet his eyes.

John nodded, looked dead ahead as they walked on.

"You didn't have to be the one to do this, you know," Hap said. "I could've gotten one of the others to handle it. Sooner or later one of them is going to have to step up anyway."

He stopped and faced the old man. "This was personal."

Hap nodded. "That it was," he said. They walked a few more steps before he asked, "Was it done the same way as the other one?"

"Yes," John said. "Exactly the same."

CHAPTER THREE

Matt lay on the bed with the towel wrapped around his waist. He slung his arm over his face, covered his eyes. Becca got up. Romy inched her way across the duvet and curled against Matt's side. He scratched behind the dog's ears.

Becca left them alone and went into the bathroom, locked the door. She stripped off her sweaty running clothes and stepped into the shower. She leaned her forehead against the tile, letting the hot water run down her back. What had she expected from him? He was only human. Was it somehow her fault?

There were two other attorneys in Matt's firm who had managed his most recent client before the file had been turned over to him. He was the go-to guy once a case actually saw the inside of a courtroom. He had a commanding presence, a certain charm that even hostile witnesses warmed to. He had the gift of persuasion.

He'd been preparing for weeks, circling their living room, practicing his opening and closing statements. As the court date approached, the meetings with his client had become more frequent, keeping him out until all hours of the night. The tension of the pending trial, prepping his client for the stand, and then late yesterday when the judge had ruled in their favor, it all had been terribly exciting, overwhelming, so he'd said. His client's patent, some kind of applicator in the cosmetic industry, the details of which his partner had handled, had been packaged and sold without permission or payment. The cosmetic company's infringement, worth millions, would have to be paid. It had been the biggest win of Matt's career. Could he help it if he'd gone out afterward and celebrated?

It wasn't his fault that his client happened to be a six-foot-tall brunette with legs so long they touched her ears. He'd confessed she'd enjoyed flashing her cleavage in his face, wearing low-cut blouses, leaning over him to look at files, touching his shoulder, brushing up against him whenever she'd had the chance. It had been building for weeks, the stress of the case, and then the big win.

Becca slapped the wet tile with her palm. She would not cry. She would not give him the satisfaction of seeing her weak.

The phone started ringing. It was the landline Matt had installed when he and Becca had first moved into the condo. She couldn't remember the last time someone had actually rung them up on it. Most everyone they knew called their cell phones.

She turned off the shower, listened to the sound of Matt's muffled voice, then the click as he hung up the phone. In the next minute, she emerged from the bathroom wearing a white cotton robe. It was too big for her petite frame, drowning her small chest and narrow hips in the bulky material. Her dark hair was short, a pixie cut, making her look young and boyish rather than like the thirty-year-old woman she was. She was nothing like the typical girls Matt had dated in the past. The other women in Matt's life had been models, beauty queens. Becca had seen all the pictures, all his previous conquests. These other women looked a lot like Matt's latest client.

Becca wasn't beautiful in the traditional sense, and she certainly wasn't a bombshell like the leggy brunette. But none of this had ever seemed to matter to Matt. He'd said it was Becca's gray eyes that he'd gotten lost in, eyes that were sharp, intelligent, kind. He'd whispered in her ear, his voice deep and sultry, confessing how her eyes held him captive, how they turned black as pitch when she was angry and lusty gray when they made love. But mostly, he'd said, he liked who *he* was in her eyes. He liked how she saw the best in him, the goodness, rather than all the other crap that made up who he was.

But now when Becca looked at him, he wouldn't meet her gaze. He looked away.

She walked past him on her way to the dresser. He reached out from where he sat on the edge of the mattress and grabbed her wrist, pulling her to him until she was standing in front of him. He buried his face in her cotton robe, his hands roaming the angles of her body.

"I'm in a hurry," she said. "I'm already late for my first appointment."

He wrapped his arms around her waist, nudging the robe open with his nose, kissing her. She didn't push him away.

Maybe she was wrong, and last night had been what he'd said, a celebration and nothing more. "I'm still mad at you." Her body relaxed in his arms, responding to his touch and in a sense betraying her.

"I know," he said.

She closed her eyes, wanting to give herself over to him. But she had to be strong. It was too soon to give in. She struggled to keep her arms at her sides, resisted running her fingers through his silky hair. "Who was on the phone?" she asked.

"Hmm?"

"Who was on the phone?" she mumbled as he kissed her stomach.

He hesitated, pulling away slightly, glancing up at her. "I don't know. He just kept coughing. I couldn't understand him."

Becca scrambled out of Matt's arms. "Coughing? Like someone-who-is-sick kind of coughing?" She yanked the cotton robe tight around her waist, her hand clutching the collar at her neck.

"Yeah. But it was probably just a wrong number." Matt closed the bath towel around his waist. He still couldn't look at her. He was purposefully avoiding meeting her eyes, but it didn't matter because it was all over his face, the guilty look of a child who had done something wrong. Her head told her all of this, but her heart refused to listen.

"Was it a Pennsylvania number?"

"Yes," Matt said. "How did you know? What's going on?"

Becca's cell phone went off. It was the clinic. The results of the ultrasound for Maggie, the three-year-old golden retriever she'd treated late yesterday afternoon, confirmed the dog had in fact swallowed a large portion of a tennis ball. She didn't want to have to cut the dog and remove it from the gastrointestinal tract if it wasn't absolutely necessary. Surgery was the last option; the belief was that no matter how minor the procedure, there was always a risk something could go wrong. Maggie had been Becca's patient since she'd been a pup, and it pained Becca to see the dog in discomfort. She couldn't put it off any longer. She had to get to the clinic.

"I have to go," she said. "It's Maggie."

"Who's Maggie?" he asked.

"Never mind." He didn't know because she had never gotten around to telling him about the dog because he hadn't come home last night. "I'll tell you later," she said, dressing quickly before racing out the door.

The veterinary clinic was a few miles from the condo on the outskirts of town. The town itself was small and largely unincorporated. One of its biggest attractions was the flea market that was open year-round. Most of the land was farmland. In this regard, it resembled Becca's hometown of Portland, another small, rural community alongside the Delaware River. The major difference between the two was that Becca hadn't grown up here. Here she wasn't known solely as the police chief's daughter.

The townspeople of Columbia knew her as one of the four veterinarians at the clinic who cared for their pets. They knew if their cat or dog or rabbit needed surgery, Becca was the vet to do it. She was the pet surgeon. That was all. And that was the point.

Her colleagues had their own preferences and specialties; one worked exclusively on large animals, another preferred reptiles and snakes, and one specialized in eye exams. But Becca performed the surgeries. She was the one who went in with her hands and fixed whatever was wrong. She took great pleasure in this, the tangible way of repairing the broken parts on beloved pets, something she wasn't able to do with the people in her life, where she failed at the intangibles, the flaws in personalities that were too big to stitch.

She pulled into the clinic's parking lot. The dogs in the kennel were awake, barking, waiting for their owners to collect them, take them home. Becca made a mental note to stop and let some of the more companionable pooches out for exercise later in the day. They were operating with half the staff most days, the sign of a struggling economy. She hated to think about all of the yearly physicals that had been canceled recently.

She entered the building through the side door, slipped on her white lab coat. "Hey," she said to Vicky. Vicky had a special kind of softness, a gentleness the animals sensed and found soothing. Becca's own unique quality was the smoothness of her voice, the confidence in her touch, her way of saying to the animal, "I won't hurt you. I'm here to take care of you."

"Is Maggie's owner here yet?" she asked.

"She's up front waiting for you."

"Okay. I'm going to check on Maggie first before I talk with her." Becca pulled the dog's chart, reviewed the ultrasound, confirmed the obstruction. She headed for the boarding room. Vicky followed. She'd been assisting Becca since her first day at the clinic. They were close in age, three years apart, with Vicky the younger of the two. She was the closest thing to a girlfriend Becca had if she didn't count the four-legged kind.

"How are you feeling?" Becca asked Maggie, stroked the top of the dog's head. She lifted the dog's eyelids to look at her pupils. With the stethoscope, she listened to the dog's heart, stomach. "We're going to help you with that bellyache, okay?" She patted Maggie's head again. Maggie responded with a thump of her tail.

"Let me talk with the owner, and then you can get Maggie prepped," she said to Vicky.

Vicky nodded. "Sure thing." She paused, searching Becca's face. "You okay?"

Becca waved her off. "It's nothing."

"What did Matt do this time?" Vicky asked and tightened the ponytail at the base of her neck. Inked on the underside of her forearm was the face of Toto, her pet schnauzer that had passed two years ago.

"Why do you automatically jump to the conclusion it has something to do with Matt?"

Vicky shrugged. "Whenever you have that look, the one on your face right now, it *always* has something to do with Matt."

"What look?"

"That one." Vicky pointed at Becca's face. "Your lips turn down, and your eyebrows knit together. It's a puss face like that cat that used to be all over the internet."

"I do not look like Grumpy Cat," she protested, but the image made her smile. She swatted Vicky playfully. "Let's get Mags ready." She turned to leave, then turned back around. "Grumpy Cat? Really?"

"Really," Vicky said.

Becca headed to the front of the clinic where Maggie's owner, Stephanie, was waiting. Stephanie stood from the bench upon seeing Becca.

"How's Maggie?" she asked. Her hair was tied in a sloppy knot, and she was dressed in yoga pants.

"The ultrasound confirmed there's a blockage. I don't recommend waiting any longer. It needs to come out."

"Now?" Stephanie asked. "I don't want to sound insensitive, but how much is this going to cost me?"

The surgery wasn't overly expensive, but depending on a person's budget, it could set them back. "We'll work out some kind of payment schedule. We really need to do this for Maggie."

Stephanie rubbed her brow. "Okay," she said. "I'll have to find some way to pay."

Once Stephanie had gone, Becca rejoined Vicky. While Vicky prepped Maggie, Becca put on her mask, scoured for surgery, donned the sterile gown and gloves.

"All set?" she asked.

Vicky nodded and handed Becca the scalpel.

Becca wiped her brow. The procedure had taken a little longer than expected, but overall, she was satisfied with the results. The piece of the tennis ball had been removed from the dog's stomach. She'd been stitched, and now she was resting comfortably in recovery.

After Becca spoke with Stephanie on the phone, she made her way out the back exit of the building. The dogs in the kennel barked their greeting. As promised, she let them out to run.

For a while she watched as they sniffed one another, marked the corner wall with their scent, frolicked up and down the runway. Occasionally, Polly, the boxer-and-bulldog mix, would stop for a pat on the head.

She watched the dogs for several more minutes until her legs grew tired from standing. She slid down the brick wall, sat on the cold cement slab. The muscles in her back ached. She never could loosen up and relax during surgery, not like some of the other vets she'd worked with in the past. They had played the radio, chatted amicably, all the while slicing and stitching.

But the tension she was experiencing now, the knots between her shoulder blades, was coming from a different source, a different kind of pressure. She pulled out her cell phone. She couldn't avoid him any longer. When the hacking cough subsided on the other end of the line, she said, "Dad, it's me. It's Becca."

🦋

Eight-year-old Becca sat next to her father in his pickup truck as they made their way down the windy country road heading toward home. It was late July, and the sun had dropped behind the mountain, but the heat was still coming off the macadam in waves. Dusk took its time, yawning across the cornfields. The windows were rolled down, and the sticky air swirled in the breeze, offering little relief. Becca's father pinched a homemade cigarette between his lips. He was forever rolling his own tobacco, rolling and smoking the cancer sticks like a never-ending assembly line. She turned her head away from the smell that lingered on his clothes, in his hair, on his breath.

"Aw, what the hell is this?" he asked, braking at the sight of a car that was half in the gutter, the other half blocking the lane. The hood was gnarled and bent.

Becca sat up straight in the seat, peered out the windshield.

He pulled to the side of the road and parked several feet behind the disabled car. "You wait here," he said. "Don't get out of the truck. Do you hear?"

She nodded, not looking at him, staring at the scene ahead, her heart pattering nervously inside her chest.

A woman scrambled out of the back seat as Becca's father approached.

"Help me," she said, flailing her arms, the fat of her triceps flapping back and forth. Sweat stained the collar of her shirt. "It's my daughter. I don't know what's wrong with her." She clung to Becca's father's arm.

"Ma'am, I'm going to have to ask you to calm down." He took her hands off of him. He used his police chief's voice, the one that sounded deeper, authoritative, in charge. Although he was off duty, wearing jeans and a T-shirt, in Becca's eyes he could very well have been dressed in his chief's uniform, the one that made everything about him feel bigger and stronger, more powerful than an ordinary man.

"I want you to tell me what happened," he said and ducked his head into the back seat of the car while the woman flitted about, her words jumbled and unclear, but Becca distinctly heard her say *deer*.

Becca pulled herself farther up in the seat, hands on the dash, straining to see what he was doing. In one swift movement, he removed a small child, a little girl, maybe four years old, from her car seat. Her face was pale, her eyes wide. Her too-short bangs were sweaty and pasted to her forehead. Becca's father turned so all Becca could see was his back, his large arms wrapped around the child's torso. He made one quick motion, and the child coughed and started to cry.

"Your daughter was choking," he said and handed the little girl to her mother as though it had been nothing.

"Thank you. Thank you. I don't know how to thank you." The woman with the fat arms clung to her daughter, kissed her daughter's cheeks over and over again. The child continued sobbing on her mother's shoulder.

Becca couldn't take her eyes off her father, her chest swelling, expanding far and wide as though she'd swallowed the whole of a summer sky. Unable to stay in the pickup any longer for fear she'd burst, she jumped out of the truck as her father walked around to the front of the woman's car. Becca came to stand next to him, close, so that his arm brushed hers as he reached under the hood.

"I thought I told you to stay in the truck," he said.

She looked up at him, having to tilt her head way back to see his face.

"Ma'am," he called, peering into the engine and ignoring Becca. "You're going to need a tow."

Becca watched him fiddle under the hood until something caught her attention out of the corner of her eye. She stared into the cornfield where the stalks had been flattened. She moved slowly toward it, lured by curiosity. Behind her, the woman rocked her child while Becca's father talked about the engine, but Becca wasn't listening to what he was saying. The blood-splattered leaves beckoned her farther and farther into the corn rows. She couldn't stop herself; she had to know, to see the animal for herself. The deer, a doe, lay on its side, panting. Its eyes seemed to lock on to Becca as if it knew she wouldn't hurt it, as though it trusted her to help.

"Step back," her father said.

Becca never heard him come up behind her. He lifted the rifle in his hand.

"No, Daddy," she yelled and pulled on his arm. "No, Daddy, please," she cried.

He shook her off. "Stand back," he commanded, pushing her away, making her stand several yards back before aiming and firing. The bullet struck the animal with a *thwock*.

Becca stared at the doe, still and lifeless, the stalks beneath it crimson.

"It was suffering," he said, taking her arm and leading her out of the field.

She struggled to get away from him, twisting and pulling. "Let me go," she cried, but he held on tight. He opened the door to the pickup and put her inside the truck once again. "Wait here."

Becca crossed her arms, the backs of her legs sweaty on the vinyl seat. The little girl and her mother played patty-cake on the side of the road while they waited for the tow truck. Becca's father continued fiddling under the hood of the wrecked car. The mother kept stealing glances at him, the woman's face aglow with appreciation and gratitude.

All the while a storm brewed inside Becca's chest, dark clouds rumbling in that summer sky she'd swallowed just minutes before, no longer clear and blue but now thundering and gray.

CHAPTER FOUR

John watched as the black smoke swirled into the fading blue sky. He was standing behind the old barn in front of the fire pit where the pile of autumn leaves blackened and burned. Behind the pit the mountain loomed, the trees covered in bright yellows and oranges and reds. A hawk circled not far in the distance.

He pulled the collar of his leather cut up around his neck. There was a nip in the air. If he were younger, he might not have noticed. The heat from the flames should've been enough to ward off the chill. But when he started to shiver despite the fire and heavy leather jacket, he couldn't blame the autumn air or his age. The cold was coming from him, from the inside, from a dark place hidden so deep he wasn't always aware of it.

Ever since he'd shot the young buck, it was as though the scars of the past had grown around his heart, their icy tendrils slowly thickening, wrapping around the muscle, suffocating whatever warmth and tenderness he had left.

"Stop being morose," his old lady, Beth, might've said if she'd been standing beside him. The thought made him smile in spite of himself. He was often surprised by how much of her vocabulary he'd absorbed through their fifteen years of marriage. She'd been smart. He'd thought of her as an intellectual. She'd had her nose in a book most days, although she'd been one hell of a partier at night.

The first time John had laid eyes on her, she'd been sitting outside of Sweeney's Bar with her feet propped on the railing, a book in her lap. The sun had started to set, casting its last rays across the top of her head in such a way he'd believed he'd been looking at an angel. She'd looked up from the page and met his gaze, creating an ache inside of him, a yearning so strong he'd thought he might explode.

A couple of the guys had walked outside. They'd started giving her shit, making fun of her for reading while her older sister, Lonnie, was inside drinking shots.

She'd closed her book and stood. "All right. Let's drink," she'd said and pulled the door open. "You fellas might want to try to keep up," she'd called over her shoulder.

John had watched as she'd tossed back shot after shot like the girl in the *Indiana Jones* movie, outdrinking every man in the place. By the end of the night, she'd been left sitting alone at a table full of empty glasses. John had been sitting a few tables away.

"Where did you learn to drink like that?" he'd asked.

"College," she'd said. "I majored in fine arts and minored in parties. Both of which are pretty much useless in the real world."

He'd nodded.

"Do you want to join me?" She'd motioned to the empty seat in front of her.

He'd shaken his head. She'd looked surprised.

"What I'd like to do is take you home." He'd crossed the room, held out his hand. When she'd touched him, every cell in his body had come alive, electric and pulsating. For the first and only time in his life, John had fallen in love.

Slowly, Beth had found her place with him and the Scions, their old ladies, their way of life. But in other ways, she hadn't. She had a certain class about her, a sophistication that had been more than just being well read. She had grace and strength, a combination very few women possessed. But she'd never looked down on any of the club members or their women. And she could have. Hell, even John had thought, although affectionately, of some of the members and their old ladies as uneducated and trashy.

And she'd never looked down on John.

Beth had died three years ago from ovarian cancer. Since then, not a day had gone by that he hadn't thought of her. It wasn't that he was lonely. He didn't mind being alone. Nor was it the frequent sex that he missed, although he did miss it more than he wanted to admit. But it was the smaller things he thought of often, how she'd toss her head back when she laughed, how she'd tuck her feet underneath his legs to keep them warm on chilly nights, how she'd furrow her brow whenever she was concentrating on something as simple as sewing a button.

But what John missed most about his wife was the easy rhythm of their days. Since she'd gone, he couldn't settle his thoughts or find a routine. It was as though he was constantly wandering, searching for something, not realizing he was the one who was lost.

He was still thinking about Beth and watching the leaves burn when the sound of a motorcycle's engine rumbled. In another moment Hap walked up behind him.

"Getting rid of the evidence?" Hap motioned toward the fire pit and smiled. Nothing amused Hap more than pulling one over on law enforcement.

"Nothing but ash now," John said. Buried deep in the burning leaves was the sack with the young buck's clothes.

"Your dad taught you well," Hap said, put his hand on John's shoulder. "He would've been proud of you. Damn proud."

John nodded. He'd taken an oath to the club, the Scions, twenty years ago, and if there was one rule he lived by, the rule his old man, Russell, had drilled into him ever since he was a small boy, it was that he put the club before himself, always, even if it meant giving his life.

"How long do you think it will take before they connect this one with the other one?" John asked.

"Don't worry. We're covered," Hap said, then added, "The boys are unloading a shipment as we speak."

"Where?"

"Frank Lars's place."

John nodded.

They both stared at the fire pit, watched as wisps of smoke curled through the air, until nothing was left of the leaves or the clothes but ash.

❦

John leaned against the side of Frank Lars's farmhouse. A pickup truck was backed up to the front door. The guys were carrying duffel bags in, stomping through the kitchen to the trapdoor that led to the root cellar.

Hap and Frank stepped onto the porch. Hap pulled a large stack of hundred-dollar bills from his pocket, handed it to Frank.

"How long do you need to store them here?" Frank asked. He smelled like manure and a little bit of body odor, having spent the day working his dairy farm. In the barn, the cows fussed, mooed.

"A couple days," Hap said. "Now that our little problem is solved, it shouldn't be too long."

A car approached, the headlights shining on the house, the porch, the men. It was a marked cruiser. One of Chief Toby Bryant's captains stepped out, put his hat on as he made his way over to them.

"Everything okay here, Frank?" the captain asked.

"Everything's just fine," Frank said.

John stayed tucked in the shadows on the side of the house, not moving from his original position, as though he were unfazed by the captain's presence. Underneath the leather cut, he could feel himself sweating.

"What can we help you with?" Hap asked.

"I was wondering if anybody here has seen a black bear hanging around the last few days?" the captain asked. "We think it's coming down off the mountain. Some folks in town are complaining about trash cans being knocked over, rummaged through, that sort of thing."

The guys standing behind the truck shook their heads. A couple of them muttered that they hadn't seen it, barely pausing as they lifted more bags, carried them inside.

"Okay, well, give me a holler if you do," the captain said.

Chitter pulled a rifle from a bag, one with a bump stock. He aimed it at the field. "Why don't you let us take care of that bear for you."

"That would be good of you." The captain looked around, stared in John's direction, paused. "Okay," he said. "Let me know when you get it." He tipped his hat, turned to go.

After the captain had gone and the last of the guns had been unloaded, Hap said, "How about a drink?"

John got on his bike, Hap on his hog. The men headed to Sweeney's Bar.

If there was one thing John could use, it was a drink.

CHAPTER FIVE

Becca sat on the hardwood chair next to her father's bed. The room was ripe with a medicinal smell. The heat was cranked up to the point of stifling. Romy lay just outside the door in the hall, her head resting on her paws.

Becca couldn't bring herself to think about the reason she'd been summoned. She couldn't bring herself to look at the shrunken man underneath the sheets and blankets. Instead, she looked at the white dresser her mother had picked out nearly two decades ago. The corners were scuffed where the vacuum cleaner had brushed against it. The knob on the lower drawer was missing. Overall, it wasn't in bad shape, but to Becca there was something sad about it. The dresser faced the bed, a constant witness to the people who slept here, but Becca didn't want to think about that either. She turned her head toward the window where the curtains drooped in the stagnant air.

Her father's raspy breath came and went in spurts. The clock ticked off each painful second at a time. She stared at the water stain in the corner ceiling and a dangling paint chip that was certain to fall if there were the slightest breeze.

Her father's lady friend, the label he'd given to all the women who'd come after Becca's mother, was downstairs. Jackie had been his lady friend for a little less than two years, and she was fumbling around in what used to be Becca's mother's kitchen a long time ago, but not so long in Becca's mind.

Becca rubbed the tops of her legs, smoothing the wrinkles on her jeans. Out of the corner of her eye, she caught movement under the sheets. She was pretty sure her father had moved his arm. He was waking up. *Look at him*, she told herself. *Look at him, and stop being a coward.*

She forced herself to turn her head and gaze at him. His shrunken and distorted body looked no bigger than a child's. His face was drained of color. His once-black hair had turned white and stuck up in sparse patches around his head.

"Becca," he said, his voice sounding hoarse, strained.

She pulled her chair closer, disturbing Romy on the floor in the hall. The dog stood but didn't enter the room.

"Hey, Dad," Becca said.

He looked as though he was trying to smile, his lips rising on only one side of his face. The other side was lax, the muscle paralyzed from a minor stroke, the medical emergency that had indirectly led them to the cancer. It was hard for Becca to imagine that had been two years ago. Then, he'd been riding his John Deere, tending his immaculate lawn, hunting, fishing, living the good life of retirement years. Of course, this wasn't something he'd said to her but rather to Becca's mother, who had later relayed the information to Becca. It had been her mother who had given Becca's father the number to the condo's landline.

"You should talk to him," her mother had said. She was living in San Francisco with her boyfriend, George, the man she had lived with since divorcing Becca's father over a decade ago.

"No," Becca had said in return.

"He's your father."

Becca hadn't responded.

"You need to let go of your anger, Bec. It's the only way the two of you can ever move on. You need to talk with him and tell him how you feel before it's too late."

Becca had imagined her mother smoothing her eyebrows while they talked, a habit she had whenever they discussed a topic she found upsetting, particularly the topic of Becca's father.

"Why? You never did. You just left."

"I know, but it was different for me. And he's your father."

"I don't care."

"Oh, honey, can you hear yourself? It takes so much energy to be angry."

They'd had the same conversation over and over since they'd first learned Becca's father had been diagnosed with cancer. Becca supposed the only reason she was here now, the only reason she was sitting next to her father's bed waiting to hear what he had to say, was because it was what her mother had wanted her to do.

He opened his mouth to talk and started coughing, a phlegm-filled, choking kind of cough. It continued for several seconds, seizing his chest, and she was suddenly alarmed.

"Dad," she said.

His hand covered his throat. She stood and spun in circles, looking for a call button or a bell. She was a vet; she was used to emergency situations and should have some semblance of what to do, but she didn't. For a moment her mind went blank. This was why she could never operate on one of her own pets. When it was personal, her emotions muddied her thoughts, rendering her useless. She reached for a tissue from the box on the nightstand, placed it to his lips. It was the only thing she could think to do. He spit the mucus clogging his throat.

The door opened, and Jackie breezed in holding a cup with a bendy straw. She was wearing skinny jeans and a tight-knit sweater with a plunging neckline.

"Here," Jackie said and put the straw between his lips. "This should help." She held the cup while he sipped the water. At the same time, she took the wet tissue from Becca's hand and tossed it in a nearby trash can.

Her father turned his head away when he'd had enough.

"Come on now, just a little more." Jackie talked to him as though he were a toddler refusing to take his medicine. "You need to keep fluids in you."

Becca's father looked at her. She could've sworn he rolled his eyes.

When he finished most of the water in the cup, Jackie smiled. "Much better," she said. "I'll leave you to your visit." She closed the door behind her.

"Does that happen often?" Becca asked once they were alone, not knowing what else to say. "Is there anything I can do?" She looked at her feet. So many conflicting feelings piled up inside of her—twisting, writhing, knotting, tangling with the anger at her core. And buried far below all these emotions, there was something else, something that made her heart ache.

He shook his head and tried to pull himself up.

"Let me help you." She reached under his arm. His bicep was as thick as her wrist. Once she got him comfortable, he looked at her long and hard, the way he used to look at her when she was a child, serious and stern. His eyes reflected a glimpse of the man he'd once been, despite the stroke and the cancer rotting his body. It was the reason he was still alive, his absolute refusal to give in. He'd stuck around a lot longer than the six months the doctors had forecast originally. Jackie might've had something to do with it.

Becca's resentment returned. How easily her feelings spiraled and churned.

He opened his mouth to speak, but another coughing fit started. She reached for more tissues. He tried to talk through it, struggled to get the words out. His shoulders shook violently.

33

"What can I do?"

He shook his head.

Jackie breezed through the door again with another cup of water. This time she placed it on the bedside table. She rubbed his back and made soothing, cooing sounds as he hacked and spewed mucus into the tissues in Becca's hand. When it was over, and air was moving more freely through his blackened lungs as best it could, he laid his head back against the pillow. It was enough to drain him of all his strength.

Becca searched Jackie's worried face.

"Let's give him a few minutes to rest," Jackie said and motioned for Becca to follow her out of the room to where Romy was waiting. But before Becca stepped into the hall, she heard her father say, "John."

She turned back around and stared at him. His eyes were closed, his head tilted to the side. It had been years since she'd heard him say John's name. Maybe she'd imagined it. She must have. And still she paused before closing the bedroom door behind her.

"Please, sit." Jackie pulled a chair from the kitchen table, the same kitchen table Becca's parents had bought when Becca had been in her junior year of high school. It had been the last big purchase her parents had made the year before they'd split. Becca had said to her mother, "You can't buy furniture together and then just up and leave."

In her sixteen-year-old mind, buying furniture had meant that her parents had been trying to work it out, because no matter how bad things had gotten, Becca had wanted her parents to stay together. Thinking back, she understood that her reasons may have been based on some primal childhood need for security, even if it had meant them staying together had been pretty messed up.

Jackie held on to the back of the chair, waiting for Becca to sit. Becca found it insulting to be treated like a guest by this woman in the place Becca had once called home.

She sat in the chair, folded her arms. "How long has he been like this?"

"Like this?" Jackie pointed upstairs. "Not long." She sat in the chair across from Becca. "I've talked to hospice. I have someone that will be coming in when I can no longer manage him on my own." She paused. "I should say *if* I can no longer manage him on my own."

Jackie touched her neck, and Becca's eyes were drawn to Jackie's ample cleavage. She forced herself to look someplace else, but everything in the room was filled with so many memories, she couldn't find a safe place to set her gaze. Romy dropped her head in Becca's lap, and she focused on her furry friend, scratching behind her ears.

"How much longer do you think he has?" she asked.

"Oh, it's hard to say. Your father is a fighter. It could be another week or two. But my guess is it'll be sooner." She sounded like a woman who had accepted what was coming. "Would you like some tea?" She sprung from her chair and put a pot on the stove.

Becca found it charming to have tea brewed the old-fashioned way. More often than not, she'd heat up a cup in the microwave.

Jackie stood by the stove; perhaps the distance made it easier for her to say what she'd planned all along. "I know you and your dad have had your differences."

"To put it mildly," Becca said.

Jackie didn't continue right away but let Becca's comment settle before she started again. "I don't know all the details of what went wrong between you two. And honestly, I don't care. I don't think it matters. What matters now is that your dad needs you. And maybe I don't know you well enough to ask this of you, but I'm going to ask anyway. I'm asking because I care about what he wants and needs. And right now, he wants his daughter with him. He needs you here."

Becca was shaking her head. Who did this woman think she was? She knew nothing about Becca or her relationship with her father. "I have the clinic, appointments, surgeries scheduled . . ." Her voice trailed off. It was a weak excuse. Her colleagues could certainly handle the workload. They were all equipped with the same surgical skills if needed.

But no. She couldn't stay here with him. Why would she? He had sent her away. And he didn't deserve her company now. He didn't deserve her. The only woman he deserved was the tart in front of her, although Becca immediately felt bad for thinking of Jackie in that way. After all, Jackie had stuck by her father all through his illness, and she didn't have to. She was fifteen years younger than he was. She could've packed her bags and walked out on him the second his health had faltered to the point where he could no longer care for himself. And the strange part about it was that Becca might've had more respect for her if she had. But of course, Jackie hadn't. She'd stayed. Becca's father had some kind of hold on certain women, a certain flaw in their character surely, but damned if Becca could figure out what it was.

"Well, what do you think?" Jackie asked. "Can you find it in your heart to stick around?" The teapot whistled. She turned to remove it from the burner.

"I don't know," Becca said. "I don't think so. I need to think about it."

Jackie poured a cup of tea and set it on the table in front of her. "Well, don't take too long. He doesn't have much time left."

Becca no longer wanted tea. She wanted to get away from this woman who asked too much of her. She wanted to tell her it was more complicated than simply agreeing to say yes, she would stay. Did she even have a choice?

"I need some air," Becca said. She needed space to think. But what she needed most was to get away from the stench of sickness, a mixture of alcohol and bodily fluids that permeated the walls and saturated the stagnant air.

Outside, she took a deep breath, stared at her father's lawn that was no longer manicured to perfection. Crabgrass and weeds had taken hold of the yard, choking out the plush, green blades of grass. The sight was at once heart-wrenching and disturbing. If she'd had any doubt, any buried hope that his condition wasn't as serious as she'd been led to believe, the state of his yard had quashed it. She looked up at his bedroom window. What had been the point of all the mowing and fertilizing, the tending, the caring, when in the end, all that was left was weeds?

She didn't know.

She had never understood her father's reasons for doing the things he'd done. She crossed her arms against the chill. Then she closed her eyes, listened to the trickle of the stream in the woods behind her father's house, remembered how the same stream ran behind John's barn on its way to feed the river.

Eight-year-old Becca picked her way through the backyard, stopped, looked over her shoulder at her father. He was standing in the drive-way next to his pickup truck, holding the rifle he'd shot the doe with the week before. She still had mixed feelings about the doe's death, about him.

She turned back around, walked into the woods behind their house. She swatted gnats from her face, steered clear of the maple tree with the beehive in it. She stomped the ground, making as much noise as possible with the hope that John was in the woods tracking deer, honing his skills as a hunter, and he would hear her.

He stepped from behind a hemlock tree. She started.

"Was that you making all that racket?" he teased. He was wearing a jean jacket, the ends frayed where the sleeves were ripped off, the word *Prospect* stitched above the left breast pocket. He had patchy fuzz on his chin and above his lip, not enough to look like a man, but too much to look like a boy anymore.

"Want to catch bullfrogs?" she asked.

"Can't."

"Crayfish?"

He shook his head.

"What do you want to do then?"

"I brought you something," he said.

She eyed him suspiciously. "How did you know you'd see me?"

"I took a chance."

"What is it?"

He reached under the hemlock tree, picked up an old barn cat lying underneath. "I thought you could use a friend," he said and handed it to her. "I know I haven't been around much. The club keeps me pretty busy these days."

The cat's fur was matted, lacked any shine to it. Its meow sounded lonely. It curled itself in Becca's arms, pushed its cheeks against her hand, looking for affection.

"You can't tell anyone where you got her. It has to be our secret," he said.

"I won't tell." Her father would be mad. He didn't like John. He didn't get along with John's father, Russell, his own stepbrother. She didn't understand why they fought with each other but thought it had something to do with Russell and his motorcycle friends and Becca's father being chief of police.

"Okay, well, she's a pretty good mouser, but you're still going to need to feed her," John said. "And maybe you can have your mom check her for fleas."

"Okay."

"Take care of her," he said. "I have to get going."

"When will I see you again?"

"I think it's best if I keep my distance from now on."

"Why?"

He touched the pocket where the word *Prospect* was written. "It just is."

She thought he looked sad about it. It made her sad too. She hugged the cat closely, searching for and finding comfort in its warm body, its purr.

CHAPTER SIX

It was dark by the time Becca left her father's house. She still didn't have any clear idea whether she would be returning. She walked into the condo and found Matt relaxing on the leather chair in front of the fireplace, sipping a glass of red wine. He was wearing one of the shirts she liked best, a simple gray T-shirt with navy-blue piping at the collar and sleeves. His legs were stretched out in front of him. His feet were bare. She recognized the serious expression on his face, the one he wore whenever he was deep in thought.

She entered the room. He immediately pulled himself up, his eyes searching hers. "How'd it go?" he asked.

She plopped onto the chair across from him. She wasn't sure if he was asking about her trip home to see her father or about the surgery on the golden retriever earlier that morning. She chose to answer the latter. "The surgery went well. No complications. She should be feeling like her old self in a few days."

Romy trotted in from the kitchen, mouth dripping with water. She pushed her nose against Matt's hand until he stroked her head, her chest, behind her ears. The dog whined with pleasure. Becca couldn't help but smile.

"I'm glad the surgery was a success." He cleared his throat. "But what about the other thing? How did that go?"

She took a moment to collect her thoughts. "He's really sick. More than I thought. I mean, I knew he was. My mother talks with him on occasion. So I knew." She paused. "I knew about the cancer. I just didn't know how bad it had gotten."

Matt looked puzzled. "Why didn't you say anything to me before if you knew he was sick? I mean, jeez, Bec, cancer?"

She touched her forehead. A headache was coming on. "I guess I didn't want to deal with it." She realized that was the absolute truth. She didn't want to deal with her father, his illness, but most of all she didn't want to deal with their relationship or lack of one. It was too damned hard.

Matt got up and knelt on the floor in front of her, taking her hands in his. "I'm sorry. This must be very difficult for you. What can I do?"

She touched his sculpted face, the high cheekbone, the curve of his jaw. Any other time she would've gotten up and walked away, unyielding in her resolve to keep him at a distance and, in a perverse way, only making him want her more. But she didn't have it in her to push him away tonight. Tonight, she needed his arms around her, holding her. When he leaned forward and brushed his lips on hers, she responded, lacing her hands through his hair, pressing her body against him, collapsing into his strong arms.

He held her for a long time, kneeling on the floor in front of her. She squeezed his back and shoulders tightly. Neither one spoke. All the anger and frustration she'd felt toward him for his failure to come home the night before slowly dissipated. She kissed his neck and ear, suddenly wanting to take back what was hers, her life here with him, and forget about her troubles across the river.

Matt scooped her in his arms, laid her on the floor in front of the fire. His kisses were deep and full of apology. She lifted his shirt over his head and pulled him to her, running her hands over the muscles along his spine, clinging to him as though it were the first time.

When they separated, she rolled to her side, stared at the crackling fire. Matt tucked his body behind her. They lay on the floor without speaking for several long minutes. It was Becca who broke the silence first.

"My dad wants me to come home," she said. "To be with him." She swallowed hard. "In the end."

The muscles in Matt's arms constricted, his body tensed up. "Are you going to do it?"

"I don't know."

"Okay." His voice was low, guarded. He was quiet for a long time. "If you decide to go, what will you do about the clinic?"

"Vicky can cover most of it for me. I'd just hate to lose the money." She wasn't a partner in the clinic yet, and she relied on her paycheck. She had student loans to pay back and credit card bills. She'd put herself through veterinary school on her own, and she took a tremendous amount of pride in that, but it had been costly. She lived from one paycheck to the next, knowing in a few years her loans would be paid off and things would turn around. Until then she made do on a tight budget.

"I wish you wouldn't worry about money. I have plenty for the both of us." Matt kissed the back of her head. He paid for the condo they lived in, prime real estate in the most sought-after address in the gated community at the top of the hill. They had spectacular views of the river and woods, man-made trails for biking and running, a community gym and pool, all contained inside the four walls of the complex. Condo living was convenient. The grounds were well kept. The place was beautiful in a manicured way.

She should be grateful to Matt. She could never have afforded such luxuries on her budget. But sometimes the walls of the condo, the whole place, closed in on her. How could she tell him without sounding ungrateful that she preferred the open air, running the unkempt trails, the slopes and turns covered with dirt and rocks, the brush and trees surrounding her, the sound of rushing river rapids or the slow trickle where the water came to rest? How could she tell him she preferred the solitude the woods and river provided, where she didn't have to maneuver around walkers or baby strollers or offer friendly hellos to neighbors? The woods were the one place where Romy could run free without a leash.

Of course, Matt loved condo living and the security of its walls, a safe place to park his ninety-thousand-dollar car. And the condo was close to Route 80, about an hour's drive to his New York City office, a two-mile drive to the private airstrip he utilized whenever he had to jet to Washington, DC.

But she didn't want to think about any of that right now. She didn't want to think at all. The day's burdens settled on her shoulders, making her weary and tired. Making love had taken the last scrap of emotions she had left. She closed her eyes. She wouldn't think about her father or why he'd uttered John's name.

❦

Sometime later, unaware of time passing, Becca opened her eyes. A blanket covered her. Romy lay a few inches from her face. The fire had long gone out, and the condo was dark. She guessed it was well past midnight. Matt was no longer curled up behind her. She lifted her head; her neck was stiff. She rubbed her left shoulder where it ached from lying on the floor.

She was about to call for Matt, wondering why he hadn't woken her to go to bed. The floor was no place to spend an entire night, not when there was a king-size bed in the next room. But before she had the chance to call his name, she heard his voice, a murmuring coming from his office.

She peeled herself off the floor, wrapped the blanket around her. The night was chilly, and the heat had kicked on. The door to his office was ajar. She peeked inside. His back was to her. He wasn't wearing any clothes, and his backside was lit by the moonlight that bled through the cracks of the blinds.

"Of course I want to see you again. As soon as I can get away. It's just not safe for me to talk right now." His voice was smooth, seductive.

Becca shouldn't have been eavesdropping, but she couldn't turn away. She stayed tucked outside the door in the shadows, straining to hear every word, invading his privacy the way she had with her father a long time ago. She picked up on something in Matt's tone, the way he softened his demeanor whenever he was talking on the phone with a woman.

Becca had noticed a subtle deepening in her own father's voice, the purring in his throat, by the time she was a teenager. She'd been standing in the kitchen doorway, and like Matt's, her father's back had been turned. His voice had been slick and velvety. Even though she hadn't been able to make out everything he'd said, she'd heard enough. She'd run from the kitchen and locked herself in the bathroom, refusing to come out. Hours later when her mother had come home, she'd found Becca standing in front of the mirror, scissors in hand, the sink full of Becca's long hair.

"What have you done?" her mother had asked. "If you wanted short hair, I could've made an appointment for you."

Matt whispered something. She craned her neck but couldn't make out what he'd said. Romy pushed past her, knocking the door wide open. Matt spun around, caught Becca standing in the doorway.

"I'll call you back," he said and hung up. Romy nudged his hand with her nose.

Becca pulled the blanket up around her neck.

He looked angry. Or was he scared? There were too many shadows across his face; it was hard to tell.

"Who was on the phone?" Her breathing was short and quick. She recognized the feeling, the hurt and confusion, the shame, familiar and yet alien at the same time.

"No one. It's not important."

"Who was on the phone?" Her voice pitched higher. The blood rushed to her head.

"It was work," he said and looked around. He was still naked, and maybe he was feeling vulnerable, because he cupped his private parts as though he was worried she was going to kick him. The thought crossed her mind.

"You're lying." This wasn't part of their routine, the way they'd sidestepped around the truth. This was something different. This was blatant. In her face. She hadn't felt such a sense of betrayal so severely, cutting through her insides like the blade of a knife, since she was a child. Or was she projecting her suspicions and anger onto Matt, when what she was really feeling was leftover childhood anger at her father?

"Babe, it's not what you think." He shook his head. "You've been dealt a blow today, and you're not thinking clearly." He took a step toward her, keeping one hand safely between his legs.

She backed up. Maybe he was right. Maybe she was confused.

"I promise you—it was nothing. Really." He stepped toward her again, and this time she didn't back away. He wrapped his arms around her. The heat from his body enveloped her. The lingering scent of sweat clung to his skin. She pinched her eyes closed.

As much as she wanted to trust what he was telling her, and as much as she wanted to believe she was overreacting, she couldn't ignore her body's reaction, the one screaming for her to flee. She froze in his arms. Her mouth went dry, the voice inside her head saying over and over again, *He was lying; he was lying; he was lying.*

CHAPTER SEVEN

Ten-year-old Becca was standing in the hallway outside of her parents' bedroom. Tears streamed down her cheeks, although she was careful not to make a sound. She was as quiet as a field mouse, watching her mother lift the sheets to her nose.

Her mother pulled the down comforter in one fell swoop. She tugged and lifted the puffy spread until it was a heaping ball in her arms. Then she flung it across the room, and it knocked the lamp off the nightstand, sending it crashing to the floor. She grabbed the sheets from the mattress, yanked hard enough to rip the corner of the fitted sheet right off. She continued pulling at the sheets, ripping and waving them in a frenzy.

She stripped the pillows of their pillowcases, dropped them on top of the shredded sheets. Her chest rose and lowered with each breath. Her nostrils flared. But instead of continuing trashing the room, she dropped onto the bare mattress and covered her face.

Becca stepped around the pile of torn sheets and sat on the edge of the mattress next to her. She put her hand on her mother's thigh. Her jeans were soft and worn.

She covered Becca's hand and squeezed it so tightly it hurt, her shame pouring from her grip, sharing her pain. Becca accepted it, welcomed it even, knowing it could be days until she'd feel her mother's touch against her skin. Becca was young, but she understood that her father was tearing her mother apart from the inside out.

"How can I show my face around town?" Her mother got up, cried, locked herself in the bathroom, refused to come out.

Becca sat quietly, patiently, listening to her mother weep. Minutes turned to hours. Her neck was stiff, her back sore from hunching over. Her stomach growled. But still, she wouldn't move. She'd wait for her mother's tears to dry no matter how long it took.

Eventually, her mother emerged, took a deep breath, and picked up the torn sheets from the floor. Her eyes were red, sunken, defeated.

Becca helped her clean up the mess she'd made. When they'd finished, her mother picked up the phone, called a friend, turned her back on Becca when she started crying again. Becca carried the ceramic shards from the broken lamp out of the room, put them in the trash can in the kitchen. Her mother would spend the rest of the day on the phone and part of the night too. The pattern would repeat for days, the calls to friends, the crying, turning her back on Becca whenever she entered the room.

❦

Becca tossed the suitcase into the back of the Jeep. Romy jumped around Becca's legs, excited about a car ride in the middle of the night. Or maybe the dog was just reacting to Becca's charged emotions. Romy barked.

"Where are you going?" Matt asked. He had slipped on a pair of shorts and a shirt and followed her outside.

"To my dad's," Becca said. She needed to get away from Matt and think. She'd learned from working with animals to listen to her instincts. And she'd been ignoring her instincts where Matt was concerned for far too long.

"Please don't leave like this," he said. "It's not what you think."

"And what am I thinking, Matt?" She opened the driver's-side door. Romy jumped in and climbed over to the passenger's seat.

"I really don't know." He tried to look innocent, his hands turned up in a placating gesture.

"Oh, I think you do," she said and slipped behind the wheel. Her hands were shaking. She looked over her shoulder and backed out of the driveway. She pulled onto the road and drove away.

For the second time in the last twenty-four hours, Becca drove across the bridge to the Pennsylvania side. She wound her way up River Road toward home. Her stomach skipped and lurched. Her thoughts scattered. The knot inside her chest felt like something close to dread.

She cut the lights on the Jeep as she pulled into the driveway, not wanting to disturb her father or Jackie at such a late hour. She remembered how the headlights on her father's patrol car used to cut across her bedroom walls when he had returned home after one of his late-night shifts. The lights would wake her up, or maybe she'd been awake all along, waiting for him. He'd sit on the edge of her bed, smooth her hair from her face before planting a big raspberry on her forehead. She'd giggle and pull the book out that she'd been hiding under the covers, waiting for him to come home and read to her. *Old Yeller* and *The Call of the Wild* had been two of her favorites, and she'd never gotten tired of listening to his voice as he read.

She clung to this happy memory as she climbed out of the Jeep. So many of her thoughts about her childhood and then later her teen-age years had become twisted and distorted, she had to force herself to remember it wasn't all bad. There had been a time when she'd believed her family had been a happy one.

Romy relieved herself in the yard while Becca pulled the suitcase from the back of the Jeep. Loud, thundering engines cut across the night air. She turned to the sound. *Motorcycles.* The Scions. Eight or nine of them rumbling down the road. When they reached Becca's father's house, they rode single file, then made a circle like you'd see in a parade. Round and round they went, marking their turf with noise, having swapped engine-muting exhaust systems for straight pipes.

Becca tried to see their faces, whether John was among them. They were yelling as though they were celebrating, perhaps rubbing something in Becca's father's face. It wouldn't be like John to do something like that, or at least not the John she used to know.

When they were gone, she patted Romy on the head. "It's okay," she said. "You get used to it."

She walked around to the side of the garage, used her old key, and entered through the back door. She put her suitcase down, stepped into the dark kitchen. Romy sniffed around a chair. She turned on the small light over the stove, jumped at the sight of Jackie sitting at the table. "You scared me," she said.

"Sorry." Jackie raised a glass to her lips. A bottle of scotch sat on the table in front of her.

"Is everything okay?" Becca asked, worried about why Jackie would be sitting alone in the dark, drinking.

"We had a rough couple of hours. He's resting now." She motioned to the bottle. "I needed to take the edge off."

"Did you hear the bikes out front?" Becca asked and grabbed a glass from the cabinet and sat across from her.

"When don't we hear them?" Jackie said.

Becca poured herself an inch of scotch. "You don't seem surprised I'm here," she said.

"You strike me as though you're the kind of person who always does the right thing." Jackie downed her drink. She set the glass on the table, filled it up again.

Becca was taken aback. It was strange to hear what someone thought of her, even if it was good. To hear it from her father's lady friend was even stranger, especially since she barely knew the woman in front of her. She hadn't given much thought to Jackie or to the kind of person Jackie might be. She'd seen her as another woman on her father's long list of women.

Besides, Becca was loyal to her mother, and it had never occurred to her to be friends with Jackie. She couldn't bring herself to care about her, even if she was taking care of Becca's father. Becca's mother felt differently, though. Her mother had been in contact with Jackie on a regular basis in the last two years. Her mother was a better person than Becca.

"I try to do the right thing." Becca couldn't say what was really on her mind. She hadn't planned on being here. She was here because she had nowhere else to go.

"It means a lot to him." Jackie tossed back another shot. "But don't expect him to tell you that."

"I won't," she said and threw back her own shot of scotch, the whiskey burning her throat and esophagus as it went down, the heat settling in her stomach like acid.

Jackie tilted the bottle in Becca's direction.

Becca held up her hand. "I'm good."

Jackie twisted the cap back on and stood. "I'm really glad you're here. But if you don't mind, I'm going to get a little sleep while I can." She tightened the terry cloth robe around her waist and walked away on unsteady legs.

Becca put the bottle on the countertop and the glasses in the sink. She picked up her suitcase. "Let's go to bed," she said to Romy, who eagerly followed her upstairs.

Her childhood bedroom was the same as she remembered—green walls, plaid comforter, white lace curtains her mother had hung when Becca was fourteen. The room smelled clean. She wiped her finger across the top of the dresser. No dust. Jackie must've anticipated her coming and cleaned the room ahead of time. She was irritated by Jackie's assumptions about her, mostly because they were true.

Romy curled up at the bottom of the bed. Becca pulled the covers to her chin and stared at the dark ceiling. It was strange lying in the bed she'd slept in as a child, comforting and upsetting at the same time. The only reason for a grown woman to return home was if she had failed in some aspect in her life. Or if her father was dying. Or both.

She rolled to her side. She could just make out the poster of Green Day on the wall. Her cell phone went off. She reached for it on the nightstand. Matt had sent her three texts. He was worried. Please text me. Let me know you made it to your dad's safely. Please tell me you're okay. She shouldn't reply. Let him worry the way she'd worried, staying up the night before, pacing their condo, wearing the carpet with fret.

She rolled onto her back, cell phone in hand, and typed, I'm fine. She was the better person. She was the sort of person who did the right thing.

But not always.

CHAPTER EIGHT

John felt a warm body next to him in bed. He rolled to his side, scooped Beth into his arms. *Beth*. He buried his nose in her hair, searching for her scent, but instead he smelled cigarette smoke and what he thought might be some kind of cheap perfume or bad hair spray. His brain was slow waking up, and the night before was fuzzy, but he knew something wasn't right. For one, Beth's smell was all wrong. Beth's hair smelled sweet like some kind of fruit, strawberries or kiwi, something natural rather than something cheap from a bottle. And the body tucked against his didn't *feel* right. This body had bony hips and protruding ribs where Beth was a full-figured woman with soft padding on all her curves.

He flipped onto his back, covered his eyes with his arm, the memory of last night seeping slowly into place one painful minute at a time. He'd gone to Sweeney's with Hap for a drink, and then the guys had surprised John with a stripper. He must've had more to drink than he'd realized and brought the damn girl home with him. He glanced at the back of her head, her bleached-blonde hair. Something downstairs fell onto the floor. Someone moaned. It was coming back to him, the guys riding their bikes here with the girls, how he'd driven straight home but the guys had stopped briefly, riding circles in front of Clint's house, a stupid stunt.

More rustling came from the rooms below.

"Wake up," he said to the blonde and nudged her shoulder, wanting her out of his bed, his marital bed that he'd shared with Beth until now.

"Come on." He nudged her again. She swatted his hand away.

He sat up. His head pounded, and the room was out of focus. It took his eyes a second to adjust. When he thought he could stand without falling over, he swung his legs to the floor, pulled on the pair of jeans that was lying by his feet. He looked back at the girl in the bed. There were bruises on her arms and one the size of a fist on her thigh. Jesus, had he done that? He didn't think he had, but hell if he could remember.

He tapped her arm. "You have to go." She was young, maybe early twenties. Too young. "Now," he said, sliding his hands under her arms and sitting her upright.

"What the fuck is your problem?" she growled. Her eyes were blackened with smeared makeup. Glitter glistened on her neck and shoulders. Hell, the glitter was all over the bed. He looked down. His chest hair sparkled.

He didn't allow his eyes to roam her body or the bed after that. Instead, he searched for her clothes on the floor, a little skirt and some kind of tiny shirt. "Here, get dressed." He wanted her out of his bed, out of his room, and out of his house. It had been a mistake. He hadn't meant to bring her here or do what he'd done. An image of her scrawny body wrapped around his cut across his mind. He pushed it away.

He kept his back to her. When she'd finished getting dressed, he escorted her downstairs. Bodies littered the couch and floor. Ashtrays and bottles cluttered the coffee table. The whole place smelled like whiskey, sweat, and cigarettes. The two spare bedrooms contained more of the same.

"Here." He put a couple hundred bucks in the girl's hand. She took the money and, without saying a word, shoved it into the pocket of her skirt.

"Well, uh, thanks," he said and pointed to the door.

"Do you expect me to walk home?" she asked.

Shit.

The toilet flushed. Chitter emerged from the downstairs bathroom. He looked like John felt. His face, pasty and damp, didn't look human. His dark curls were matted and stuck to the one side of his head. His left eye drooped.

"Hey, darlin'," Chitter said, then turned to John. "You got any coffee?" He sat in the only empty chair in the living room and turned on the TV.

The girl sat at the kitchen table while John put a pot of coffee on. He swallowed two aspirin and chased it with a large glass of water. He refilled the glass from the faucet and set it along with the bottle of aspirin on the table in front of her.

"Thanks," she mumbled.

He stared at her.

"What?"

He pointed to her arm and the black-and-blue marks. "Did I do that?"

She covered them up with her hand. "No," she said. "You didn't. But don't you be asking me who did. You hear? Mind your own goddamned business."

John tossed up a hand, a signal he wouldn't ask her any more questions, but the notion some punk had struck her enraged him, and a familiar protective instinct flared inside his chest.

"Hey, John," Chitter called from the living room. "You might want to get in here."

The rest of the guys were rousing, and some of their girls too. Clothes were sorted, and everyone dressed. They surrounded the TV when the local news came back on, the volume on as high as anyone could stand it. Yellow crime scene tape marked off the area behind the reporter. She was talking about a body that had been found next to one of the cement columns under the pedestrian bridge.

"That didn't take long," Chitter said and glanced in John's direction.

"Shut up," John said. Chitter should've known better than to say anything in front of the girls, even if it was just some stupid innocuous remark. Business was never discussed in the presence of non–club members.

The reporter shoved her microphone in the face of an elderly man whom John recognized from town. The man's name was Paul. He owned the antique store along Route 611 and what was also Delaware Drive. John had gone into the store once or twice with Beth and not since.

Paul told the reporter he'd been out with his grandson on the river fishing when they had spotted the body. The camera zoomed in on the grandson's face, but the boy hid behind Paul's leg. Paul rubbed his grandson's back, comforting him as the camera lens swung back to the reporter.

The front door flew open, and Hap stepped inside. "Jesus Christ, it stinks in here."

Some of the guys looked over their shoulders at Hap, then turned back to the news.

Hap looked at the TV, then at John. "Get these girls out of here," he said to the other members. "Now."

Chitter and some of the guys grumbled, but they did what they were told. They collected the girls, including the one John had found in his bed, and escorted them out of the house. Hap was the oldest member of the club and the one most respected. No one questioned Hap's orders.

In the next few minutes, their motorcycles fired up, making it impossible to hear the TV. But once the guys had gone, John found the silence was worse.

"I'll send over a couple of prospects to clean this place up," Hap said and poured a cup of coffee. He handed it to John.

John took it. He felt numb on the inside, void of any emotion as he stared at the TV and the pretty news reporter who was trying to get one of the police officers to answer her questions.

"No comment," the officer said.

The station was about to cut away to another segment when there was a commotion coming from behind the yellow tape.

An officer yelled, "Hey, Parker. You're going to want to see this."

CHAPTER NINE

Detective Parker Reed squatted next to the body. His stomach turned. He was sure the color had drained from his face. "What exactly are we looking at?"

"A field dressing," Nathan said. He moved a flap of skin with his gloved hand. "Gutted like an animal. And see this." He pointed to an area on the skin in the upper chest. "That's from a bullet." He turned toward Parker. "Do we know where this happened?"

"No." Parker's mouth was slick with warm saliva.

"Well, you might want to start by looking for this guy's intestines, his heart, liver."

"Right." Parker stood, covering his mouth with the back of his hand.

Nathan smiled, shaking his head.

Parker had seen other dead bodies on the job from gunshot wounds, car wrecks, and drownings. And once he'd seen the body of a burn victim. But this was his first case as lead detective, and he'd never seen one carved up like an animal, dumped into the river like a piece of trash.

He swallowed hard. "How long was this one in the water?" he asked.

"Not that long. I'm guessing less than twenty-four hours," Nathan said, looking back at the body, puzzling out the injuries.

Parker hesitated, collected himself, pulled it together, before he headed up the bank and ducked under the crime scene tape. The local news van was parked near the bridge. A small crowd had gathered. The reporter was interviewing Paul and his grandson live on camera. She caught Parker's eye.

"No comment," he said, deflecting her. He continued walking. The reporter returned her attention to Paul, never missing a beat.

Parker stopped next to his unmarked cruiser where Bill was standing, scratching his head. Bill had been sent from headquarters to assist Parker until they found him a permanent partner. Parker worked out of the field station. Headquarters was located in Bethlehem, a forty-minute drive away.

"What do you have for me?" Parker asked Bill.

"I talked to a few people, but no one knows anything. No one's come forward about a missing person," Bill said.

"Let's check with the Jersey police too. Maybe someone reported a missing person on their side." It had been less than twenty-four hours, and the chance of a missing person report having been filed was a long shot, but they had to start somewhere. The sooner they identified the victim, the closer they'd come to finding out who had done this.

"It's like that other one," Bill said, keeping his voice down. "That other body they pulled from the river back when we were just a couple of kids."

Parker didn't say anything, but that was exactly what he was thinking.

CHAPTER TEN

Becca called the clinic that morning from her old bedroom, her hair damp from a shower. She explained the sudden family emergency.

"Take care of Maggie, and call me if anything changes," she said. "I'm just over the bridge. I can be there in fifteen minutes."

"Okay, but don't worry. Mags will be fine," Vicky reassured her.

"And call me with any questions or if there's a surgery one of the others isn't comfortable doing."

Vicky was silent.

"Vick?"

"I will. I promise."

"Okay, I know," she said.

"I'm really sorry about your dad," Vicky said. "Why didn't you ever say anything about it before?"

"My dad and I aren't exactly close. We kind of lost touch in the last few years."

"A falling out?"

"Something like that."

"Well, you're there now," Vicky said. "Maybe you could look at it as an opportunity."

"I don't know. Maybe some things are better left alone." It was what her mother might've said at one time had she been asked the same question. It used to be her mother's way, to keep the peace and not upset the balance of things, but was it Becca's way? She thought it was. Besides, she didn't want to have the conversation she was too afraid to have with him. She didn't want to hear the answers to the questions she couldn't bring herself to ask him.

Becca hung up the phone. She rubbed her forehead. Last night when she'd blurted out that she was going home, it wasn't something she'd thought through. And now that she was here, she felt trapped, a sink-or-swim situation.

Romy nudged her hand with her wet nose. "Do you want to go for a walk?" She scratched behind the dog's ear.

Becca opened the bedroom door, and the dog raced out of the room.

"Becca," Jackie called. "Is that you?"

She dropped her head, resigned to answer. She took a moment before replying, "Hey," and peeked into her father's bedroom. Jackie was sitting on the bed with him, her arm around his thin shoulders. They were watching the news.

"Come in," Jackie said. She was wearing another small shirt, the V-neck pulled tight across her chest. She leaned over to whisper into Becca's father's ear. "She decided to stay," she said and squeezed his shoulder.

Becca averted her eyes, uncomfortable with their closeness, their touching each other, although it wasn't the first time she'd seen him cozy with another woman who wasn't her mother. She suddenly wished she hadn't come home at all. But she crossed the room to where he lay in bed with his lady friend. "How are you feeling?" she asked.

He cleared his throat as a way of answering. Jackie motioned for her to sit in the chair next to him. His once-large hand was a fist of bulging knuckles and veins. He held his wrist at a bent angle. The stroke had twisted his joints into arthritic formations. He stared at the small television.

A headline flashed on the screen: *Breaking News*. A local reporter Becca didn't recognize was standing next to Paul, the owner of the antique store Becca used to explore with her mother when she'd been a kid. The reporter asked Paul questions. A small boy clung to Paul's leg.

Jackie turned the volume up.

"We saw the body down there." Paul pointed toward the riverbank where the yellow crime scene tape had blocked off the area. "He was caught against one of the cement columns, facedown. I could tell by the way he was laying there in the water, you know, it wasn't a rescue we needed to be concerned about. I mean I knew he wasn't . . ." He looked away from the camera.

"You're saying you could tell the man was already dead from where you were standing on the riverbank?"

"Yes, ma'am. There was no question in my mind." He rubbed his eyes with the back of his hand. "Now I told you everything I know. I've got nothing more to say." He backed away from the camera, looking over his shoulder, taking his grandson with him.

The dread Becca had felt the night before when she'd crossed the bridge to home swarmed her chest. She remembered seeing something herself in the river yesterday. Her father reached toward the TV, pointing with his crooked finger. He started shaking.

"Dad, what is it?"

Jackie was on her feet. "Is it the pain?"

He clutched the sheet in his fist, the crease between his eyebrows deepening into the angry face Becca remembered from when she'd been a teenager, the same face he'd made on the occasion she'd come home after curfew. But it hadn't been anger emanating from his coiled muscles that had frightened her. His wrath had never been more than a lot of hollering and the threat of punishment. Her father had done a lot of things, but he'd never hit her.

So no, it wasn't seeing her father angry that she found so unnerving. It was the thread of fear she saw behind his eyes.

"Okay," Jackie said and held up a needle, the morphine squirting from the syringe and into the air. She stuck his arm, but not before taking a moment to glance at Becca.

Once they had him calm again, Jackie said, "That came on sudden. It usually doesn't happen like that so quickly." She smoothed her frizzy hair away from her face.

"What's that smell?" Becca asked.

"Oh." Jackie rubbed her forehead. "I think he went to the bathroom."

"What do you mean he went to the bathroom?" Becca looked at him. He was staring at the wall, humiliation all over his face.

"All right," Jackie said and pulled the covers down. "You can help me change him."

"I don't think I can," she said, embarrassed for him, for herself.

Jackie glared at her. "Yes, you can," she said. "It will go much quicker with two of us."

"But I've never done this before."

"It's easy."

She didn't want to, but she said, "Okay," and released a slow breath. "Tell me what you want me to do."

Her father kept his eyes cast on the wall. He wouldn't look at either one of them, and Becca had to admit she couldn't look at him either. For him to be reduced to this, to this state. She stared at a spot on the bed, forcing herself not to look at the parts of his body a daughter shouldn't see, but she couldn't help but see, loathing herself the second she did. She wanted to run out of the room. God, the smell was awful. *Oh, Dad.*

Jackie was quick, changing the soiled diaper and replacing it with a clean one while Becca helped raise his bottom. When they'd finished and the blankets had been pulled back up to his chest, Jackie picked up the remote to turn off the television as the news came back on.

"Wait," Becca said, touching Jackie's arm, stopping her from hitting the button.

Becca recognized the man behind the reporter and standing next to an unmarked cruiser. It was Parker.

CHAPTER ELEVEN

Sixteen-year-old Becca sprawled out on a flat rock by the river. She was wearing shorts and a bikini top. The hot sun kissed the exposed areas of her skin. A small pool of sweat collected in her belly button. Every now and again she dipped her toes into the cool water for a little relief from the heat, then kicked her feet in an attempt to get Parker's attention.

"Don't splash," Parker said. "You'll scare the fish." He cast his line upstream, letting the current carry the lure downstream in hopes of hooking a shad. The shad were making their way upriver to spawn, according to Portland's local fishing association.

"I'm not splashing," Becca said. She extended her legs, letting her feet dangle over the side, careful not to spray the water as it dashed by. School would be letting out in another three weeks. Their junior year was almost over, and the long, lazy days of summer stretched before them.

She dipped her feet farther into the water, the current carrying her legs in its hurry to pass by. Parker hadn't caught a single shad in the last two hours, and she was getting hot from sitting in the sun waiting.

"Pick up your pole and help a guy out," he said.

"Fine." She sat up, grabbed her fishing pole. "But if you catch something the second I cast my line, I'm pushing you in."

Parker couldn't seem to catch a fish unless they were competing. He thrived on the thrill of the catch, but he lived to one-up her. Whether it was a race to see who could make it to his pickup truck first or who could eat an entire hot dog in the least amount of bites, he challenged her on everything. Sometimes she wondered what the heck he had to prove. They'd been friends all through high school.

She tied a lure she borrowed from his tackle box to her line. It was white with a red head, the same lure Parker had on his line. If they were going to see who could catch a fish first, she wanted to make sure the competition was fair and that there wouldn't be any debate later on about which kind of lure they each had used.

She glanced at him as he slowly reeled in his line, looking at him in that new way that seemed to have happened overnight. Heat pricked her neck, cheeks, remembering the way he'd covered her hand on the gear shift on the drive over. He'd been teaching her how to drive stick. His skin had been warm and dry. And then he'd left his hand on top of hers. He'd never held her hand before. She'd lost focus, taken her foot off the gas. The truck had slowed; the engine had groaned.

"Easy," he'd said, explaining how to downshift.

They'd bucked forward, then stalled.

He'd removed his hand, and she'd instantly missed the warmth of his touch. She'd turned her face toward him, felt his breath on her lips. She'd closed her eyes, leaned forward, expecting him to kiss her. This was it, the moment she'd been waiting for, when he would see her as more than a friend.

He'd pulled away suddenly. "Let's get to the river," he'd said and grabbed the stick shift.

She'd kept her eyes on the road after that and couldn't look at him. She'd been confused, her emotions mixed up and conflicting. Why didn't he want to kiss her? All she'd thought about the last few weeks was what it would be like to press her lips against his, taste what it was like to be the girl who had finally captured his attention.

She watched him now. He was shirtless, his skin tan and smooth. The muscles in his back and arms flexed each time he cast and pulled. There was a soft patch of dark hair below his belly button. His abdominals were ridiculously toned.

"What?" he asked, catching her staring.

"Nothing," she said and cast a little way downriver from where he was standing. It was a poor cast. She reeled the line in to try again.

Parker stepped on a rock farther out in the river where the water crashed and sprayed. She wished he wouldn't go out so far where the current twisted and churned. He didn't seem concerned. She couldn't recall anything that had ever frightened him—not Dead Man's Curve, the fastest stretch of rapids, where people had been known to get crushed against the rocks and where he kayaked several times a year; nor had he been afraid of sitting on the rail of the pedestrian bridge, the site where jumpers had lost their lives and where he'd dangled his legs over the side of the forty-foot drop.

"Look, no hands." He'd waved his arms around, tipping closer and closer over the edge.

"Stop," she'd yelled and grabbed the back of his shirt, pulling him onto the bridge. "Don't joke around like that." He'd frightened her to near tears. "You could have fallen." She'd punched him in the arm. "You could have." She'd pointed to the sign: JUMPING FROM THIS BRIDGE CAN BE FATAL AND TRAGIC.

"But I didn't," he'd said. "Race you." He'd taken off running over the bridge to the Pennsylvania side. She'd shot after him.

Thirty minutes into their little fishing competition and neither one had a bite, although Becca wasn't paying much attention to her line, keeping her eyes on Parker and the rapids, gripping her pole so tightly that her hands hurt. Finally, he made his way back to the water's edge, mumbling under his breath the entire way.

"What did you say?" she asked, relaxing now that he stood next to her.

"Nothing. I wasn't talking to you."

She looked around. "Then who were you talking to?"

"The river."

She gave him a funny look.

"What? Don't tell me you've never talked to her before?"

"Her?"

He shrugged. "The river. I talk to her all the time."

"What do you tell her? The river, I mean."

"Stuff I can't say to anyone else."

"Like what?" Becca wondered what it was he could tell the river but he couldn't say to her.

"I don't know. Just stuff. She's a pretty good listener." He continued. "Right now, I told her I wish I could figure out where she's hiding the shad."

"Oh." Becca looked down, away. She'd been hoping he was talking to the river about her, how he thought he was falling in love with her. A stupid, teenage-girl wish. "Does she ever answer you?" she asked.

"She's good at keeping secrets. But sometimes if you listen real close, she'll whisper what she thinks you need to know."

"Yeah, okay," Becca said, shaking her head.

"You don't believe me? It's true. I don't know all the science behind it, but some people are convinced that water has a certain kind of intelligence."

"Come on."

"I'm serious. Some say she's a reflection of our souls and that she thinks and feels just like us."

"Do you really believe that?"

"I do."

After their exchange, they continued fishing in silence. Several more minutes passed without a hit. Parker put his pole down. He stared at the water, his hands on his hips.

"You know, if you miss the shad's line by a few inches, you're not going to catch them," Becca said, offering a realistic explanation. Shad swam in single files rather than in big groups. If you were in the wrong spot, it was all too easy to go home empty-handed. Parker liked the challenge, but it also had the potential to put him in a bad mood.

"That's not it. But I think I know what the problem is." He pointed to the river. "I think she's picking up on your sour mood, and that's why we're not catching anything."

Her sour mood? She didn't argue. Maybe he was right. Maybe she was in a bad mood. Lately she didn't know what was wrong with her. Her emotions swung one way and then another and then back again. She laid her pole next to his. While he fiddled with the tackle box, she scooped a handful of water and watched it run through her fingers and down her arms. She thought about what he'd said about the river, how the water had a kind of intelligence, kept secrets, was a reflection of their souls. Maybe it wasn't all that crazy of an idea talking to her, saying the things Becca felt in her heart, things she didn't know how to say to the people who hurt her.

She checked Parker's back was turned. She wasn't sure what made her do it, but she put her face close to the rushing water, whispered the one secret she'd kept hidden, the truth she'd kept tucked inside: "I think I'm falling in love with him."

When she looked up, Parker was staring at her.

They carried their fishing gear along the path, avoiding the poison ivy growing on either side of the trail. They walked up a hill, wound their way through the woods, and came to the clearing where his truck was parked. A warm breeze blew. They stashed their fishing poles and tackle box in the bed.

"Now what?" Parker asked. "Do you want to head over to the diner?"

They walked the two blocks to town. The diner on Delaware Drive was the closest restaurant around. Most of Parker's and Becca's classmates hung out at the counter and back booths after pep rallies or sports games to grab milkshakes and root beer floats. Families celebrated birthdays there, and couples toasted anniversaries. Truckers who traveled on Route 611 stopped for home-style meals served with a healthy dose of fat and grease.

Becca's father's police cruiser was parked out front. She looked through the window, catching him whispering into the ear of a young waitress, touching her, his hand lingering by her waist. The waitress leaned into him, smiling at whatever Becca's father had said.

Becca looked away, turning her back on the diner and her father. She was about to tell Parker to take her home, to take her home this instant, when Chad, one of Parker's buddies, pulled up next to them. Parker leaned into the passenger-side window.

"You up for a game of football? All we need is one more to make it four on four." Chad waved to Becca. "Hey, Bec."

Parker turned to her. "Want to come?"

"No, but you go. I can walk home."

"I can drive you," Parker said. "Unless you still want to get something inside."

"I'm not hungry. You go ahead with Chad. I'll walk," she said, insisting.

"Are you sure?" he asked.

"I'm sure. I'll catch you later."

Parker shrugged and hopped into Chad's pickup. Becca was left alone on the street. Sometimes she really hated living here. She couldn't go anywhere without bumping into someone she knew, without running into her father. She kicked a pebble as she walked. The hot sun burned the tops of her shoulders.

She continued walking down the block, when she heard yelling, glass breaking. It was coming from the alley near Sweeney's Bar. The hollering grew louder. People came out of the shops along the street to see what was going on. Becca followed the crowd. She stopped next to Mr. Dave, the butcher. Harley-Davidsons lined the alleyway. In front of Sweeney's Bar, two Scions circled each other like boxers in a ring. The smaller, younger-looking Scion had a gash above his brow. Blood dripped down the side of his face. The larger man threw a punch. They both were swinging; some hits landed on their faces, some missed. There was something in the big man's hand.

Becca stood, frozen, her heart like a bird's wings flapping inside her chest. She should've been frightened, and she was, but she couldn't look away. She'd never seen this side of human nature, so raw, violent.

Becca's father parted the crowd. He was hard to miss. He was tall and broad shouldered and carried his presence as though he were ten men. The two Scions stopped fighting when they saw him. The large man dropped a broken beer bottle from his hand. Blood dripped from his fingers.

"What seems to be the problem?" her father asked. His hand rested on his gun belt, his chief's hat pulled low on his forehead.

The door to the bar swung open. Russell and John stepped out. John had shaved the beard he often grew during the winter months, and he looked as though he'd had a recent haircut. He wore the leather cut that identified him as a member.

"There's no problem here," Russell said and leaned against the bar's porch railing. He lit a cigarette, took his time blowing the smoke from his lips. "Just a couple of boys working out their differences. You remember those days, don't you, Clint? Raising your fists to me, trying to be the bigger man."

There was a moment when the crowd collectively held its breath as Russell and Becca's father stared each other down. Becca could feel her father's anger toward his stepbrother as though it were a living, breathing thing.

Captain Toby Bryant came running down the alley. "What's going on, Chief?" he asked, stopped next to Clint.

"I am the bigger man," Clint said to Russell, turned away from him. "Take him to see Doc Reed," he said to Toby about the Scion with the cut above his brow. "He's going to need stitches."

The crowd dispersed then, bumping into Becca as they passed by her. Russell continued smoking his cigarette, an amused smile on his lips. John caught sight of Becca. She couldn't read his face. Becca's father grabbed hold of her arm, led her down the alley and away from the bar.

CHAPTER TWELVE

John and the full-patch members were seated around the table in the back room of Sweeney's. Hap was at the head of the table, drumming his fingers on the wood. It wasn't typical to hold church on Saturday, or even Sunday for that matter, not their kind of church anyway. Most club meetings were held on Wednesday nights. It was a club tradition. But Hap thought it was important to have a sit-down tonight. He was troubled by what he'd seen on the news, surprised the state police had come on the scene so quickly. Hap figured the local police would've handled the body, at least initially.

"It would've been better if it had washed up on the Jersey side of the river," Chitter added. "It would've taken some of the heat off us."

"You mean off me," John said. "I own this one. The club doesn't have to worry. I'm prepared to take the fall." He said what the other members needed to hear.

Hap shook his head. "We took steps to make sure you were covered."

John wanted to ask what steps, but maybe it was best he didn't know.

"The problem is"—Hap leaned forward—"the chief was tossed out at the scene. There's no way he can bury evidence if he wasn't there to collect it."

John kept still. It wouldn't serve him to show any emotion one way or the other. He'd done what he'd had to do for the club and for Beth, for Beth's goddamn niece. The young buck hadn't known what he was getting into. Was that supposed to be John's fault? Sweat dripped by his temple, but he'd be damned if he'd be caught wiping it away and allow the guys to see him nervous or scared. And he was scared. Old man Russell wasn't around to protect him. And although John loved Hap like a father, he wasn't up for the job. John could see it all over Hap's pale face, the way he touched his chest as though it hurt like hell. It wasn't Hap's heart that was the problem but more his liver, shot to hell from years of drinking.

John was struck by something Beth had told him not long after she'd gotten sick from the chemotherapy and the cancer. He'd been telling her she wasn't alone, she had him, that he'd be by her side every step of the way. She'd touched his cheek, smiled a sad smile. "It's my body, my sickness, and I'm alone with it. You can be here with me, hold my hand, wipe my brow. But I'll still be alone with it."

He'd argued with her, adamant she'd been wrong. She would never be alone, not while he was alive. But now, he finally understood what she'd meant. The club members would have his back without hesitation, but he had pulled the trigger. It was his actions that set him apart, his consequences to face. His life. The club was a beast of its own making. Every member was expected to sacrifice himself for the group as a whole. And that was exactly what he'd done when he'd killed the young buck. He'd sacrificed himself.

No matter how much he'd yearned to be a part of the club, a member who had fought to belong, a man who had prided himself with friends who had vowed to give their lives for him as he would give his life for them, in the end when it came right down to it, he was all he had. It was what Beth had been trying to tell him, to show him what it meant to be truly alone.

The realization cut through his muscles, slicing straight to his bones. He thought he might fall out of the chair and curl up on the floor and cry. Not for himself but for Beth. It tore him apart to imagine the pain she'd felt, how he'd been powerless to help her, how he hadn't been able to understand what she'd gone through, how much she had really suffered.

"John," Hap said.

"Yeah." He shifted in his seat, pulling himself out of his thoughts. His forearm sparkled with the stripper's body glitter. He'd thought he'd scrubbed most of her scent away, but the damn glitter was everywhere. The stuff would cling to his skin and hair for days. He rubbed his arm. The sight of it pissed him off, a reminder of another mistake.

"I asked when you think they're going to retaliate." Hap's stare bore through him as though he were searching for a weakness.

"The kid was skimming off the top from everybody. If we didn't get to him, someone else would have."

"Maybe we should've let them," Chitter said. He lit a cigarette. A skull tattoo with devil's horns covered his forearm. His hair was a mass of dark curls except for a bald spot by his temple where he'd been struck by the handle of a gun. He'd been left with a scar, a white, raised patch of skin where the hair no longer grew. He was lucky it hadn't been a bullet.

It had happened several years back. The club had organized a run, a party across the bridge on the Jersey side with the Crew, another chapter with whom they did business. It had been a typical event, bikes and booze, old ladies and sweeties. Chitter, being who he was and having the sixty-nine patch on his cut to prove it, had been caught with one of the Crew's old ladies. A fight had broken out, fists and brass knuckles. When they'd tired themselves out or passed out, they'd found Chitter unconscious on the ground, with a gaping head wound but alive.

"Too much booze and women, and you turn into a bunch of Neanderthals," Beth had said. She'd been holding an ice pack to

Chitter's skull. "I don't think you'll need stitches," she'd told him. John had rubbed his jaw where he'd taken a punch. "Dumb asses," she'd said and smiled at both men. John had pulled her into his arms, kissed her. It had been so long ago, but *Christ*, it felt like yesterday. Even Chitter's scar reminded him of Beth.

John shook his head. "No," he said to Chitter. "This was personal. We agreed I was the one who would handle it."

Hap continued strumming his fingers on the table. In the bar the sound of balls cracking on the pool table filled the silence. A girl's voice rose above the noise. The door to the back room flew open.

Chitter jumped to his feet. "What the hell?" he said.

Candy, Beth's niece, burst into the room, pointing her finger at first Chitter and then Hap, stopping on John. She was crying; mascara blackened her eyes and ran down her cheeks. Her lip was still swollen from where the young buck's fist had struck her mouth.

"You," she said to John. "You did this." She lunged at him, punching her small fists on his arms and chest. He didn't protect himself and let her hit him. He turned his head away. She was swinging at him with everything she had, landing blow after blow and barely making an impact. She was too thin, and there were track marks on her arms. John suspected she was using heroin or maybe cocaine. Either way, she was addicted to something, and he suspected the young buck had had something to do with that too.

Chitter grabbed her by the waist, pulled her off John. "Come on," he said. "It's time for you to go." She swung and kicked, trying to get at John, to break free from Chitter's grasp.

The men in the bar were laughing. "Ain't she a wild one," one of them said.

"Don't just stand there," Chitter said, struggling to keep a hold of her. "Someone grab her legs before she kicks me in the balls."

She was screaming obscenities, calling out names directed at John, but he didn't allow himself to fully hear everything she was saying.

"How could you? You bastard!" she hollered. Her voice carried through the bar. "Murderers! Every last one of you!"

Chitter and two other members dragged her outside before returning to the bar and meeting room. Candy raced back in, banged on the door. "Uncle John," she cried. "How *could* you?" she wailed. "I loved him. Do you hear me? Uncle John. You bastard!" she shrieked. "I loved him!"

"Get her out of here," Hap said, and Chitter motioned for one of the guys to take care of it. Candy's hollering and sobs finally stopped when she was put on a bike and driven away.

John kept his eyes on the table, his hands on the bottle of beer Chitter had put in front of him. Chitter slapped John's shoulder. "Crazy bitch," he said.

John took a long swallow, but otherwise, he didn't move. He stayed in his seat across from Hap. He'd done the right thing. He'd promised Beth he would watch over her niece. He'd done it for the club. He'd done what he'd had to do. And he would do it all over again, he decided, no matter how sick it made him feel inside.

CHAPTER THIRTEEN

"Who's Parker?" Jackie asked.

"He's an old friend," Becca said and turned toward the bed where her father gripped the blanket. His skin was drained of color; pain etched the lines on his face. She stepped forward, wanting to comfort him, then stopped. She didn't know what to do. She found herself clinging to the familiar, to the angry knots in her heart that she'd pulled tight for so many years, and yet desperately wanting to show him the compassion that was inside of her too.

She reached for his hand.

He pulled his hand from hers with more force than she thought he was capable of in his current condition. "No." He was angry suddenly. "No." His voice was scratchy but strangely strong. He flailed his arms. If Becca hadn't moved away, he might've struck her. "What do you know?" he hollered. "Why are you here?"

"Maybe I should just go." Becca pointed to the door and quickly walked out of the room. She rushed down the stairs with Romy at her side. At the bottom of the steps, she put her back against the wall. Her cell phone, which she'd stuffed into the back pocket of her jeans, buzzed. She pulled it out, read the text message from Matt. How are you? How's your dad? Can we talk? I'm sorry. I miss you.

Jackie came down the steps after her. She slowed after seeing Becca at the bottom landing, leaning against the wall. She touched Becca's arm, and it took all Becca had not to move away. She was angry at Jackie for asking her to come back here, for asking her to stay here with her father. Who the hell was she to make such a request? Why had her father summoned her home in the first place?

"It's the morphine," Jackie said. "It changes him. His personality. It causes anger and confusion, and you know how your father is. He likes to be in control. And right now he's not. He doesn't have control over anything. Not this disease or his body. Try not to take it personally."

Becca folded her arms, aware of her defensive posture. But she couldn't help it. If her father wanted her to feel guilty for not being with him sooner, for not coming when she'd first learned he was ill, he could forget it. On the surface she looked like a horrible daughter. But it wasn't that easy. It was complicated between them, or at least it was complicated for her. The child in her refused to forgive him for what he'd done. If anyone should feel guilty, it should be him for what he'd done to her mother.

"I have to answer this." She held up her phone and walked into the kitchen. Matt, the condo and its walls, her job at the clinic, all felt so far away and out of reach. She'd been gone for less than a day, but it felt so much longer. She started to type a reply to Matt, to anchor herself in her old life, and stopped. Romy pushed her warm body against Becca's leg. She bent down, buried her face in Romy's fur, having turned to animals for comfort ever since that day John had given her that scruffy old barn cat.

Jackie entered the kitchen. "Why don't you get out of here for a while and pick up a few things for me in town?" She pulled a grocery list from underneath a magnet that was stuck to the side of the refrigerator and handed it to her.

Becca took the list, thankful for the chore to get her out of the house. "Want to go for a ride?" she asked Romy. The dog jumped and pranced around her legs. She grabbed the leash and headed for the door only to stop and turn back around. "How do you do it?" she asked. "How do you stay here with him?"

Jackie gave her a sympathetic smile. "You get used to it. It becomes the new normal," she said. "Besides, believe it or not, I stay because I love him."

Becca nodded. She believed it all right. She had never met a woman who didn't love her father.

🦋

The day was cool but not unpleasant. The autumn sun shared its warmth through the Jeep's windows as Becca drove the few miles to town. She passed mostly woods and the occasional cornfields that were ready for harvest. The woods continued on her right, and the river flowed somewhere to her left. The mountains squeezed in around her, the trees with their brightly colored leaves like a blanket around her shoulders. She wound her way along the back roads. A car full of teen-agers blew by, music blaring from the speakers. Romy poked her head out the passenger-side window, tongue hanging out, curious at her new surroundings.

Becca stopped at the stop sign at the edge of town. To her right was the diner. She suddenly craved a vanilla milkshake. She wondered if Gloria was still behind the counter pouring coffee and root beer floats, talking about her youth and days gone by. Gloria had been consid-ered ancient back when Becca had been a teenager, and the thought of someone replacing Gloria behind the counter wasn't something she'd considered until now. She'd cut herself off from the people here, even the ones she'd cared about, including Parker.

She pulled into the parking space in front of the local grocery store that sold fresh produce and meat from local farms. Across the street, not far from where Becca had parked, there were several police cars along with the local news van. A few townspeople had gathered, but by the looks of it, most everyone had gone home. It was as though someone had held up a sign reading, NOTHING TO SEE HERE, FOLKS, or more likely, NOTHING YOU WANT TO GET INVOLVED IN. If the people in Portland knew how to do one thing, it was to turn their backs, to look the other way, especially if it didn't concern them, especially if it involved the Scions.

She spotted Parker. He was still standing next to the unmarked cruiser. She and Romy got out of the car, walked down the sidewalk, closer to where he was talking with a uniformed police officer. At six feet two, Parker was the second-tallest person she knew. Her father was the first. It made it easy to locate him in a crowd. She took a few more steps and stopped, unable to take her eyes off of him. He must've felt her stare, or maybe it was what she wanted to believe, because he looked her way. Romy stayed close to her side.

Parker touched the police officer's arm as if to say, *Give me a minute.* He made his way across Route 611 to where Becca was standing, waiting, fiddling with the leash in her sweaty palms.

"Hey," she said in a rush. "I can't believe it's you." She resisted the urge to throw her arms around him, sensing hesitation on his part.

"It's been a long time," he said. "Who's this?" he asked about Romy and patted the dog's head. Romy licked Parker's hand, then sniffed his scuffed, muddy shoes.

"Her name is Romy," she said. Romy was a good judge of character, and Becca was glad to see her take to Parker so easily. He continued to pet the dog in silence.

"So, it's been like, what?" She quickly calculated the years since she'd last seen him. "Twelve? Thirteen years?" He looked the same, maybe a little older around the eyes, mouth. His hair was clipped shorter than she remembered, but it still maintained the hint of unruly waves. Stubble covered much of his face. He was the same old Parker, a little rough and unkempt, but in a good way.

"At least that many," he said. His tone was cautious and not at all like how he used to talk with her. "What are you doing back in town? I hope it doesn't have anything to do with your dad. I heard about the cancer." He looked over his shoulder at the police officers milling around. The crime scene was farther down the riverbank. The news reporter was leaning against the back of the van, talking to her cameraman.

"He's not doing great, so yeah, I'm staying with him for a while at the house," she said, wanting him to know she was here and she would be, for a little while anyway.

He nodded. "I should get back."

"So you're a cop now?" she asked, pointing to the scene. She'd heard rumors off and on, tidbits of information about him online from former classmates that he'd gone to the police academy after graduating college and that he hadn't married. But she rarely checked social media sites anymore; the gossip, the photos, the sharing of people's daily lives all felt overwhelming, exhausting to keep track of.

"I'm a homicide investigator," he said. "State police."

Now that he said what he was, she was struck by how much he looked the part. She'd only ever met two detectives in her life, some twenty years ago, back when she'd been just ten years old. They'd worn the same dark suits with white shirts. She wondered if Parker had a gun strapped to his side underneath his jacket like the two men who had visited her house looking for her father.

"It was good seeing you." He gave Romy one last pat. "Tell your dad I was asking about him." He paused. "You look good," he said and turned to walk away.

"Parker. Wait," she called.

He turned back around.

"Meet me for a drink later? We can catch up?" she asked, hoping more than she should that he would say yes.

He didn't answer right away, and she became uncomfortable in his silence. *Please*, she quietly begged. She didn't know what she wanted from him, but he used to be her best friend and something more, at least to her, and it hadn't been until she'd seen him that she'd realized just how much she'd missed him.

"Sure," he said. "But I don't drink. I'll meet you at the diner for a milkshake." He glanced back at the scene. "It might be late by the time I get off work."

"I'll wait," she said and watched him walk away.

❦

Becca walked through the grocery store feeling as though time had stood still and she was back where she'd started, the girl known throughout town only as the police chief's daughter. She'd lived and breathed an identity that had been wrapped around who her father had been rather than who she was—although back then she hadn't always been sure who she was, questioning everything from her short hair, her choice of a boy for a best friend, her preference for the company of animals rather than people.

She passed the bins in aisle three where she'd shucked corn with her mother. She turned the corner and waved at Mr. Dave behind the meat counter. His apron was smeared with blood from the slab of chuck roast in front of him.

"Becca Kingsley," Mr. Dave said. He peeled the nitrile gloves off his hands. It occurred to her that what she'd seen on John's hand the other morning by the river had been a nitrile glove.

"It's good to see you," Mr. Dave said. "Say, how's your dad?"

He wore the same expression she was coming to expect from the people around here, one of pleasant surprise at her sudden return and then concern that the reason for her visit had to do with her father and the possibility he'd taken a turn for the worse. It was kind of them to care about their old police chief. It was. But some small part of her wanted to know why no one had asked what she'd been doing since she'd left. Why hadn't Parker asked?

"He's doing okay," she said, feeling bad that her reply was vague, but how was she supposed to tell him that her father was dying?

"You tell him I asked about him. And everyone in town is looking forward to seeing him again real soon."

"I will," she said, in a hurry to get away.

She picked up the items on Jackie's list—medicated swabs, aspirin, soap, deodorant, milk, and bread. She was back in the Jeep in less than ten minutes. Romy barked in gratitude. Becca put the supplies on the floor behind the seat, taking another look across the street at the area marked with yellow tape. She'd been so excited to see Parker, she'd almost forgotten about the body they'd pulled from the river.

"Hello," she called to Jackie after setting the bags on the kitchen countertop. Romy had stayed outside in the front yard with the new bone Becca had purchased at the last minute before she'd exited the grocery store.

She called another hello, and after not getting a response the second time, she slowly made her way upstairs. She was careful not to make a sound, creeping along the wooden floor, placing her feet on the less creaky boards. Every movement she made felt as though she were taking a step back in time, as though she were sixteen again, sneaking into her bedroom long after curfew.

Her father's voice carried down the hall. "No," he barked. He sounded gruff, stronger than any of the other times she'd heard him speak in the last two days. She paused, steadying herself against the wall.

"You have to calm down," Jackie said. "She doesn't understand. You need to give her a little time."

"No," he said.

Hearing his voice, the one she remembered from her childhood when he had been vigorous and full of life, made her feel young and weak and powerless, as though she were ten years old again.

She took two steps backward, inched her way back down the hall. When she reached the stairs, she raced down the steps and flew out the door that led to the garage. She passed her father's old pickup truck and his beloved John Deere riding mower. She leaned against the outside wall of the garage like she used to do as a kid, catching her breath, gazing into the backyard where the woods met the overgrown grass and weeds.

There was a time when Becca used to sit in this same spot with her old dog, Sheba, and watch her father mow. It was the only time she remembered ever seeing him relax, the lines on his face softening. He'd been at peace in the yard, comfortable in the yellow bucket seat. The motion of the ride had been soothing, the humming motor blocking the noise inside his head. He'd told her mother all of this at one time when Becca had been foolish enough to believe her parents' marriage had been a good one.

She crossed her arms. The large oak tree at the edge of the yard dropped several acorns, the sound of which forced another memory, one that was more like a slap in the face, quick and sharp. She'd been standing in this same spot when she'd noticed Russell underneath the tree. Sheba had growled, a low belly growl, her way of sending a warning.

Becca's father had been cutting grass but cut the mower when he'd spied Russell too. The two men had stared at each other. After a moment, her father had climbed out of his favorite yellow bucket seat and approached him.

Becca had been too far away to hear what they'd said, but she remembered the look on her father's face when he'd turned around. His face had been drawn and pale. It was the only time Becca had ever seen her father scared. His stride back to the mower had been shaky at best. And still, he'd climbed back into the seat and finished cutting the grass as though nothing had happened.

Becca had never asked her father what had transpired between him and Russell. Her father wasn't someone who answered other people's questions, not her mother's, and certainly not his daughter's.

❧

Two days after Becca had watched her father and Russell talking at the edge of their yard, her father walked into the kitchen holding a handgun. He laid it on the table next to her bowl of cereal. This wasn't unusual. She was used to guns around the house, lying on the countertops, in the hall closet, on the nightstand by her parents' bed. She'd never touched them. She'd never even been tempted to put one finger on the cold hard steel. Her father had explained to her at an early age the kind of power a gun wielded, how the weapon could be the difference between life and death. And hadn't she seen it for herself firsthand? She was ten years old now, but she'd never forgotten the doe he'd shot in front of her, the helpless, injured, innocent doe.

He drank a large glass of water before putting the cup in the sink. He turned around. "Follow me," he said and picked up the gun.

She lagged behind, silently begging, *Please don't shoot the groundhog; please don't shoot the groundhog; please don't shoot the groundhog.* Her father hated animals digging in his yard. She had seen the rodent the other day burrowing in his manicured lawn. She'd run after it, chasing it away for its own safety. Then she'd quickly filled in its hole. She thought she'd saved its life, but it was possible it had come back to do more damage.

She stepped outside. A target had been set up in the backyard. He looked at her. She didn't understand.

"You need to learn how to shoot."

She shook her head and crossed her arms, her armpits damp.

He ignored her. "We'll start with this." He checked the small Ruger was loaded before he held it out to her. She wouldn't take it.

"Go on," he said. "You're old enough to understand the responsibility of it."

"I don't want to."

"You have to."

"Why?"

"You need to learn how to protect yourself."

"From what?"

He didn't answer. She'd known he wouldn't. She wanted to tell him he was wrong. He was wrong about so many things. But a young girl didn't talk back to her father. At least not this young girl.

Finally, he said, "No country girl worth a spit doesn't know how to fire a gun."

He knew just what to say to get to her, to weaken her resolve. She wanted nothing more than to show him that she was worth so much more than spit.

"Take it," he said, daring her to.

She lifted the gun from his hand. It was heavy and bent her wrist. He helped her by holding her arm straight until she got used to the weight of it, the feel.

For the next two hours, Becca learned about guns, their parts, how to aim, how to shoot. It became their routine that autumn. Every Sunday morning during the months of October and November, while the rest of her classmates slept in or attended church services, Becca and her father shot targets.

She'd never again feel as close to him as she had on those Sunday mornings, standing next to him, smelling the smoke on his clothes, the soap on his skin, breathing in his father smell.

CHAPTER FOURTEEN

Parker hung his jacket on the back of his chair at the station. He'd canvassed the entire area by the river where the body had been found, walked up and down Delaware Drive, talked to business owners, locals. He'd handed out his card, hoping someone would come forward with any information about the homicide, who the victim was. They still hadn't identified the body.

It was turning out to be a long day.

He turned on his computer. Bill dropped a box onto Parker's desk.

"What's this?" Parker asked.

"The file on that first case we talked about." He rolled down his shirt sleeves, buttoned the cuffs. He reached for his sport coat.

"Where are you going?" Parker asked.

"Lieutenant Sayres requested me back at headquarters. They got a string of shootings in Easton he wants me to work."

"You're kidding."

"Afraid not." He tapped the box full of files. "Good luck," he said and left.

"Hey, Sarge," Parker called to his sergeant, whose office door was open. "When am I going to get a permanent partner?" There were supposed to be two investigators assigned to the station. As of now, Parker was it.

Sarge didn't even glance in Parker's direction, continued looking at the computer screen when he said, "I'm working on it."

"Yeah, yeah." Parker opened the box that Bill had dumped on his desk. He pulled out the top folder, the case name, River Body; the date, October 1994.

Parker had been just a kid when the body had been pulled from the river, but it wasn't something he'd ever forgotten. In a small town like Portland, everyone remembered where they'd been, what they'd been doing when the discovery had been made. It had been something the locals had talked about behind closed doors for years.

He opened up the file. After all this time, he was going to get an inside look at the case. He read the first report. The victim had been a thirty-four-year-old male. He'd had a criminal record, several arrests for armed robbery and auto theft. Died of a gunshot wound to the chest fired from a .30-06 rifle. The body had been stripped, gutted with a five-and-a-half-inch large-blade knife, then dumped in the Delaware River. He'd been discovered on the riverbank on the Pennsylvania side by a couple of kids who had been out fishing. Neither the gun nor the knife had been found. The victim's clothes had never been recovered. No witnesses had come forward. No arrest had been made.

Primary suspect: Russell Jackson, deceased.

Parker searched the box, found the photos of the victim's body. "Jesus," he said, flipping through them. They looked an awful lot like the body they'd pulled from the river today. He set the images aside, checked his phone for the time, then grabbed his jacket from the back of the chair.

"Where are you off to?" Sarge asked.

"Autopsy."

"You're late," Sandra said. She was standing at the autopsy table in her lab coat and gloves, her curly hair tucked under a cap, the victim's body laid out in front of her. She wore a mask. She could've been a surgeon, she'd told Parker once, but she'd preferred patients who couldn't complain.

"Sorry, lost track of time," he said, smearing peppermint oil on a mask, covering his nose and mouth. After a minute, the oil did nothing to block the smell.

"What's this, our second date?" Sandra asked. "And I'm already hearing excuses."

He smiled behind the mask. She was teasing him, of course. This was his second autopsy; he'd preferred to skip them on the other cases he'd worked, relying on her detailed reports. But this was his first case as lead, and he felt he should be here. "What did I miss?" he asked.

"Single gunshot wound to the chest. I found the bullet. It's in the evidence bag over there." She motioned to the tray behind her. "Is he still a John Doe?"

"Yes." Parker picked up the bag with the bullet. He'd have it sent to ballistics. "Any identifying features?"

"Barbed wire tattoo around his right bicep. Piercing above his left eyebrow. A small birthmark on his lower back."

Parker took notes. "What about the gutting?" he asked.

"Yes, that's interesting," she said. "The blade entered here." She pointed to the lower abdomen just above the genitals. "Worked its way upward." She gave a detailed analysis of how the killer had carved his victim, the organs he'd removed—heart, lungs, liver, stomach, intestines. Parker listened, his own stomach queasy.

She continued. "I'm not a hunter, but it appears to be the same technique as a field dressing."

"Any idea about what type of knife was used?" He was thinking about the original river body case.

"Well, I can tell you that it had a gut hook."

"Like a hunting knife."

"Yes. If you give me more time, I can get you the length of the blade."

The knife in the first case was a large blade but had no gut hook. So different knives then. "Okay," he said, having gotten what he needed at this point. He'd get the rest from her report. "I'll let you finish up." He couldn't get out of the room fast enough. Sandra had said he'd get used to the smell, wouldn't even notice it after he'd been on the job a few years. Parker wasn't so sure about that.

He tossed the mask into the trash on his way out the door, headed to the crime lab with the bullet, thought about the knife again. He wondered if he was looking at a copycat killer.

CHAPTER FIFTEEN

John walked out of Sweeney's feeling worse than when he'd walked in. His head pounded from the beer Chitter had given him in addition to all the alcohol he'd drunk the night before. His arms hung at his sides, and sweat leaked from his pores. He could smell himself, a mixture of alcohol, body odor, and adrenaline. After Candy had showed up at the club meeting screaming accusations, all he'd wanted to do was get on his bike, ride home, collapse in bed.

But he'd stayed seated out of respect for Hap and church. He'd waited until club business had ended. All the while his insides had churned, a swirl of stomach acid and dread.

Hap came up behind him. "I'll have one of the guys keep an eye on Candy," he said and stuck a toothpick between his teeth.

John appreciated the support even though he didn't believe Candy was a threat, not really. "She's young, but she's not stupid," he said. "She knows not to go to the police." He glanced at Hap. "Lonnie will make sure she keeps her mouth shut." Candy's mother and Beth's sister, Lonnie, was the old lady of one of the members in the Jersey chapter. She understood this was business.

Hap nodded.

John stepped off Sweeney's porch and strode to his bike, brushing his graying hair from his eyes. If he didn't get a haircut soon, he was going to have to tie it back in a ponytail. Maybe he could get one of the old ladies to cut it. He wasn't ready to see himself as a gray, long-haired biker. He was still a few years away from fifty, but damn if it didn't feel like it was closing in fast.

He slipped on the half helmet he wore. Some of the younger members preferred the full-face helmets, but John liked the feel of the wind in his face. He didn't even mind the occasional smattering of bugs in his mouth and eyes.

He started his motorcycle and headed for home. What he needed was a little time away to be alone and sort things through, to go over one more time the steps he'd taken, the precautions, making sure he hadn't left any evidence behind. But what he really needed was to come to terms with what he'd done. *And sleep.* If he had more sleep, he could think more clearly. He wondered if he'd ever have a restful night again.

He wove his way around the back roads, avoiding Route 611, Delaware Drive, and the cops, taking his time so as not to draw attention to himself. He was almost home when he passed by Clint's house and spotted a Jeep in the driveway. He slowed, catching sight of a dog lying in the overgrown grass in the front yard.

He continued downhill and made a U-turn in the middle of the street. He hadn't seen another vehicle parked outside Clint's house in over a year. He wondered if the cancer had finally taken him. He'd heard the rumors in town about Clint's illness, the diagnosis made not long after he'd retired as chief of police. The Scions kept tabs on all the cops, and the old chief was no different.

John passed Clint's house again, and this time he was certain he recognized the German shepherd in the yard. He sped up the hill, made another U-turn for a third pass. Sure enough, outside the garage not far from the dog, he saw Becca. He was so surprised at seeing her that he didn't realize he'd eased up on the throttle, almost coming to a complete stop.

She'd spotted him, of course, but what had he expected, riding past the house three times on a loud motorcycle?

Her dog lifted its head, tearing itself away from a bone. When Becca stepped toward John, he gave the bike some gas and sped away. An uneasy feeling picked its way up his spine. He didn't like that she was on this side of the river.

He didn't like it at all.

He fed the bike more juice until he was going too fast to decelerate in time to stop. He blew by his driveway, easing up on the throttle once again. He turned back around and headed toward home. An old pickup truck was parked alongside his house, the rear fenders rusted and full of holes. He grumbled, cursing under his breath.

He got off his bike and opened the side door to the kitchen. One of the club's prospects was in his living room cleaning out ashtrays and wiping down the table. John had forgotten his place had been trashed last night, littered with booze and smokes and strippers. He dropped onto the couch, legs splayed in front of him. The place had been straightened up a bit and no longer had the funky party smell. He eyed the prospect. The kid looked to be twenty, maybe younger.

"I'll get out of your way," the kid said, a nervous waver in his voice.

John cocked his head. "Are you afraid of me, Prospect?"

"A little," the kid said.

John laughed a strange, maniacal laugh and not his usual light-hearted sound. The kid looked down and all around, anything to avoid looking John in the eyes. He didn't blame the kid. After all, John was the enforcer in the club.

"That's good," he said. "A little fear is a sign of respect. It will serve you well around the other members." He rubbed his chin. "It may even save your life." He wasn't sure what he'd meant by the last part. Maybe it was simply that having a little fear about something made a person cautious, made a person think twice before taking action. But the trick, he reminded himself, was listening to that fear, the very thing he'd failed to do and pulled the trigger anyway.

The kid swallowed. "Yes, sir."

John stood and put his hand on the kid's shoulder. The boy was sturdy. He had some muscle to him. That was good too. He would need it sooner or later to defend himself or the club.

"Let yourself out when you're done. I'm going to lie down." He headed for the stairs, then turned back around. He didn't mind the kid being frightened of him, but he didn't want the kid to think he was an asshole. "And thanks for cleaning up. I appreciate you helping me out." He motioned to the kitchen and the soon-to-be-cleaned living room.

The kid smiled, his one cheek rising higher on the left side. It was the first John had noticed the right side of the kid's face sagged as though it lacked muscle tone. John shook his head. A bunch of misfits, that was what the club had turned into. Society's castoffs, juvenile delinquents, guys with strange appearances or personalities or oddities. It was what had attracted his father, a Vietnam vet who no longer fit into mainstream society, to the club. It was only by default that John had been sucked into the life. He'd never felt he'd had a choice.

His legs were heavy as he dragged himself upstairs, collapsed on top of the bed. He thought about Becca. He needed to find out the reason she was back, what she was doing here. He closed his eyes. Maybe her father had died like he'd thought earlier, but the club would've heard about it if he had. Her return couldn't be a good sign. He never should have allowed her to see him by the river. He'd made a mistake, and if there was a loose end, a weak link, she was it. But he couldn't change the fact that she'd been there. It was far too late for regrets.

The question he needed to answer now was what he was going to do about it.

CHAPTER SIXTEEN

Becca paused outside the diner and gazed at the stars. How different they looked on this side of the river—clearer, brighter, more brilliant somehow—which wasn't logical and was borderline ridiculous, but she saw what she saw. As much as she wanted to forget her life here, she couldn't forget that it had once been home. Even the air was wetter, sweeter, from the breeze coming off the water.

Across the street, she could just make out the yellow tape marking off the area where she'd first spied Parker. For a moment, Becca allowed herself to think about the body in the river. For as long as she could remember, drownings had occurred in the Delaware. There were places in the river that were deep, unpredictable. Rapids rushed and slowed only to rush again, crashing over rocks and debris. There were long stretches of winding white foam where only the highly skilled in white water rafting could manage. And yet, every year, someone less skilled, someone inexperienced in the river's undercurrents, got sucked under, never to resurface. It only took a second for a tragedy to occur.

She wasn't being melodramatic about the dangers on the river. She'd seen what it could do, how one second you could be floating in your inner tube, soaking in the warm sun, taking in the green leaves of summer, the perfect blue skies, the rapids pulling you along, and in the next second, the current was dragging you under, plunging you deep into the abyss, the inner tube continuing downriver without you.

It had happened when she'd been young, only fourteen years old, tubing with Parker and his parents. They'd been in the water for less than an hour. The river stage had been three feet, which had been considered good conditions for a recreational outing, the stage being the elevation of the water above a fixed point, not to be confused with the depth of the water since the depth varied with drop-offs, holes, shallows, and ledges.

It had been a gradual float downriver, a leisurely trip. They'd been heading around a bend. Parker and Becca had been a few tube lengths behind when his mother's inner tube had taken an unexpected turn. In a second she'd disappeared, pulled right out of the center, vanishing underwater. Parker's dad, a big, tall guy like his son, had stretched his long arm into the cycling current, grasping her hair by the fistful. With some effort, he'd yanked Parker's mom's head above the water, ripping a clump of hair from her scalp in the process.

They'd made it to the riverbank, where his mom had collapsed in the mud, her scalp bleeding where the hair had been torn out. Parker's dad had asked her questions, checked her scalp, examined her. When he'd finished, he'd dropped on the ground next to her. It had been several minutes before anyone had spoken.

"Mom," Parker had said.

"I'm okay." She had patted his arm.

Parker and Becca had stared at one another, scared and relieved at the same time. As for Parker's mom, her hair eventually grew back, but the patch where it had been yanked from her scalp was white, wiry, compared to the rest of her soft brown locks.

Tonight, Becca stood outside the diner hoping to see Parker again. A small family approached. Becca stepped to the side to let them pass along the narrow sidewalk. They continued across the street on their way to the pedestrian bridge. Another couple lingered outside the storefront window of Paul's antique shop. Most people walking the little town at night were tourists who came down off the mountain, leaving the bigger resorts farther north in the Poconos to shop in the smaller gift stores for postcards and trinkets, to buy fresh produce, or to walk the bridge. But the biggest business in town was the rental shop where people came from all over to rent kayaks, canoes, and tubes to risk a day on the river.

An older couple exited the diner. She said hello, letting them pass before entering. The place smelled like she remembered, rich with butter mixed with a sweet, syrupy scent. The floor was the same red-and-white-checkered pattern. The red vinyl seats were faded and cracked from heavy use. She slid onto a stool in front of the counter. A young girl wearing a white apron and collared shirt, her face smattered with pimples, asked Becca if she would like to see a menu.

Becca shook her head, not recognizing the waitress.

"Does Gloria still work here?" she asked.

"Oh, no." The waitress shook her head. "She died a few years ago."

Becca looked at her hands in her lap. "I'm sorry to hear that."

"Were you a friend of hers?"

"I guess I was. I used to hang out here a lot when I was a kid."

"You're from around here?"

"I used to be," Becca said, leaving out any further details. She was sure the waitress didn't want to hear how Becca had been sent away against her will, but then later by choice, how she'd fled to college never to return. Until now.

"On second thought," she said. "I will look at a menu."

The menu hadn't changed; even the tasty drinks remained the same. She ordered the vanilla milkshake for old times' sake and checked her phone. It was closing in on eight thirty. There was another text from Matt asking for her to call him. He said he wanted to talk, but he could wait until she was ready. He only wanted to know that she was okay.

She put the phone down and eyed the door. She continued the pattern for the next hour, checking the time, ignoring Matt's text, staring at the door. She sipped the milkshake on and off, tapping her foot on the stool.

She'd told Parker she would wait, but after another thirty minutes had passed, she wondered if she'd been stood up. It wouldn't be like Parker to do something like that, not the old Parker anyway. She couldn't be sure what the new Parker would do, the new Parker she'd seen today dressed in a television-show-detective suit. Everything about him being a cop bothered her suddenly. She couldn't bear to think he might've turned into her father. Maybe she was better off not knowing if he had. Maybe she was being unfair. Maybe she should get up and leave, say she'd waited as long as she could if they ever happened to cross paths again.

She turned to make her exit when the door swung open and Parker stepped inside. He strode to the counter, confident and sure, sliding onto the stool next to her.

"Hey, Pam," he said to the young waitress. "I'll have the usual."

After an awkward moment, he angled his head slightly in Becca's direction. "So," he said. "You're back."

"I'm back. For now, anyway." They'd covered this already.

Pam set a root beer float in front of him. She looked back and forth between Becca and Parker before walking away to clear a dirty table.

Becca picked up her milkshake, sipped the vanilla cream from the bottom of the glass. A long silence stretched between them. She hadn't expected him to throw his arms around her, thrilled to see her again, not after his lukewarm greeting that afternoon, but she hadn't expected things to be so uncomfortable either.

"You know," she said, "I tried searching for you online on all the usual sites, Facebook, Instagram, but I couldn't find you."

"That's because I'm not on any of them. I don't think you'll find a whole lot of guys in law enforcement on the internet unless it's job related." His words were clipped, cool. He sounded like a damn cop.

"Well, I tried to find you anyway."

He didn't say anything. Then he played with the whipped cream in his float, sucked it through the straw. He looked like the Parker she remembered, the seventeen-year-old boy who had been one of the best wide receivers their football team had ever had, who had tried out for the track team every spring for no other reason than that he'd loved to run.

"So how long have you been a detective?"

"I was promoted three months ago."

"You're kidding. Congratulations."

He smiled, and for the first time since he'd walked through the door, she started to relax. His smile said he was the same old Parker hidden somewhere inside the new one.

"Thanks," he said.

"You're a rookie." She punched his arm like she used to do.

"I'm a sucker for long hours and low pay." He looked tired. His clothes were rumpled. She'd forgotten he'd been working all day and much of the night. He looked beat.

They both turned toward their drinks and sipped the cream, shoulder to shoulder, some of the earlier tension peeling away.

"But seriously, how did you end up a detective?"

"I worked patrol for a while. It was the next logical step. I guess I thought I'd be good at it, protect and serve the community where I grew up. Give something back," he said.

His answer sounded rehearsed, generic. It was obvious there was more to it than he was saying, but he wasn't willing to share it with her. She let it go. "So what happened today?" she asked. "How did the guy drown? Tubing? Kayaking?"

"Who told you it was a drowning?" He looked her over in the new cop way he'd acquired in her absence.

"I just assumed. Are you telling me it wasn't?"

"I'm not at liberty to discuss it."

"My dad never talked about his job either."

"I'm sure he had his reasons."

"I'm sure he did." She played with the straw. Knowing cops the way she did, she knew she wasn't going to get anything more out of him. "Aren't you going to ask me what I do?" she asked.

"You're a vet," he said.

She was surprised he knew.

"I never said I didn't go on the internet."

Pam returned. "We're closing up soon," she said.

Parker reached into his pocket for his wallet.

"Let me get this," Becca said and tossed a few bills onto the counter.

Instead of getting up to leave, they stayed where they were, and Becca tried to think of something else to say. She couldn't come up with anything, and maybe Parker couldn't either, because he remained quiet. Pam appeared with a mop and bucket.

"I think that's our second cue," he said.

Becca twisted in her stool to stand, her knees bumping into his. His long legs had always taken up more space than she'd allowed for.

Parker held the door open for her. They stepped outside. She became uncomfortable again, feeling awkward standing so close to him on the narrow sidewalk. She stared at her feet. She didn't want to go home, but she couldn't think of anything else to say. She couldn't think of anywhere else to go. She was about to suggest they go for a walk, but he cut her off.

"I have an early day tomorrow," he said. "It was good seeing you." He turned toward his unmarked cruiser, calling over his shoulder, "You look good."

"You said that already."

"Then it must be true." He smiled his old Parker smile, waving as he folded his long legs into the driver's seat.

She watched his taillights head in the opposite direction, heading downriver, farther away from town. She wondered where he lived now. She should've asked him. She wanted to see him again, realized she had no idea how to contact him. And he'd never asked how to contact her, but if he wanted to, he could find her at her father's house.

But she suspected he wouldn't.

Maybe it was just as well.

Becca got in her Jeep. Before she started the engine, her cell phone vibrated. It was another text from Matt. I miss you.

She smoothed her brow, not knowing whether she missed him too. She'd been pulled in too many directions in the last two days for her to sort through her feelings, although some of her anger toward him had lost its edge. She was going to have to talk with him sooner or later, make sense of it all, but not yet. She typed a reply. We'll talk soon.

She tossed the phone aside. Funny how she finally had his full attention now, when she wasn't sure she wanted it anymore.

CHAPTER SEVENTEEN

John was sitting on the couch in front of the television. He was staring at a blank screen. He'd missed the morning news. Maybe it was for the best. Maybe it was better if he didn't know where the cops were in their investigation. Ignorance was bliss, after all. He would only drive himself crazy watching, listening for information about what the cops did or didn't know. Then again, maybe it was better if he knew. Maybe he could *fix* things before they got out of his control.

At least his head felt clearer than it had the last two days. He'd slept well, considering. His dreams had been mixed, visions of Beth, her cheeks full and sun-kissed gold, the way she'd looked before she'd gotten sick. She'd been talking to him in dreamland, her voice soothing to his ears. She'd been telling him about *her* dream, about drifting on the river, floating along the current under a clear blue sky. She'd been at peace, and this in turn had made him feel at peace. But every so often an image of a body, a man's body, had flashed behind his eyes, the man's insides hollowed out, the river carrying the corpse farther downstream.

"No!" John had screamed, unsure if he'd said the word out loud, or if he'd only hollered it inside the dream that had turned into a nightmare.

Still, he felt rested. And now that he was awake, his mind focused, he thought about Becca, seeing her at her father's house the day before.

He would have to decide how to handle her if he needed to, how her father had handled her the first time.

John remained staring at the blank screen on the television, deep inside his thoughts. He wasn't sure how long he'd been sitting there, but long enough for his joints to stiffen. He ran his hand across his forehead. There was no mistaking Becca might've seen something. But how much had she seen? How much did she know about what had happened? And how was he going to find out?

He turned his head toward the sliding glass door that led to the back porch and the view of the barn, the woods, and the mountain. He heard what sounded like dogs barking. He stood from the couch, went to look outside.

He saw movement behind the barn, flashes of orange and black. A herd of men, voices muffled, following the dogs' cries, moving as a unit between the trees and brush. He counted at least a dozen of them and who knew how many dogs.

A sinking feeling almost dropped him to the floor. This wasn't good. No, this wasn't good at all. They were search dogs, and damned if it wasn't the state police.

CHAPTER EIGHTEEN

Becca knocked on her father's door before stepping into the room carrying a tray. She set it on the nightstand. Jackie had given her instructions on what her father might eat—soup, Jell-O, pudding.

"I'll be surprised if you can get him to take even one bite," Jackie had said. "But you're welcome to try."

"He needs to eat. Otherwise, he's going to starve."

"It's not unusual for him to stop at this point."

Becca had shaken her head. "I'll get him to eat something. You should get out while you can." She'd insisted Jackie take a few hours off and get out of the house, reenter the world of the living for a while. She'd even gone as far as suggesting Jackie meet a friend or get her hair done or go for a walk in town. Becca hadn't been thrilled with the idea of being alone with her father, but it was only right for her to help out when she could. "If I'm going to be here, you might as well let me feel useful," she'd said. After much hesitation, Jackie had finally agreed.

"And his meds," Jackie had said, flustered. "I've given him a healthy dose for the pain. He shouldn't give you much trouble." She'd grabbed a notepad and written down his medication and dosage, and then they'd exchanged cell phone numbers. "Text me if anything happens, you know, if . . ."

"I will. Don't worry. He's not going anywhere while you're gone."

Jackie had surprised Becca by pulling her into a tight embrace. "Thank you," she'd said. "For coming. For being here for him." She'd pulled back to look in Becca's eyes. "And for being here for me."

Becca hadn't known what to say. Her reasons for coming home had not been as altruistic as Jackie believed.

She forced herself to look at him now. She worked hard at keeping her face neutral as she gave him a quick once-over, tried to ascertain his mood. He'd slept much of the morning and afternoon.

He was sitting up in bed. He seemed to fluctuate from good to bad to worse and back to good again. Romy lay in the hall outside the bedroom door.

"I brought you some dinner," Becca said.

He coughed the hacking cough.

"You have to eat," she said in a tone she might've used on a child. "Jackie went out for a while, so I'm going to help you."

He looked upset.

"She'll be back soon." She paused. "Give her a break. She deserves one."

She turned on the news. Then she pulled up a chair and dipped the spoon into the split pea soup, one of her father's favorites, held it to his lips. He wouldn't open his mouth.

"Come on," she coaxed.

He stared at the TV.

"Please, Dad. You have to eat, even if you don't want to."

He continued ignoring her.

"Please. If you won't do it for you, then do it for me."

She held the spoon to his mouth a second time. After a long hesitation, he opened up. He was like a little bird, stretching his lips like a beak, taking tiny slurps. She caught a drip on his bottom lip with the spoon, dabbed the corners of his mouth with a napkin. He watched her, his eyes never leaving her face. She continued to feed him through the local sports and weather, although most of the soup never made it down his throat. She wiped the green drops from his face. He pressed his cheek into her hand, his skin thin and dry. *Dad.* She yearned to tell him all the things she'd never been able to say to him, but she couldn't find the words, not the right ones or even the wrong ones.

Breaking News flashed across the screen, and the moment for her to speak up was lost. The same female reporter who had broken the story about the body that had been found in the river was once again standing near the pedestrian bridge. The police had identified the victim, released a photo. It must've been taken by a family member or friend at some kind of outdoor gathering. The guy was sitting on top of a picnic table holding a beer. He looked to be in his early twenties. His head was shaved, his left eyebrow pierced. There was a barbed wire tattoo around his right bicep. A picnic basket sat on the bench by his feet.

The woman reporter spoke in a soft, sympathetic voice. But before Becca could feel too badly for the guy or empathize with his family over their tragic loss, another photo popped onto the screen. This one was a mug shot of the victim, Judd Cafferty, who went by the nickname Caff; he was a longtime resident of the state of New Jersey. The reporter's voice became more businesslike as she dispensed the facts, how he'd been in and out of prison the last five years for mostly drug-related misdemeanors and one felony for armed robbery.

The reporter continued. It wasn't another case of accidental drowning as Becca and the townsfolk in Portland had first been led to believe, although Parker had hinted this much to her already. The victim had been shot and gutted, his body dumped in the river. The Pennsylvania State Police were asking anyone who had any information concerning the crime to contact the number at the bottom of the screen.

Becca was so engrossed in the news report that the spoon in her hand with the split pea soup was left hanging in midair. Her father grabbed her wrist with his crooked fingers, spilling the green soup onto the white sheets, knocking the spoon out of her hand. It landed with a clatter on the hardwood floor by her feet.

"I'm sorry," she said, trying to free her wrist from his strong grasp while using her other hand to pick up the spoon. "I wasn't paying attention."

He yanked on her arm.

"Ow," she said as he continued to pinch her skin with his tight grip, forcing her to look at him. There was a look of desperation in his eyes, a kind of panic in his glare. It frightened her.

"What is it, Dad?"

His grip weakened. She pulled away from him, rubbing her skin where his fingers had left red marks.

His words came out deep and slow, as though every syllable uttered was a tremendous effort. "There's something you need to know, decisions I made a long time ago."

Becca leaned back in the chair, turned her head away. She didn't want to hear a deathbed confession, if that was what this was. She didn't want to know the intimate details of her parents' marriage, his reasons why he had done what he'd done to her mother, why he'd sent Becca away. And yet a deep down part, a buried part, longed for an explanation.

"Dad," she said. But before she could continue, the phone on the nightstand rang, the one from the landline. "I'll get it." She sprang from the chair.

"Becca?" Parker asked.

She rushed from the bedroom, closing the door behind her. "Your timing couldn't be more perfect," she said as she made her way down the hall and stairs to the kitchen, Romy at her heels.

"Oh, yeah? Why is that?"

"It's my dad, but never mind. I don't want to talk about it. I'm just glad you called. I was hoping we could get together again." She was talking fast, aware of a nervousness she wasn't used to feeling, not since she'd first met Matt. But this was Parker, and right now, she needed a friend.

"Okay." He hesitated. "I'll be fishing off my dock tomorrow morning. I'm a couple miles down the river from town. It's the first cabin on the left about two miles after Dead Man's Curve."

So he lived close by. It made sense since the commute to the police station was less than thirty minutes. The entire time she'd been living in New Jersey, Parker had been just across the river. It brought a smile to her lips. She didn't see the river as separating them, but rather as the very thing that connected them.

"I'll be there," she said.

There was a long pause on the other end, as though he had something else he wanted to discuss, the real reason for his call. When he didn't say anything, she asked, "What's going on?"

"You know what? Don't worry about it. It can wait until tomorrow," he said. "See you then."

She was about to hang up when he said, "Oh, Becca. I start at five a.m."

She groaned. But she'd be there.

She let Romy outside, and then slowly she made her way back to her father's bedroom to clean up the mess she'd made with the soup. She pushed the door open. He was staring at the TV, watching some commercial about erectile dysfunction.

"Let me clean this up," she said, scrambling to wipe the dried pea soup off the sheet. When it was clear the stain wouldn't come out without a good washing, she hurried from the room and returned with a clean sheet. In a flurry of activity, she changed out the dirty sheet with the clean one, then picked up the dinner tray. "Do you want me to leave the pudding?" she asked.

He didn't respond, keeping his eyes on the screen, avoiding looking at her. She could tell he was angry with her for not listening to what he had to say earlier. Well, she was angry with him, too, for wanting to tell her things she wasn't ready to hear.

"I'll check on you later," she said and walked out of the room.

❦

Becca was ten years old, lying awake in bed, staring at the dark ceiling. It was after midnight, twelve hours since her father had left the house after the two detectives had come looking for him, twelve and a half hours since her father had snuck a woman into her parents' bedroom. She heard her father's car pull into the driveway. She wondered if her mother was awake, if her mother was waiting up for him like Becca was.

She leaned on her elbows and listened. The garage door closed. He was in the house, making his way quietly up the stairs. His boots clicked on the hardwood floor in the hallway. She lay back down but kept her eyes on the bedroom door. He paused outside her room, his silhouette visible in her doorway. She closed her eyes, hoping he would think she was asleep and go away and, at the same time, hoping he wouldn't. She didn't open her eyes again until she heard the tapping of his boots, the sound fading as he walked away.

"Hell of a night," her father said, which meant her mother was awake too. "The state police were all over my ass today. That's why I'm so late getting home."

Becca sat up, straining to hear.

Her mother didn't respond.

"You know," he said, "I always thought Russell and I were so different, that the only thing we shared was a mother. But maybe I was wrong. Maybe we're more alike than I ever wanted to believe."

"He's in a motorcycle gang. You're chief of police," her mother said. "You couldn't be more different."

"I suppose," he said. The mattress squeaked. It sounded as though her father had sat on the bed to take off his boots, get undressed. "But I did something today I thought I'd never do as chief."

"What is it, Clint?" her mother asked. "What did you do?" Becca didn't believe her mother was asking about his job or Russell or what the state police had wanted from him, but rather her mother was asking about the other woman she'd smelled in their bed.

"I can't tell you. But if there's any trouble, I mean if anything happens to me, I want you to know I did what I had to do. They left me no choice."

"What are you talking about? Who left you no choice? What could happen to you? I don't understand."

"It doesn't matter," he said. "I can't undo it. What's done is done." The new sheets rustled, clean and crisp and washed hours after her mother had yanked off the old ones in a fury.

In the next minute, her mother said, "Don't touch me."

Silence stretched. It continued to stretch far and long.

Becca's eyelids grew heavy. She struggled to keep them open. It wasn't until sometime later that she woke to the sound of her father's pleas drifting down the hall.

"I'm sorry," he said. "Please," he begged. "I promise it will never happen again."

Her mother didn't say anything, and Becca wondered if her mother believed him, or if she also knew that he was lying.

CHAPTER NINETEEN

Becca pulled her Jeep alongside Parker's cabin and cut the lights. The sun lurked behind the horizon, not yet high enough in the sky to make an appearance. The more sensible people were tucked soundly in their beds with another hour or two of luxurious sleep ahead. Even Romy was curled in a ball on the floor in Becca's room. But this was typical Parker, waking before the rest of the world, hoping to catch a big fat fish.

It was nice to know some things about him hadn't changed. She hoped she would discover that a lot more about him had stayed the same, because what little she had seen of cop Parker she didn't much like.

She stepped into the cool autumn air, followed the stone path that led to Parker's front door. The cabin itself was covered in cedar shingles. Dark-green shutters framed the windows. His place looked to be straight from a fairy tale, warm and inviting. She stepped onto a recently swept porch, the broom propped against one of the two rocking chairs. The cushion on the chair closest to the door looked worn and used. The other cushion looked brand new, as though no one had ever sat on it. It was a sign Parker didn't get much company. The thought made her sad and strangely happy. Maybe it meant he didn't have anyone special in his life, or maybe it meant he didn't invite a lot of people to visit him. He liked being alone almost as much as Becca did. And they both knew *how* to be alone, unlike most people Becca came into contact with. It was something they had in common.

Matt happened to be one of those people who preferred company. He sought out crowds, looked for reasons to be on display. He thrived on attention. She imagined it was another aspect of his personality that made him such a good litigator. She shuddered at the thought of standing in front of a courtroom and having everyone's eyes and ears on her. The idea was terrifying. She pushed it away.

She knocked on the front door. She stood there waiting for what seemed like a long time. After another minute when he didn't answer, she peeked in one of the windows, seeing only shadows of furniture in the dark. She knocked on the door again, but when there wasn't an answer a second time, she made her way around to the back.

She stepped onto the deck. Wooden stairs led down the bank to the river. At the bottom of the steps, Parker stood on a large dock. His movements were fluid and relaxed as he cast his line and slowly reeled it in. He paused as though he was listening for something. He must've sensed he was being watched, turned to catch her looking down at him. For a moment neither one of them moved. When he raised his hand and waved, she skipped down the stairs to greet him.

"Where's your pole?" He kept his eyes on the water as he cast the line a second time.

"I don't have one."

He raised an eyebrow. "There's an extra one on the deck. Help yourself."

She walked back up the stairs and found the fishing pole outside the back door, a chugger already tied to the line. It was a top water popper Parker used for catching largemouth bass. So bass it was.

Parker continued casting the line and reeling it in. Twice he had a bite but failed to hook the fish. He was using a chugger similar to the one he'd tied to the fishing line on her pole. They fished for a while in companionable silence.

The river was quiet, spreading out in front of them like a calm lake. Farther upstream the rapids crashed over the rocks at Dead Man's Curve. But Parker's cabin was far enough away from the noise and the fast-moving white water, making his home a prime piece of real estate.

Every now and again, she would catch him glancing at her out of the corner of his eye. Finally, he said, "I wasn't sure you'd come."

"Oh, come on. You know how much I used to love waking up before the sun to fish with you."

"I know how much you used to complain about it."

"But I always showed up, didn't I?"

"That you did," he said, looking at her so intensely she had to look away.

He recast the line, eyes back on the water.

"How are your folks?" she asked.

"They moved to Florida a couple of years ago. Dad loves the deep-sea fishing. Mom likes walking the beach. They're happy. I try to get down and visit whenever I can."

"Tell them I asked about them the next time you talk to them. I think about your folks sometimes and how they always included me in everything, in all your family activities."

"I'll tell them," he said.

They continued fishing, careful with one another in the conversation that followed. Parker caught her up on old classmates, how Chad worked for the local electric company and had married Krissy, his high school sweetheart. They had two kids, with another one on the way. Some of the other guys Parker had played football with had stayed local and lived in the Slate Belt area.

He shrugged and said, "Nothing really newsworthy, I guess."

She wanted to ask him why he hadn't married, whether there had ever been a girl in his last year of high school or later in college, whether there was a girl now, but she couldn't work up the nerve. They were still feeling each other out, working out the distance, the awkwardness between them. Plus she didn't want to talk about her relationship with Matt. She didn't want Parker to know she'd been living with someone for the better part of five years. He would ask the same questions she'd asked herself more often than not. Why hadn't they gotten married? Why hadn't Matt asked her? Would she have said yes if he had? Why had she put up with his lies?

The sun was beginning to rise, warming her face and chest through the windbreaker. Parker checked his watch. He put his pole down.

"I'll be right back," he said and took the stairs two at a time, his strong thighs easily carrying him up the steep incline. He returned a few minutes later with a thermos and two mugs. He poured them each a cup of coffee. They sat across from each other on teakwood chairs.

"Thank you." She raised the mug before taking a sip.

"You're welcome." He leaned back, his legs sprawling out in front of him and taking up much of the space between them. "So how's your dad doing?"

She gave it some thought before answering. "When I got here, it was like he was on his deathbed. Jackie, his nurse." She looked down at the mug in her hand. "His nurse and *lady friend*," she added. "She thought he had maybe a week, two at the most. But I don't know. He seems a little better. Not great or anything, but it's like he got a second wind." She sipped the coffee. "I don't know how else to explain it. He's just not ready to let go."

"Maybe it's because you came home."

She laughed a little bitterly. "I don't think so. You give me too much credit." She looked out at the calm water, thinking relationships were a lot like the river, sometimes tranquil and other times tumultuous. She and her father were more like the white water rapids tumbling over rocks, navigating bends, riding the currents, unable to stop as they barreled into Dead Man's Curve.

She continued. "My dad and I fought a lot. I'm not sure how much you knew about that."

"I suspected as much." His voice was barely above a whisper.

"When he sent me away, I was so angry. God, how I hated him for it." She stared at the river, the myriad of red and orange leaves covering the trees along its banks. When she turned her gaze back to Parker, he was staring at her in that intense way he had. "What?" she asked.

"Your dad. He knows a lot about this town and the people."

"I suppose. He knows a lot of the women, that's for sure."

"Yes," Parker said in a careful voice.

"So?"

"Do you think he'd be up to talk with me? He might be able to help me with something, answer some questions I have."

"Is this about the guy that was found in the river?" She sensed a change in Parker, a shift to the new Parker, the one she didn't recognize.

"It might have something to do with it," he said, eying her over the rim of his mug.

"I saw the news last night. They said the guy was from New Jersey. And bodies from the cities turn up in the river all the time."

"True."

"So what's different about this guy?"

"I can't tell you," he said.

"Well, can you tell me what this has to do with my dad?"

He shook his head. "Just tell your dad I'd like to talk with him."

She felt protective of her father suddenly for reasons that weren't entirely clear. And she felt hurt, too, thinking Parker had an ulterior motive for asking her here.

"Is that why you called the house? Hoping to talk with my dad? And then asked me here to get an in with him?"

Parker looked stunned. "Jeez, Becca, when did you become so paranoid?"

It was her turn to feel stunned. Was she being paranoid? Had living with Matt all these years made her suspicious of everyone? Or had that been her father's doing?

Parker stood and grabbed his fishing pole. "I have to get to work," he said. "You can stay here as long as you want. The view is spectacular, if I do say so myself. Or not. It's up to you." He turned and scaled the stairs with his long, strong legs, leaving her alone on the dock.

CHAPTER TWENTY

John drove his motorcycle alongside Hap's hog. The bikes' engines were thunderous in the quiet hours of the early morning, but John wasn't concerned about waking the people in town. The locals were accustomed to the sound of their bikes. He imagined most would sleep through the noise; others might stir only to roll over, forget what they'd heard.

They continued on Delaware Drive, turning left onto Turkey Ridge Road. The sun was peeking over the mountain, casting long shadows on the macadam. They were headed to Saddle Creek Road at the northern end of town, passing a smattering of houses along the way, a mix of stately homes with long elaborate driveways tucked deep into the woods, paired with the odd couplings of trailers stacked on cinder blocks, most abandoned, some that were not.

They rode up and over a one-lane bridge. John's stomach lifted and dropped as though he were riding on one of the small roller coasters at the town fair where his mother had taken him when he'd been a boy. He hadn't thought about his mother in a long time. She'd been a good mom as far as he could tell, making sure he'd been bathed and fed, buying him ice cream, taking him on rides. But she had her moments when she'd been sharp and hard, a tough love kind of woman.

Then again, the same could be said for most of the old ladies in the club. You had to have a thick skin, a roughness about you to withstand the kind of hard-core lifestyle the members adhered to. The club had rules, some of them unfavorable to a woman's point of view, like the strippers and sweeties made available to all members whether the members were married or not. Rules were followed or punishment was fierce. There were no exceptions.

John leaned with the bike, taking a sharp curve before turning into the driveway of a two-story home. The white siding was faded and the shutters in need of repair. The paint on the picket fence was cracked and chipped. John supposed the police chief's salary wasn't all that much, considering.

He pulled his motorcycle next to Hap's hog and cut the engine. Immediately, John missed the vibration, the rumble, the power of the engine between his legs. He got off his bike reluctantly and removed his helmet before following Hap onto the front porch. Hap knocked twice on the screen door. He turned to John and said, "He had to hear us pull up."

John had an image of Toby answering with a rifle aimed at their chests. He grabbed Hap's arm, pulled him out of harm's way.

Hap shook him off, knocked again.

A shuffling sound came from inside, and in the next second, the door flew open. Toby stood behind the screen, wearing an old pair of work pants, the fly and button undone. He was shirtless. His chest sagged and looked like what some of the girls at the club had described as man boobs. His cropped hair stood up in the back of his head.

"What can I do for you boys?" Toby asked.

John sensed fear in Toby. He was no Chief Clint Kingsley, that was for sure. John wondered if Toby had it in him to do what they were about to ask of him.

"We need a favor," Hap said.

Toby's wife walked into the room behind him. She was short and round and wearing a dingy yellow robe. "Toby, honey, who is it?" She pulled the collar of the robe tight around her neck.

Toby turned his head and said, "Go on back to bed, Mary. It's nothing for you to be concerned about." He stepped onto the porch, closed the front door behind him.

John leaned against the railing. Hap stood next to him, a little more hunched over than usual. The old man looked tired, the stress of the last few days weighing on him and the club. Toby crossed his arms and looked back and forth between them. He was short for a cop, for a *chief*, John thought. Short and shaped like a doughnut. He wasn't exactly emanating a position of authority. The zipper and button of his pants hanging open wasn't helping the image. John felt another pinch of doubt rising up in him, his confidence that Toby would be up to the task slipping away as each second passed.

"I don't like you coming to my home," Toby said, puffing up his flabby chest. "Whatever this is about can be handled down at the station."

"No," Hap said. "I'm afraid it can't. Walls have ears. And you don't want anyone to hear what we have to say. Zip up, man." He pointed below Toby's waistline.

Toby looked down, embarrassed. He quickly zipped and buttoned his pants. "What's this about? I don't want to hear it has anything to do with that guy we pulled from the river."

"I'm afraid it might," Hap said.

Toby took a small step backward. "Shit," he said and ran his hand down his face.

"What do you know about it?" Hap asked.

"Not much. The staties took it over the second they heard about it."

"Why? What did they find?" Hap asked.

Toby snorted. "You want me to tell you what evidence they have?" He was shaking his head. "They don't tell me much, that's for sure.

Once they take over, I'm out of the loop. And Parker—Detective Reed, that is—he might be one of us." He meant a local. "But that's not going to matter much. These kids today aren't like us, loyal to our own town, if you know what I mean."

"Just tell us what you know," John said, talking for the first time, irritated with Toby's jabbering.

Toby stared at him. After a second, he said, "Yesterday with the dogs. They found some of the guy's blood. They know where he was shot and gutted and dumped into the river."

Hap leaned on the railing next to John. "Well, we might have a problem then," he said. "But it could go away with your help." He nodded at Toby. "Maybe you could fix it for us so it goes away."

Toby put up his hand to stop Hap from continuing. "I'm not doing anything illegal," he said. "I've looked the other way on more than one occasion with the strippers and the gambling and whatnot. But this? Uh-uh."

"It's a simple request," Hap said. "It shouldn't be too hard, even for you."

"No," he said. "The state police are involved. It's out of my hands. What do you expect me to do?" He rambled, whined. "I've got a wife. A kid."

"All we need you to do is make sure John's name is on that police report. You know the one I'm talking about. A couple of your men arrested some of our boys a few nights ago for partying in the streets. I believe they were charged with disturbing the peace."

"They didn't leave my men any choice but to haul them in. There were too many witnesses, too many tourists around."

"I've got no problem with what your men did. They did exactly what I wanted them to do. And John was one of the boys they arrested. Isn't that right?"

Toby stared at Hap with a blank expression on his face. Then it slowly changed as he started to understand it had been the Scions' intention all along to create a disturbance, to have a bunch of the members arrested, to lock them up for the night for disturbing the peace, to give John an alibi. "Shit," he said again and dropped into the chair on the porch. "You set it up."

John remained quiet, watching Toby's reaction carefully. He was more than a little uncomfortable putting his trust, *his life*, into Toby's hands.

"So what do you think? Do you think you can make John's name appear on that police report?" Hap asked.

Toby didn't say anything for a long time. "Would you have asked Clint to do the same if he was still chief and not me?"

John was starting to understand what he hadn't before. It wasn't that Toby had a problem with helping them per se, but rather he was struggling to overcome his captain status. It had been five years since he'd taken over Clint's position and become chief. But people still treated him as though he wasn't in charge, asked him for things Toby seemed convinced they wouldn't have asked if it were Clint wearing the chief's badge. But Toby's thinking was wrong. His question showed how little he knew of Clint, his former boss and friend.

"We would ask the same of Clint," John said, his tone confident. At one time he'd asked so much more from Clint, more than Toby or the town could've possibly known.

"And what do you think Clint would say?" Toby asked. "I'll tell you what he would say. No, that's what he would say. He'd wash his hands of the whole mess and let the staties take care of it like he did twenty years ago when that first body washed up on shore . . . " His words trailed off.

Hap raised an eyebrow. "I don't believe that case was ever solved. Was it?"

"No," Toby said. "It wasn't."

"And why do you think that is?"

Toby shifted his weight in the chair. "Are you saying Clint had something to do with it?"

Hap shrugged.

John looked at Hap, a look that said they were heading in a direction that John didn't want to go. Of course, John wasn't thinking about Clint, but rather he was thinking about Becca, Clint's daughter. The more removed she was from him the better.

"So what's it going to be?" Hap asked, narrowing his eyes and leaning in close to the chief. "Are you going to help us out or not?"

CHAPTER TWENTY-ONE

Becca stayed on the dock when Parker went into the house to get ready for work. She watched the sunrise, in no hurry to rush back to her father's bedside. The fresh air moved through her lungs easily. A damp breeze blew from the water despite the warmth of the sun's rays slipping through the branches of the trees. She hugged herself against the chill. She'd forgotten how quiet early mornings on the river could be, how peaceful.

Her life on the other side of the river had left very little time for stopping, sitting, being still. Her mornings were spent running with Romy, focused on the trail, her pace, monitoring the dog, making sure the dog was getting the exercise she needed, resting and racing with the dog's natural rhythm. And more times than not, Becca's thoughts were on the animals in her care at the clinic. She made a mental note to call Vicky later to check on Maggie.

And then there was Picasso, the cat who had chewed an electrical wire, shocking and burning the inside of his mouth, lucky to be alive. Which reminded her of Lucky, Matt's cat, although Becca couldn't remember the last time Matt had actually fed the cat or cleaned her litter box. Becca missed the feline rubbing against her legs, the sound of her purr, her soft kitty fur.

Eventually, inevitably, she circled back to Matt, how he would hate sitting here, motionless, taking in the scenery. If he were beside her, she imagined he would be staring at his phone—texting, calling, working—missing the beauty around him.

She had let him take control of how she'd spent her free time outside of the clinic, whether it had been jetting to Washington, DC, for some benefit dinner or driving into New York City to catch a Broadway show. It had been exciting, extravagant, uncomfortable.

She'd forgotten how much she missed her time away from the rest of the world, alone with only the river, the woods, and its animals for company. She'd forgotten what it was like to feel the kind of peace she felt on the inside when she'd been still. She'd forgotten how she'd once shared this feeling with someone, with Parker.

She turned, sensing his presence at the top of the stairs, feeling his eyes on her; he was watching her from the back deck. He didn't say anything. In the next moment he was gone. She heard his car starting, the tires crackling on the gravel driveway, the sound disappearing once the wheels hit the blacktop. She reached down to pet Romy and then remembered she'd left her at home.

Her gaze returned to the river. She was left with only the sound of water lapping against the shore, the occasional bird calling to anyone who was listening.

After leaving Parker's sometime later, she turned into the driveway of her father's house. As she was pulling in, Toby was pulling out. He stopped alongside her, rolled down his window.

"Becca," he said.

"Hey, Toby, or should I say Chief?" He looked older than she remembered, heavier in the face and neck, creases by his eyes. It wasn't that aging was surprising, but his expression was disconcerting. "Is everything okay?" She motioned toward the house, her father.

"Sure, he's, well, he's . . ." He lifted his hand from the steering wheel. "What can I say?"

She understood it was hard for Toby to see her father so ill. Her father and Toby went way back, having worked side by side for over fifteen years.

"It's good to see you home," he said.

She nodded and was about to take her foot off the brake when he added, "You be careful, you hear?" and pulled away.

"Yeah, okay," she said, watched him drive down the road, wondered what the heck he'd meant by that. She parked her Jeep by the garage and got out. Romy greeted her, tail wagging, prancing, licking Becca's hands and face when she stooped to pet her.

"You can come next time," she said, feeling bad about not taking the dog fishing with her, but she'd been worried about the casting, Romy getting hooked by a lure. Now that she'd seen the size of Parker's dock, she knew it could easily accommodate a dog. She kissed Romy's head and stood, but she wasn't ready to go inside the house just yet. She needed a little more time before she faced her father for another day.

"Let's go for a walk," she said to Romy.

She trekked through the crabgrass and the weeds of what had become of the backyard, moving in the direction of the woods. Romy jumped and ran in front of her, stopping to sniff the ground, a rock, a leaf, following a scent known only to dogs. It didn't take long for Becca to find the path at the bottom of the mountain, the one that crossed the stream where she'd spent many hours playing when she'd been a kid, the same one that led straight to the river.

The leaves were starting to fall from the trees; yellows and reds and oranges blanketed the ground. Squirrels scurried along branches, their cheeks packed with nuts, preparing for the winter months ahead. She and Romy walked on, pausing when they came upon John's old barn. Romy stopped, ears perked, teeth bared.

"It's okay, girl," Becca said, reassuring the dog and herself. "I know the man who lives here." John's farmhouse was on the other side of the barn.

"Come on, we'll walk around." She started to lead Romy away, but after taking a few steps, she paused, glanced over her shoulder, catching sight of the farmhouse, a single motorcycle parked outside.

She started moving faster than she had been before, covering the ground in long strides as much as the thick brush would allow. Romy trotted on the right side of Becca a couple yards away, putting Becca between the dog and the barn.

Becca continued to pick up her pace. Something in the back of her mind, something she wasn't ready to acknowledge, drove her forward with a kind of fury. She started running. She was used to running in the woods and dashed through the scrub. Twigs and small branches whipped her arms and legs, most of them missing her face. She had to watch her footing on the rocks and branches and uneven terrain.

She ran a half mile, maybe more.

It was hard to gauge distance when you were surrounded by maple and oak trees, pines, ferns, and brush, all blending into one colorful, autumn-enhanced visual. Her heart pounded; her breathing was heavy. The collar of her shirt was damp underneath her windbreaker. She heard the river. Her pace slowed as she approached a small clearing. Romy panted beside her after racing ahead and then doubling back.

Becca was certain she'd never been to the clearing before, but she knew it was there like she knew about all of the places along the river where kids weren't supposed to go. There were certain areas they stayed away from, locations considered off-limits where the Scions congregated for outings, hangouts, meetings of unknown business. No one had to tell them to stay away from these places. It was just another part of growing up in the town, as much a part of the area as were the tourism and tubing, the fishing and hunting, the bears and wolves.

At the thought of bears and wolves, Becca searched the wild grass, the weeds, all yellowing from the cool autumn air. A section looked to be stomped down, walked over repeatedly by several large animals.

She'd never been afraid of being alone in the woods before, but she sensed something strange in the air, something charged and not quite right. She listened for any sound. Other than the rushing rapids, all was quiet. A chill flitted across the back of her neck, making the hairs rise.

Romy was preoccupied with the scent of whatever or whoever trampled the ground. The dog lifted her head into the faint breeze, sniffed the air. Not far from where Romy stood, Becca spied a piece of yellow police tape dangling from the trunk of an oak tree.

She'd stumbled onto what was left of a crime scene. She took several cautious steps forward, approached the riverbank. Her thighs strained to keep her balance and control her forward momentum downhill. She came to a stop at the bottom near the water's edge.

The rapids thundered by, the noise drowning out the sound of her own breathing, of Romy's panting. She hesitated, not wanting to look but looking anyway, across the river to the Jersey side. She recognized the path she and Romy ran every morning, the path that curved toward the river where she would catch John watching her.

She was standing where he'd stood.

"Becca."

She jumped, spun around. Parker was half walking, half sliding down the bank toward her. He was wearing his gray detective suit. The bottoms of his pants were dusty and dirty. His jacket flapped open, exposing his sidearm.

"What are you doing here?" he asked in a loud, scolding tone.

"Romy and I were walking." She had to shout to be heard over the rapids.

Parker shook his head as though he couldn't believe the shit he had to deal with. "You have to go," he shouted. "You can't be here."

"Why?" She batted a mosquito away from her ear.

"Because you can't."

She glanced across the river at the path she ran every morning.

"This is a crime scene, Becca. You and your dog have to leave."

"It doesn't look like a crime scene anymore." The police tape hanging from the tree had been cut and no longer blocked off the area.

"Well, it is. It's ongoing." He rubbed his eyes. She'd been with him not three hours ago, and already she could see the wear of the day on his shoulders and in his face.

"What happened here? What's going on?" She took a step closer to him.

He shook his head, refusing to answer her. He looked around, craned his neck as though he was listening for something.

"What's going on?" she asked again.

"I told you before I can't talk about the case." He took her by the elbow. Romy danced around them as though she wanted in on their game. "You have to go now. I've got a team coming. They'll be here any minute."

"What team?"

"We're dragging the river." He tried to lead her back up the riverbank.

She pulled her arm away. They stared at one another. Becca saw concern in Parker's eyes, worry, and something more, a dogged determination. Romy stopped jumping around their feet.

"What are you dragging the river for?" she asked.

The sound of voices drifted through the woods before drowning in the rapids.

"Just go home, Becca," Parker said and walked away, making his way back up the bank.

She backed up slowly, taking hold of Romy's collar and pulling the dog with her. She took off running. Romy raced ahead, thinking they were playing some kind of new game.

Becca ran upstream away from Parker, the police, and the spot along the river where John had stood. Her feet sank in the soft earth where the water met the shore. John was a Scion. She'd always known he was Scion. And she'd seen him by the river the day before the body had washed up against one of the bridge's columns.

She raced on. Her legs and hips absorbed the pounding of her feet, her body taking in the shock. When it became too rocky at the water's edge, she had to slow her pace so as not to fall. She turned and ran up the riverbank and into the woods. Romy ran several feet ahead of her, leaping over small shrubs, graceful and strong.

Fear chased Becca. Adrenaline pushed her forward. He'd been wearing nitrile gloves, hunting gear. The body in the river had been shot and gutted. Parker had to be searching the river for the murder weapon—a gun, *a knife*.

She darted around trees, jumping over roots and fallen limbs. She didn't stop until she reached the path alongside the stream, the path to home. Romy slowed to a trot, panting. Becca's cell phone went off in her pocket. She recognized the clinic's ringtone.

"Hello," she said, out of breath, her head buzzing from the exertion. Romy drank from the trickle of water at her feet.

"It's Vicky. I wanted to let you know Maggie went home today."

"That's great." Becca wiped her brow. The clinic. The golden retriever. Matt. Her thoughts were muddied. Parker. The crime scene. Her father. All of it tangled together in her mind. Nothing was clear. "That's great," she said again.

"Are you okay?" Vicky asked.

The trees tilted to the right. The ground swayed left. "I'm good," she said. Her words echoed in her ears. "Thanks for letting me know about Maggie." Romy lifted her head. Water dripped from her jowls. Becca's vision blurred.

"Is there anything else?" she asked.

"No, that's it. Are you sure you're okay?"

"Yeah," Becca said and closed her eyes to make the dizziness in her head go away. "Yeah, I'm good." She couldn't make sense of it all, but in her gut she knew she had seen something and wished she hadn't.

CHAPTER TWENTY-TWO

Becca was sixteen years old. It was late July and her last summer in Portland, although she didn't know it at the time.

She was hanging back from her friends as they crowded around Parker's pickup truck. They were deciding where to go for a party that night. Chad's older brother had hooked them up with a half keg, and it was just a matter of deciding whether they would park their trucks in a field for a good old-fashioned country tailgate or look for a less conspicuous spot.

"Max Headroom," Parker said, picking a well-known hangout along the Appalachian Trail where someone had spray-painted a large rock with the faded caricature of the computer-generated TV host from the eighties. It was the perfect place for kids to drink, smoke, and engage in the kinds of activities their parents had warned them about.

Parker continued. "Otherwise, we're going to have to pile everyone into pickups to get to the field." He pointed to Chad and two other guys on the football team with trucks.

"What's wrong with piling into pickups?" Chad asked.

"It will draw too much attention," Parker said.

"But we're with the police chief's daughter," Chad said. "No one's going to question what we're up to. Right, Becca?"

She didn't answer.

Chad's girlfriend, Krissy, clung to his arm. Her eyes were outlined in black, her lips shiny pink. "Let's just go down to the river," she said.

Becca folded her arms, tired of the same old debate, where to party, who was driving, who was hooking up with whom. She was sick to death with the routine of her life in the small town, sick to death with the same arguments with her high school friends, the same troubles with her father.

"Let's just go to the river," she said, jumping into the ongoing discussion, feeling the rebelliousness rise up whenever she thought about her father. She supposed her friends knew this about her, knew she'd take more chances with getting caught doing the things they shouldn't be doing, if for no other reason than to shove it in her father's face. They went along with it, of course, pushed her even, knowing in the end her father would bail them out.

Eventually, after some continued reluctance from the others, they agreed the river would be perfect. The moon was full. The air was thick with the heat of the day, the humidity, a typical night in July. It would be cooler by the water. Chad would meet them down by the pines, a place where the riverbank was wide and a row of hemlocks lined the backdrop to the woods. Couples would lie behind the pines on a blanket of needles, invisible to the others partying by the water. Girls in Becca's class lost their virginity behind the trees.

Becca wasn't one of them.

She and Parker were just friends. He'd made that pretty clear when he'd failed to kiss her that time in his pickup truck earlier that spring. Things between them had gotten weird after that. She was hurt. She was the girl the guys wanted to be friends with but no one wanted to date. She didn't mind most of the time, but somewhere hidden beneath all those confusing feelings about love and sex, she wanted to be the girl who was desired, the girl who was capable of capturing Parker's attention.

The keg was hidden in the woods, and they had to walk back and forth with their red plastic cups for refills. Someone made a circle of rocks to sit on. Music from a boom box blared Tim McGraw's "Angry All the Time." Parker had grown quiet, holding the same cup of beer for the last hour, skipping rocks across the river. He'd gone off on his own more and more as the summer had worn on, putting distance between them.

Becca herself had been moody, feeling out of sorts and bored. She'd started drinking one beer after another, losing count of how many she'd had and not caring. Mosquitoes buzzed around her legs, biting the skin on her calves and thighs. She didn't bother batting them away. Nothing felt right. Tim McGraw's wife was angry. She was angry. She wanted to leave, but where was she supposed to go? And now Jenna had joined Parker by the river. Parker had started talking to Jenna more and more lately, a girl a year behind them in school. Becca was angry about that too. Her thoughts were fuzzy, her arms heavy. The red plastic cup slipped from her hand, splattering beer onto her feet and ankles.

"Watch it," Krissy complained, moved away.

Becca gazed in the direction of Parker. He was standing close to Jenna, moving her hair away from her face. It looked as though he was going to kiss her. And then he did kiss her. *He kissed her.* What did Jenna have that Becca didn't? How could he have kissed Jenna and not her? She marched toward the keg to refill her cup to get stupid drunk, to numb the pain. But instead, she kept walking, winding her way up the riverbank and through the woods. She had to get away. She couldn't watch him with another girl. It hurt too much. Several times her feet tangled in brush, and she had to rip the plants and vines away with her hands. She couldn't find the path.

She came to the railroad tracks that ran through town. She followed them, tripping over the ties, the alcohol making her off-balance. Not far in the distance, Delaware Drive came into view, the streetlights illuminating the strip of town and the small shops that lined the street.

Tourists walked up and down the block, their voices carrying in the night air. A large group of men and women holding cameras headed for the pedestrian bridge to take pictures of the moon on the river, the Delaware Water Gap as their backdrop.

But down the alley not far from where the antique store sold trinkets, the diner served tasty root beer floats and vanilla shakes, the sports store rented tubes and canoes and kayaks, was the darker part of town where there weren't any streetlights, where the music played fast and hard, where the Scions congregated in Sweeney's Bar.

Becca walked toward the dark alley, leaving the shops, the tourists, the street, the light behind. She didn't think about what she was doing, not really, taking tentative steps toward the bar, her curiosity about the Scions, John, drawing her ever closer. Several motorcycles were parked out front, the chrome shiny in the moonlight. A lone figure stood on the bar porch. Becca jumped when whoever it was struck a match.

"Come a little closer," the woman said and lit a cigarette. "So I can see you."

"Me?" Becca asked and looked over her shoulder. She was the only one in the alley. The noise of the town was all but gone, faded into the humid air. The music that had been playing inside the bar had stopped. Men's voices bellowed in between laughter.

"Yeah, you. Ain't no one else out here but us." The woman took a long drag of the cigarette, the end of the butt illuminating her face. She looked young but also old too. Weathered, Becca's mother would've described her if she'd been there. Her mother would've said the woman was someone who had taken some hard knocks, lived a hard life.

Becca stepped onto the porch. Her legs a little unsteady from the beer she'd drunk. The woman was wearing a white tank top and a black miniskirt. The neon sign in the window flashed red and blue lights across the woman's tattooed arm.

"You want a drink?" The woman took another long drag from the cigarette, then flicked it into the alley.

Becca knew she wasn't thinking clearly and that she should turn around and walk away. The bikers' bar was no place for the police chief's daughter.

"Sure," she said and followed the woman inside.

The door banged shut behind her. A large bearded man at a nearby table turned toward them. He reached out and grabbed the woman Becca had followed into the bar, wrapping his large hand around the woman's wrist.

"Have a seat," he said and pulled the woman onto his lap as though she were some kind of rag doll. She didn't protest and wrapped her skinny, tattooed arms around the man's neck, kissing his cheek and ear and lips.

Becca lingered by the back wall, abandoned. A couple of men were playing pool. A stack of money was piled high by one of the corner pockets. The tables and bar were crowded with bikers dressed in jeans and leather and tattoos. The women all looked the same with their teased, bleached hair and cheap clothing. The place wasn't anything like Becca had expected, although she couldn't say what she'd thought it would be like. But this place . . . this place was dingy and smoky and smelled like a boys' locker room, wet and stale. It didn't make her want to leave, though. Someone belched. Becca caught the scent, turned her head away.

Not far from where she stood with her back against the wall, she spotted a woman sitting alone. She wasn't like the other women. She was wearing a plain T-shirt, and her reddish hair was tied in a ponytail. Several empty shot glasses littered the table in front of her, but she didn't appear drunk. Becca thought the pretty woman would be the safest person for her to approach. Now that Becca was here, she figured she might as well get what she had come for.

She skirted around a couple of men, trying to be inconspicuous as she made her way to the pretty woman. She was five steps away when someone grabbed her forearm.

"Aren't you a cute thing," the guy said, smiling, his teeth stained brown with nicotine.

"Thanks," she said and tried to pull her arm free.

"Where are you going?" He squeezed her tightly. His fingers were covered in skull rings. "Come on, sit. Have a drink."

"No, thanks," she said, feeling afraid for the first time since she'd stepped inside. "I'm meeting a friend."

"Sit." He kicked out a chair. "I don't bite. Not unless you want me to." He laughed, and then his face turned serious. "Come on, doll. Sit."

Becca's mouth went dry as she lowered herself into the chair. He released her arm, handed her a beer. She sipped from the mug. One of his friends grabbed a chair, turned it around so that it was facing backward, dropped down on it in front of her.

"Look who we have here," he said. "The police chief's daughter, all grown up." He was wearing a leather jacket full of patches. One of them was the number sixty-nine. He caught Becca looking at it.

"You know what that means, don't you?" He wriggled his tongue.

Becca's legs started shaking.

"It's Becky, right?" the guy with the patches asked.

"Becca," she said, clearing her throat.

"Well, Becca, what do you say we go for a little ride? I bet you could give us something extraspecial," he said, laughed, punched the guy with the rings in the shoulder.

Becca's heart pounded. The guy with the skull rings stood. The other guy with the leather jacket full of patches slipped his hand under her arm, pulled her up. *No*, she wanted to yell. She was supposed to holler, *No! Stop!* The music started blaring. A guitar riff sliced the air. Who would help her? Who would hear her if she screamed? She felt as though she were being dragged, her feet barely touching the floor as the guy with the patches pulled her through the bar, the crowd, and headed for the door, the guy with the rings on their heels. No one stopped them. Not many had been paying attention, and the ones who were smiled, laughed, joked, a blur of stained teeth and talking heads. Surely the other women would see what was happening and save her. But as they got closer to the door, the woman from the porch, the one who had invited Becca inside, tossed a condom at her. It hit Becca in the face before falling to the floor.

"You can't be too careful now, honey," the woman said.

Becca yanked her arm free and reached for the condom, stalling, anything to stay inside the bar with the others. The warnings given during school assemblies, the pamphlets passed around classrooms, the health teacher talking about what to do when you were confronted with the exact situation Becca had now found herself in, raced through her mind. *Don't let them take you to another location. Fight. Run. Find help.* But no one said what you were supposed to do when fear overwhelmed you, paralyzed you, when you were frozen in a state of panic. Later, she imagined they would say she was compliant, a participant in the horrible acts that she believed were about to be bestowed upon her tender body.

This time the guy with the skull rings grabbed her upper arm, pulled her toward the door. Becca tried to wriggle from his grasp. Then his buddy with the patches clutched her other arm. At the same time, John appeared as though she'd summoned him telepathically, as though he'd heard her private cry for help.

"Not tonight, fellas." He removed the guys' hands from around Becca's biceps. He was taller than she'd remembered, much taller than he'd looked from a distance.

"What the hell?" the guy with the rings said. "We were just having a little fun. Weren't we, doll?"

"Not with this one, you're not," John said.

"What? You scared of her daddy?"

Becca folded her arms, curling in on herself. She stared at the sticky floor, feeling small and like a little girl. She'd been foolish to come here, when all she wanted to know was what it was like inside the bar, and who these men were that the town feared, respected, looked the other way rather than get involved in whatever business the members were conducting. She wanted to know what John's life was like, why he stopped coming around, watched her from a distance.

"Is there a problem?" the pretty woman asked, wrapping her arms around John's waist.

"There's no problem. Isn't that right, fellas?" There was something about John's expression, a look that said he shouldn't be messed with.

The guy with the rings flipped over a chair. Several of the men at the bar and surrounding tables turned to see what the commotion was about. For a second, Becca thought she was about to be tossed into the middle of a bar fight.

"Fuck this," the guy said and walked away.

"Later, *Becca*," the guy with the patches whispered in her ear before he walked away too.

John looked around the bar at the crowd. Anyone who had turned to see what was going on had turned away and continued with their conversations, drinking, playing pool.

"I'll wait here," the pretty woman said. She kissed John on the cheek before disappearing in the crowd.

"Let's go," he said and escorted Becca outside.

"Where are we going?" Becca asked and followed him off the porch, wondering if maybe she should be afraid of him too. It was clear he was in a position of power over the other members. He was feared.

He straddled one of the motorcycles parked in the alley. "I'm taking you home," he said.

She slid onto the back of the bike. The engine rumbled between her thighs.

"Hold on to me," he said.

She grabbed his waist, his muscles hard beneath the leather jacket he wore on a hot night in July. She pressed her head against his back and closed her eyes, smelling the leather mixed with sweat.

The motor revved as he shifted gears and took off down the road. She felt like she was flying, soaring through the night, hanging on to a man she trusted more than her own father.

John pulled into Becca's driveway and cut the engine. Becca slid off the back of his bike. She was about to thank him for saving her when her father flew out the front door of the house. He stopped short when he saw them.

"Get in the house, Becca," he said.

She knew by his tone she was in deep trouble. It was well past her curfew. She reeked of alcohol and cigarettes. Not to mention the fact that she'd come home on the back of John's motorcycle.

"Thanks for everything back there in the bar," she said.

John nodded.

"Now, Becca," her father said, his final warning.

She dragged her feet, making her way toward the house. The motorcycle's engine revved as John drove away, racing up the road. She wasn't two steps in the house when her father stormed in behind her.

"I better not ever catch you on the back of his motorcycle again," he roared. "You stay away from him. Do you hear?" He pointed his finger in her face. "You don't ever go near him again!"

"Why? What's the big deal? It's not like he's a pervert or anything. It's not like he's *you*."

Her father's expression changed. He no longer looked angry but more hurt than anything else. In a calmer voice he said, "I want you to go upstairs to your room and pack your bags. You're leaving for boarding school in the morning."

"What? No!"

Her mother appeared on the steps. "Clint, you're being unreasonable."

"Stay out of this, Jane."

"Mom, you can't let him do this."

"Clint."

"Jane, I'm warning you. Stay out of it." He turned to Becca. "It's for your own good. I won't hear another word about it. I should've sent you away to school years ago. But you're going now, and that's final."

"I hate you!" Becca screamed, pushing past her mother, racing up the stairs to her bedroom, slamming the door behind her.

She heard her mother say, "Don't you think you're overreacting? So she came home on John's motorcycle."

"You don't understand," her father said.

"Then explain it to me."

"I can't."

"Can't or won't?"

"Both. She's leaving tomorrow. End of discussion."

Becca didn't speak to her father during the two-hour drive to Philadelphia. She still didn't talk to him after her bags were unpacked from the car and sitting on the floor in her new room, a suite that she'd share with two other girls at the start of her senior year of high school. He didn't make eye contact with her or her mother. He left them alone while he went to talk with one of the school officials, the one he'd made a deal with, called in a favor, in order to get his daughter enrolled on such short notice, a month before classes would officially begin.

"It doesn't seem so bad," her mother said, looking around the flat, the sparse furniture, the beige cement walls. "Think of it as a fresh start. A new beginning." She almost sounded envious.

"I don't ever want to see or speak to him again," Becca said about her father.

"I know you feel that way right now, but I'm sure your father has a very good reason for doing what he did."

"Yeah? And what is that?" She kicked a box, plopped onto the mattress, crossed her arms.

Her mother shook her head. "I don't know. Honestly, I don't understand why he does the things he does sometimes."

"I hate him," she said.

Becca's mother joined her on the bed, wrapped her arms around her. "Sometimes I feel that way about him too."

After hanging up with Vicky, Becca emerged from the woods and walked up the yard, one shaky step after another. She leaned against the outside wall of the garage. Her legs were weak, her insides hollowed out. It happened on occasion, mornings she pushed her legs too hard, running on an empty stomach without any fuel. There were times when she would have to stop and throw up the water she'd drunk that was sloshing around her gut. But this wasn't one of those times. Overexerting herself wasn't causing her to be nauseous.

"Becca," Jackie called and stuck her head out the garage door.

"Over here." She pushed off the wall, wiping her lips with the back of her arm. Her mouth tasted vile and dry. Her tongue burned with the remnants of stomach bile that had never quite made it all the way out.

"I checked your room earlier, but you'd already gone." Jackie was wearing a light-blue terry cloth warm-up suit without a bra. She looked Becca up and down.

"I went for a run," Becca said, explaining her ragged appearance.

"Your dad has been asking for you."

"Okay," she said, with the understanding it was her turn to sit by his side. "I'll go up in a minute." She walked into the kitchen. Romy raced ahead. She poured fresh water into the dog's water dish, set it on the floor along with a bowl of food. Romy dove in.

Becca drank greedily from her own glass of water. Jackie sat at the table picking at her cuticle, inspecting her long fingers and clipped nails.

Becca's father coughed. Both Becca and Jackie looked toward the ceiling to his room upstairs.

"I'm going," Becca said, leaving Jackie and Romy in the kitchen. Slowly, she made her way up the steps and down the hall. The bedroom door was wide open.

"Jackie," he called.

"No, Dad, it's me." She sat in the chair beside him.

He nodded, closed his eyes. She thought he was going to sleep and she would only be expected to sit by his bedside, relieved not to have to talk. She needed time to think things through about John, about what she'd seen at the river. But he opened his eyes, poked his finger to his chest.

"What is it, Dad?"

His lashes were wet. His bottom lip trembled. He turned his head away as though he couldn't bear for her to see him cry.

CHAPTER TWENTY-THREE

"Wait here," Russell said.

He left with a rifle in his hand, walking in the direction of the woods, taking the path near the stream, the one that ran north away from town and eventually connected to the Appalachian Trail. John waited a few minutes before setting out to follow him. He was sure-footed and comfortable in the woods, as silent as a predator stalking its prey. If his father knew he was tracking him, he never let on.

Russell drifted off the path and away from the trickling stream. John kept close, hiding in the brush, ducking behind trees. He was so quiet he startled a deer that had crossed in front of his path. Russell jumped and swung around, the rifle aimed and ready to fire. When his father saw the small doe, he lowered his weapon. Russell was a good hunter, and the doe would've been an easy kill, but John's father respected two things—one was nature. You never shot and killed an animal for sport. You did it to survive, to eat the meat and take your place inside the food chain.

The only other rules his father lived by were those of the club, the Harley-Davidson manual his bible. If you listened to Russell explain it, he was a man of principles, and he wasn't above killing another man if that man went against the very things that Russell believed in.

John continued following his father, trekking farther and farther away from the path, closing in on the edge of the woods that backed up to a yard. It didn't take him long to figure out Russell's plan was to confront Clint. But Russell didn't walk up the lawn to where Clint was riding on his John Deere lawn mower, making neat little rows in the grass, mulching the autumn leaves, bagging them. Instead, he lingered by a large oak tree, leaning his shoulder against it, his rifle by his side.

John inched his way closer until he was about twenty yards from where his father stood. He hid in the shadows of the sweeping limbs of a hemlock, keeping out of sight. The air was filled with the scent of pine. He stepped closer to the tree, peering at his father through the opening of the branches. The needles poked the exposed area of his skin around his neck and wrists. Despite the crisp autumn air, moisture gathered underneath his arms. A bead of sweat dripped down his back. A surge of adrenaline pulsed through his veins. The lawn mower's engine continued to hum.

He had a terrible thought.

What if his old man picked up the rifle and aimed it at Clint? John wouldn't let him. He wouldn't allow his father to kill his own stepbrother. And then something much, much worse crossed his mind. What if his father was waiting for Becca to come outside? He never should've told him what she'd seen in the barn. She was just a kid.

He started to shake, a small tremble deep inside his bones. "Steady," he whispered and raised his rifle, peering through the scope, a direct shot at his father's right shoulder. *Please, Dad, don't do it*, he pleaded silently. *Don't make me shoot you.* Tears blurred his vision. He wiped his eyes on his upper arm, keeping the rifle raised the entire time.

The sound of the lawn mower stopped suddenly. The silence was deafening. Clint had spotted Russell leaning against the tree at the edge of the woods. He climbed off the mower, leaving it sitting in the middle of the yard, and made his way over to John's father. If Russell was going to take his shot, it would be now, but he left the rifle at his side. He smoothed his long beard and watched Clint as he approached.

John kept his rifle pointed at his father, but he looked away from the scope and stared at the two men.

"What's this about?" Clint asked, glancing at the rifle by Russell's side.

"We've got ourselves a situation," Russell said.

"How's that?"

Russell stroked his beard again. "I'm going to need you to bury some evidence for me."

"Is this about that body we pulled from the river?" Clint asked.

"Maybe."

"I don't think this is a conversation we should be having," Clint said and turned to walk away.

"You're going to want to hear me out, Clint." Russell was calm, his voice sounding as though he was nothing but a reasonable man.

John removed the last drop cloth that was covering his old man's chopper. It had been years since he'd last seen the bike. It had sat in the corner of the barn, untouched, next to several bales of hay ever since Russell had dropped over of a heart attack at only fifty-five years old.

John hadn't been able to sell the bike after he'd lost his father, but he hadn't been able to ride it either. Instead, he'd wrapped it in several layers of cloth to preserve the black paint and chrome and stashed it away.

He rolled the bike to the open space near his workbench to get a better look at the engine. Any gas in the tank was sure to have turned to pine tar. He tried to start it. The engine sputtered and coughed. The bike wasn't happy with the neglect, and it was letting John know, whining the way an old lady would if she wasn't getting the proper attention.

He grabbed the tools he would need to take off the spark plugs, lube them, check the oil filter. He worked for the next hour, going through the steps to get the engine up and running. He didn't think too hard about the reason he'd suddenly pulled Russell's chopper from storage. But seeing the bike, working on it, made him feel close to his old man, and he needed to feel close to him for reasons he wasn't ready to accept.

John had always looked to his father to guide him and help him make the hard decisions he'd had to make.

He removed the gas tank to check for rust. He didn't find any, which was a good sign. He drained what was left in the tank into another container. While he waited for the fluids to bleed, the sound of tires on gravel drifted into the barn. His body stiffened. It felt as though his blood had stopped flowing through his veins. If it had been a motorcycle, he would've heard it coming from a good distance away. He might've even been happy for the company. But a car, the engine of a cruiser, could only mean one thing.

A door slammed. He waited for the second car door to close. They wouldn't send just one cop to arrest him. He strained to listen for the sound of more tires, more police cruisers.

He stood and waited, wiping his greasy hands on a towel. Toby walked into the barn, his chief's hat in his hands. John blew out a slow breath.

"Chief," he said and bent over the gas tank, fiddling with the line where the fluid dripped. "What brings you by?" His blood started flowing again, although he was pretty sure it had never stopped but rather paused, waiting for whatever would happen next.

Toby leaned against the workbench, hat in hands, his sidearm jutting from his hip. "That report we talked about," he said. "It seems your name is on it after all."

John glanced at him. Toby's lips were pulled tight, his fat neck red and bulging under the collar of his uniform. John crouched next to the bike. "It makes sense, seeing I was arrested with the others that night."

Toby slipped his finger under his collar, loosened the shirt pinching his skin. "I don't know what kind of deal you or your old man struck with Clint, or how long it's been going on, and I don't care. I told him I'd do this one time for his sake and one time only. Am I making myself clear?"

"What kind of deal do you think I have with Clint, Chief?"

Toby tossed up his hands. "I don't want any trouble with the Scions, John. We've coexisted in this town for a long time. Even peacefully, if you ask me. You keep to your business, and you stay out of ours. Hell, I think it's been good having you here. It's kept out most of the other riffraff and whatnot that other small towns have to deal with. We're lucky we don't have that here, and I suspect it's because of you and your friends."

"I'm touched you feel that way."

"Don't be." Toby pointed a finger at him. "I'm a decent man trying to make a decent living. I care about the people in this town." He lowered his voice. "I can't be a part of anything illegal."

John wiped his hands on the towel again, staining the cloth black with more grease. "You're getting all worked up over nothing."

"Am I?" Toby asked. "They dragged that damned river today." He leaned in close, lowering his voice again. "They're looking for the murder weapon, John. And they're coming back tomorrow and the day after that and the day after that. They're not going to let this one go."

John concentrated hard on keeping his face neutral. He looked down at the greasy towel in his hand, stared at the black stain as though he were transfixed by the filth while he tried to wrap his mind around Toby's news. He was determined to keep his voice even when he asked, "And what does any of this have to do with me?"

"I hope nothing," Toby said. "I hope it doesn't have anything to do with you at all." He put his hat on and walked out of the barn.

John didn't move as he listened to the sound of the police cruiser's engine, the rumble fading as it drove farther down the road. When he was sure that Toby had gone, he searched his workstation, pulling open drawers he hadn't touched in decades, finding screwdrivers, pliers, wrenches, and tweezers. He rummaged through each one, knocking the contents onto the floor in his haste.

When he couldn't find what he was looking for, he slammed each drawer shut with all the strength he could muster, nearly knocking the workbench on its side. He swept his arm across the top of the desk, sending a lantern, a notebook, pencils, and a small toolbox careening to the floor. He focused on breathing in an attempt to harness his temper to keep from making another mess he would only have to clean later. He clenched and unclenched his hands, spying the cabinet where his father used to keep the white cotton cloths.

Slowly, he pulled open the top drawer, bringing his anger under control. Inside the drawer was a pile of pristine white cotton cloths folded with an exactness bordering on obsessive compulsion. He filled a bucket with dish detergent that he got from the house and set out to clean Russell's chopper. He was meticulous about his job, taking care not to rub any dirt into the paint or chrome for fear of leaving scratches. The bike wasn't as dirty as one would expect after it had sat in a dusty barn, because John had covered it thoroughly, protected it with care and attention, the same focus he gave to the job now with gentleness and affection.

As he worked, his thoughts returned to Becca. There was no getting around the fact that she was the weak link in an otherwise airtight job. The cops could drag the river all day every day for all John cared. Let them find the rifle or the knife or both. It didn't make a damn bit of difference. They'd never be able to trace either weapon back to him.

But Becca was a different kind of threat. She was a witness, an innocent, unknowing bystander.

When the paint sparkled and the chrome glistened, John filled the gas tank from the pump outside the barn, the one he paid to have filled every few months. He was self-sufficient, and the less he mingled with the locals, even those at the occasional gas pumps, the better.

He slid onto his old man's chopper, fired it up, turned onto the open road. The roar of the engine between his legs, his hands gripping the handlebars where his father's hands had been, made him miss his old man in ways that he hadn't in a long time.

He rode past Clint's house. Becca's dog was lying in the front yard. It lifted its head as John passed by.

He accelerated, revving the engine. He didn't slow down until he reached the edge of town and pulled into the alley, parking the chopper outside of Sweeney's.

The place stank of testosterone and alcohol and strippers. It was a familiar, comforting smell. He felt himself relax. The guys surrounded the bar. They were in a good mood, slapping each other on the back, laughing, toasting each other with shots. John sat at the other end of the bar and away from the celebration. Lou, the bartender, poured him a shot and a beer and set them down in front of him.

"There he is," Hap said, making his way over to John. He placed a hand on John's shoulder. "The man of the hour."

The guys raised their shot glasses to him, then tossed the whiskey back.

Hap lowered his voice. "The shipment went off without a hitch. It was the easiest transaction we've had in months, now that our little problem was removed, thanks to you." He laid a stack of bills two inches thick on the table. He put John's hand on top of the pile. "You earned it." He slapped him on the shoulder and made his way back to the guys at the other end of the bar, joining them in another round.

John squeezed the wad of bills in his hand. He thought he might be sick.

CHAPTER TWENTY-FOUR

The sparse patches of hair that had stuck up on Becca's father's head had fallen out. Pieces lay on the pillow. A few strands sprinkled the tops of his shoulders. His eyebrows, once dark and fierce, were thin and gray. The five-o'clock shadow, the scruff that most women had found attractive, according to her mother, had vanished completely. His skin was dry and blotchy and paper-thin. The crevices around his mouth and eyes made him appear to be a much older man of seventy or eighty rather than a man of sixty.

His hand, bent and misshapen, resting at his side, twitched. His fingers and wrist were nothing but bone. When she'd been a little girl, she'd feared his hands, big and strong, gripping her upper arms, scolding her for sneaking into the basement and playing with his fishing lures, fearing she could've been injured by their sharp hooks.

"Dad," she said.

He opened his eyes for a second and closed them again.

The phone rang. She thought about answering it, but after two rings it stopped. Jackie must've picked it up, not wanting to disturb them.

"Dad," she whispered. "I need to talk with you."

He turned his head away. Jackie opened the door.

"Becca," she said. "You have a phone call."

The last person to call her here had been Parker. "I'll be back," she said to her father and rose from the chair to take the call on the kitchen phone, thinking maybe Parker could answer some of her questions. But she would have to be careful not to say too much to him, not to appear too interested. She wasn't ready to divulge what she had seen by the river, not until she was sure she understood it herself.

❦

"God, it's good to hear your voice," Matt said.

Becca was surprised to find Matt on the other end of the line. She plopped onto one of the kitchen chairs and dropped her head in her hand. She'd been hoping to speak with Parker, and not just because she wanted to ask Parker questions about his case, but because she just wanted it to *be* Parker.

"Why are you calling me on this number? Why didn't you call my cell phone?" she asked, not meaning to sound surly. Romy trotted into the kitchen, pushed her nose against Becca's leg. She reached down to pet her. Romy lay on the floor at Becca's feet.

"I was afraid if I called your cell phone you wouldn't have answered it." He continued before she could reply. "Look, whatever you think I'm guilty of, you're wrong. But whatever it is, I'm sorry. I'm sorry a thousand times. Please give me a chance to explain, to make it right. Please, come home."

Becca covered her eyes. It was much more complicated than her simply going back to New Jersey and picking up her life where she'd left off. She'd seen John by the river. She was involved in something here. But how could she explain it to Matt when she wasn't sure she understood it herself?

"I have to stay with my dad. I have to see this through," she said and realized she meant it.

"Okay," Matt said. "I get it. You need to be there with him." His voice was soft, soothing. "Maybe I could come to you. I want to support you. I want to help you through this."

A part of her wanted to say yes, *come*. She could use his strong arms around her. But in the end, his presence was just too big, his personality too consuming. He'd suck all the air out of the room with his smile, usurping all the oxygen, claiming whatever space she had left to breathe for himself. She'd wither under the weight of his beautiful eyes. She understood these things about him, these things she loved and hated equally.

"I need some time," she said. "But I promise to call you and keep you updated on how things are going here. Because you're right, we need to talk. And we will. Just let me get through this with him."

"But you're coming home, right? When this is over?"

"I'll call you." This was the longest she'd kept her distance from him, kept herself closed off from his pleas of forgiveness.

There was desperation in his voice she hadn't heard before when he said, "I miss you. I miss you so much."

"I'll be in touch." Becca hung up the phone. She turned and jumped, surprised at finding Jackie standing behind her. Romy had gotten to her feet, nudged Jackie's hand until she petted her.

"Everything okay?" Jackie asked.

"Everything's fine," she said. "How's Dad? Is he awake?"

"He's knocked out. I'm betting he'll sleep for a few hours."

Becca nodded.

"It's good he's sleeping, you know," Jackie said. "He's resting, and that's more than he's been able to do in a very long time. The treatments." She paused. "The chemo was killing him. He couldn't sleep. He was sick all of the time. His feet and hands were covered in an itchy, painful rash. His mouth was full of blisters. He couldn't eat or swallow."

They were quiet. Jackie was the first to break the silence.

"Well, anyway. It's good he's sleeping soundly," she said and walked out of the room.

Becca wasn't about to wake up her father, not after what Jackie had said. She grabbed her car keys from the kitchen counter. Romy pranced, believing they were going for a ride.

"I can't take you with me," she said and kissed her on the nose. "They don't allow dogs where I'm going."

Romy looked dejected. She barked when Becca left without her, and Becca felt bad. She promised to make it up to the dog with a new toy or extra playtime.

She hopped in her Jeep and raced down the road.

CHAPTER TWENTY-FIVE

Parker sat on a stool in the pub not two miles from the station. It was a favorite hangout for the guys in his troop. The pub was a place for them to meet, shake off the job before they went home to their families. Parker didn't drink, nor did he have family to go home to, but he often dropped by for a club soda to show he was one of them. He was a team player.

Tonight was different, however. He'd gotten a call from a retired detective, a Rick Smith, who had handled the first river body case, the name the case had been given long before Parker had joined the force. He was sitting at the bar listening to an old Hank Williams Jr. song about a tear in his beer. He ordered a second club soda when Rick Smith slid onto the stool next to him. Rick wasn't wearing the standard dark suit and bland tie that Parker and the other detectives donned, but he still looked the part in jeans and sweatshirt. There was a look about cops, detectives, an air of confidence, craftiness, a complete lack of emotion on their faces that was expected on the job. Parker believed he'd mastered these skills, aware of the shift in his personality, the toughness the job required settling deep inside his bones, taking up permanent residence. It was only when he'd been alone with Becca that he'd felt the mask slip away, felt himself slide into the old Parker of his youth, free and easygoing. The moment hadn't lasted long, and he'd recovered, but it had been there. He'd felt it when he'd been sitting next to her, along with other emotions he wished he hadn't.

"Thanks for meeting me." Rick signaled Benny, the bartender, for a beer.

"What's this about?" Parker asked. Detectives were often protective of their cases, holding them close, keeping outsiders and intruders from telling them how to do their job. But Parker was willing to hear Rick out. It was Parker's first big case, and he had a bad feeling about it.

"Tell me what you know about the case, and I'll tell you what's not in the file," Rick said.

Benny placed a mug of whatever was on draft in front of Rick, interrupting their conversation. "Good to see you," Benny said. The two shook hands. "How's retirement treating you?"

"Boring as hell," Rick said. "I'm not going to lie. I miss the work but not enough to come back." Benny was called to the other end of the bar. Rick turned toward Parker, looking at him closely. "You're a bit green to be the lead on this one, aren't you?"

Parker took a drink of club soda. "I'm the perfect man for the job."

"Why's that?"

"I was born and raised in Portland. If the people in town are going to talk with anyone, it's going to be with me."

"You may have a point," Rick said and took a long swallow of beer. "Damn funny town of yours. Most people like to talk; they like the attention. But the people in your neck of the woods, they don't say a word. You ask them a question, and they stare at you as though they don't speak the same language. Why do you think that is?"

"They're private people," Parker said, trying to keep the defensiveness he felt out of his tone. He couldn't help it. He had a loyalty to his hometown that had never left him. Maybe it had to do with the way he had been raised with a sense of responsibility, devotion to the small, tight community that for the most part had been a safe place to grow up. Maybe that was why he'd transferred to the field station at the first opportunity, to be close to the people who knew him best, to live his life quietly alongside the river and leave behind the day-to-day problems that came with the job. There was truth to this, but there was also a deeper reason for why he'd returned, one he was just starting to figure out.

"If you ask me, they don't talk because they're scared," Rick said.

Parker didn't reply. He didn't have to. There was a certain look on the faces of the people in town that he'd recognized on his own father's face. He'd been a boy when he'd first become aware of his father's activities where the Scions were concerned. It had happened one night when Parker had been up late, past his bedtime, when there had been a knock on their back door. His father had opened the door to find a rough-looking guy on their stoop. The guy had had his hand pressed to his abdomen, blood pouring through his fingers.

"In here," Parker's father had said, leading the man in the leather cut and tattoos to his office on the side of the house where his private practice had been located. He'd directed the man to lie on the table. The door to the examination room had been left open a crack, and Parker had peered in, watched as his father had worked, cutting the clothes away from the guy's wound, blood splattering the front of his father's white lab coat that he'd thrown on over his pajamas at the last second.

The man had been sweating, his face a putrid white. "The mother-fucker stabbed me," he'd said.

"Don't say anything more," his father had said, working frantically to stop the bleeding. "I don't want to know." In another hour, his father had had him stitched up, and then he'd left the examination room where the man had lain resting, waiting for his ride.

His father had returned to the house and poured himself a shot of whiskey.

Parker had stepped out of the shadows. His father had jumped. His hand had been shaking.

"Why do you help them?" Parker had asked, wondering why his father had bothered to help men like the Scions.

"Everybody deserves care," his father had said. "Even criminals," he'd added.

Parker's father had never reported the incidents to the local police. He'd treated the members of the club without questions whenever they'd appeared on their doorstep, sometimes at all hours of the day and night, with open wounds, busted-up faces, gashes on their heads, swollen knuckles, and broken fingers. Parker believed his father had been afraid to turn the men away, to turn them in out of fear of what they might have done to him if he had, when all Parker had wanted to do was put them behind bars.

"Tell me about your case," Rick said.

Parker didn't see any reason why not. He'd stick to the facts. "The victim was a young guy from Jersey. He had some priors, the biggest being a felony for armed robbery. There are rumors he was involved with a motorcycle gang in Jersey. It's not clear what his connection to them might be. Nothing in the system to confirm one way or the other."

Rick drank from the mug. "And what about the body?" he asked.

"Shot and gutted and dumped in the river."

"And washed up on our side."

"Don't they always," Parker said.

"Any problems with the Jersey State Police wanting to take it over?"

"They won't touch it. We found some of the victim's blood on our side of the river a few miles upstream from where the body washed up. No question it's ours." He thought about the clearing in the woods, the spot along the river where the dogs had picked up the scent, the blood where the guts had been discarded. They believed an animal had come along and devoured them, an animal that had gorged itself, had a taste for human flesh.

"What else have we got?" Rick asked.

We? Parker thought, but he let it go. He'd answer Rick's questions, expecting Rick to hold up his end of the bargain and divulge the information he had on the first case, information that wasn't in the original file.

"The victim was shot with a .30-06 rifle, same make and model as the first case but different gun, according to ballistics. The knife was a common hunting knife that any number of hunters in the entire Slate Belt area carries. We're dragging the river for both." They'd searched every inch of the crime scene and surrounding woods. Maybe they'd get lucky in the river. Ever since he'd been a young boy, Parker had believed the river had her own kind of intelligence and that she'd held secrets, and all a person had to do to hear them was listen.

He was listening.

"We dragged the river too," Rick said. "What felt like every inch of it at the time. Never found the rifle or the knife. But it was the knife that interested me the most. The field dressing was his signature. If we would've found the knife, we would've had him."

Parker had the same thoughts.

Rick continued. "We knew the Scions were involved. We had our suspect, the enforcer at the time, a guy by the name of Russell Jackson. We searched his place. We even tore apart his barn. I was so sure we'd find something." He shrugged. "But we didn't."

Parker nodded. Rick wasn't telling him anything he didn't already know.

"I don't suppose you have any witnesses?" Rick asked.

"None yet." Parker stared at his glass. Condensation dripped down the sides, making a small puddle on the bar. He'd talked to a few potential witnesses, made a full sweep of the town, but so far no one had given him anything to go on. He was waiting for the local news media to move on and forget about his case before he tried again, knocking door-to-door. Only then would he have any chance of getting some information out of the locals. But Rick was right; people were scared.

Rick finished his beer and signaled Benny for another. He waited until his mug was refilled. When Benny stepped away, Rick picked up the mug and asked, "Do you know Clint Kingsley?"

"Yes." Parker cleared his throat. "He was the chief of police until about five years ago."

"Yeah, well, he was the first cop at the scene on the first case. He handled the investigation for the first seventy-two hours before we got wind of it, of the implications of what the case entailed. You know how important those first forty-eight hours are, so you can imagine my partner and I weren't too thrilled about taking it on after seventy-two hours."

Parker didn't reply. Something told him the bad feeling he'd had earlier was about to get worse.

Rick continued. "He was annoyed. He didn't seem to want us involved, and at the same time, it was like he didn't want any part of it either. I thought it was a little strange, but like I said, the people in your town were a little peculiar around that time. No offense."

"None taken," Parker said and grabbed an ice cube to suck on.

"When we finally got around to his office, his whole demeanor changed. He went from being annoyed to downright uncooperative. He wanted to know why we were so interested in the case. He said it was small-town stuff and he was perfectly capable of handling it. Then he goes on to tell us that since it was so small town, he hadn't even finished his report and he needed some time. He said he was waiting for the medical examiner's report. We told him not to worry about any of that, to just hand over whatever he had, we'd take it from there. But no, this guy insisted he finish his report and all but threw us out."

"Maybe Clint just liked to keep the town's police matters under his control. It was his job, after all," Parker said. He refused to believe Becca's father was incompetent or crooked in any way.

"Maybe. But the report we got was shit. Hell, he could've typed it up while we were standing there. There was nothing in it. I always suspected we didn't get the original report from him, but I could never prove it. So we followed him for a while."

"You tailed him?"

"Yeah, for a couple of weeks, to see what would turn up. Like I said, we didn't have the rifle or the knife. We just didn't have enough evidence to make an arrest. We knew the chief was the younger stepbrother of our guy, Russell. We were hoping he would lead us to him."

"And?" Parker asked. The muscles in his arms tensed.

"And nothing," Rick said. "Clint was clean. I'd even go as far as to say he was a good chief."

Parker's body relaxed.

"So that makes the flimsy report and his behavior all the more confusing." He paused. "Well, there was one flaw in his character. Hell, nobody's perfect."

"And what was that?" They were talking about Becca's father, a man Parker had looked up to most of his life, and his curiosity about Clint, his curiosity in general, had gotten the better of him.

"Let's just say he liked women."

Parker had heard the rumors before, how Clint had been seen around town with different women while he'd still been married to Becca's mother. There was always some truth to gossip. Parker had wondered about it back when he and Becca had been in high school, but she hadn't liked to talk about her father, and Parker hadn't pried.

"And how is any of this supposed to help my case now?" He wondered what he was supposed to do with all of this noninformation. Russell Jackson was dead, so he couldn't be responsible for this crime. But his son could be the copycat killer. Parker knew John Jackson had stepped in as the enforcer, taking his father's place in the club. But what Parker hadn't been able to find was what had eluded Rick on the first case, the hard evidence to make an arrest.

"Clint knew something," Rick said. "All these years later, and it still keeps me up at night. He knew something. He wears a badge same as us, but he wasn't talking. Why? Who was he protecting? Russell? The history we dug up on them was that they'd never gotten along. It didn't seem likely that Clint would protect him, not for something this big." He paused. "Well, that was my gut feeling anyway."

The door to the bar swung open, bringing a draft of cold air into the place. Both Parker and Rick turned in their seats to see who had walked in. Parker recognized the pixie cut, the slight build, the big, careful eyes of the girl who had once been his best friend.

Rick was eying her closely. Parker's pulse picked up. After what Rick had suspected about her father, Parker felt an overwhelming need to protect her. The best way he knew how was to pretend he hadn't recognized her. He turned back to the bar, hoping she wouldn't spot him.

"Hey," Becca said, tapping him on the shoulder.

Parker turned around, feigning surprise. "Hey," he said. "What are you doing here?"

"I was looking for you," she said, touching the small stud in her right ear. "I stopped by the station. They told me to check here."

"Aren't you going to introduce me?" Rick asked, keeping his eyes on her.

Parker didn't like the way the retired detective was looking her over. "Sorry," Parker said. "Becca, this is Rick Smith."

Rick seemed to be studying her face. "You look familiar," he said. "Have we met before?"

"No," Becca was quick to say—too quick, which made Parker think she was lying.

"Are you sure? I never forget a face, and yours is definitely familiar," Rick said.

Behind where they were sitting, some of the guys hooted and hollered over the hockey game they were watching on TV.

Parker used the brief disruption as an opportunity. "Sit," he said to Becca and pulled the stool out on the other side of him, putting himself between her and Rick.

No one said anything. Parker didn't know how he was going to get Rick to leave, but then Rick stood. "Well, that's it for me." Before he walked away, he said to Becca, "I'm sure I know you from somewhere. It'll come to me sooner or later. Probably in the middle of the night. Don't you hate when that happens? I can never get back to sleep." He stared at her a second more.

She kept her head down, didn't reply. Parker wanted to shield her from Rick's glare.

"Okay," Rick said. "It was nice meeting you, Becca." He slapped Parker on the back. "Keep in touch."

CHAPTER TWENTY-SIX

Becca was ten years old. She was outside skipping rope at the end of her driveway. Sheba was darting around the yard, carrying her favorite toy, the kind that squeaked every time she bit down.

"Forty-one, forty-two, forty-three." Becca counted the jumps with each swing of the rope. Her goal was to make it to one hundred without missing.

Her mother was volunteering again at the nursing home across town. She'd been spending more and more of her free time there, out of their house and away from Becca's father. Her mother read to the patients from their favorite books and magazines, and occasionally she styled the women's hair or applied a little makeup to their cracked and withered faces. She'd said it made them feel better, like somebody cared. It made them feel human. But mostly, her mother had said, it made *her* feel good.

Becca's father's truck was parked in front of the garage. He'd chased her outside when he'd come home, eager for her to leave the house, demanded she play outdoors. He'd said he'd let her know when she could come back in. The weather was pleasant enough, so she didn't mind so much, although the wind bit at her ears. She'd made it to sixty-six when her foot caught the rope just as a dark-blue sedan slowed and pulled into the driveway, coming to a full stop beside her.

She blinked.

The driver's-side window went down. "Do you live here?" the man in the sedan asked.

"Yes, sir," she said and looked back at the house. She wasn't supposed to talk to strangers. Should she run and get her father? Or would he be angry at her for interrupting him? Sheba had stopped playing with her toy, although it was still in her mouth. She stood in the middle of the yard and stared at the car, eyes and ears alert.

The man in the sedan must've sensed her hesitation. "It's okay," he said and flashed his badge. "I'm a police officer. You can call me Jim, and this is my partner, Rick. Is that your dad's truck? Is he home?"

Because her father was chief of police, she knew the other cops in town by name, but she had never heard of Jim or Rick. These two weren't from Portland. They weren't wearing the typical police-blue uniforms her father and the other Portland officers wore.

She took a step back.

"What do you say you take us inside," Officer Jim said and got out of the car. He was tall and thin, in a suit and tie. He looked important. Sheba barked.

"My father's home, but he doesn't want to be disturbed."

"Oh, yeah? Why's that?"

By this time Officer Rick had gotten out of the car. He was wearing a suit too, and when he put his hand on his hip, Becca saw a gun strapped to his side.

"He has company," she said.

Officer Jim smiled. "Is that so?" He turned to his partner. "Maybe we should go in and see who it is."

"We're not here to get involved in small-town domestic shit," Officer Rick said. "Just tell him we're here," he said to Becca.

She didn't want to go inside and get her father, but she didn't believe she had a choice. Sheba sniffed around the two officers' legs. Officer Rick bent down to pet her.

Becca stepped through the front door, dragged her feet up the stairs. The mattress in her parents' bedroom creaked. "Dad," she called and knocked. There was more creaking, heavy breathing.

"Dad," she hollered and kicked the door. The room grew quiet. Then there was the sound of muffled voices and shuffling around.

In the next minute, her father pulled open the door. "What the hell?" He stepped into the hall, yanked the door closed behind him. He was shirtless, and the button of his pants was undone. "I told you to wait outside."

She stared at her feet. He smelled funny. "There are two police officers outside waiting to talk with you. They're not from around here."

He pushed past her and entered her bedroom to look out her window. "Shit," he said and grabbed Becca by the arm. "Go on and tell them I'll be out in a minute."

She went back outside. Sheba was lying in the driveway, chewing the handle on Becca's jump rope. "He's coming," she said to the two officers, looking at her feet once again, ashamed and confused about what her father was doing with another woman in her parents' bedroom. It was wrong. She knew it was wrong, but what was she supposed to do about it?

The two officers leaned against the side of their sedan and waited.

It was another few minutes before her father approached them from the garage, fully dressed. "What gives you the right to barge into my home?"

"We're here for the river body case." Officer Jim, who turned out to be Detective Jim Cronen, flashed his badge. "We'd like your cooperation."

"I'm still the goddamn police chief around here. You want to talk with me, then you come to my office."

"We were already there. One of your boys told us we could find you here," Detective Smith said.

"Well, hell." Becca's father ran his hand over his head. "You want the case? No problem. It's yours. But don't come to my home the next time and bother my family, you hear?"

The detectives exchanged a look, shrugged.

"Give me an hour, and I'll meet you downtown." Her father walked back toward the house, pointing his finger in Becca's direction. "Don't go anywhere," he said to her.

She was back on the detectives' radar. Instead of getting into their car and driving away, they called her over.

"Do you play in these woods around here along the river?" Detective Smith motioned to the area around her house. Her house was the only one on the street, if you didn't count the farm five miles up the road or Russell's farmhouse a mile down the road in the other direction.

"Yes, sir." The woods were her playground, along with the farmers' cornfields. The river was her watering hole.

"You didn't happen to see anyone in the woods in the last few days or by the river, did you? Maybe it was someone you knew, or someone who looked like they might be hunting when they shouldn't be?" Detective Smith asked.

She looked Detective Smith in the eye. She was angry at the detectives for forcing her to go into the house to get her father, madder still at her father for all the ways he hurt her.

"No, sir," she said. "I didn't see anything like that."

She lied.

❦

Becca looked over her shoulder. She waited until the retired detective was gone before she spoke. "I know him," she said, her voice barely above a whisper. Parker smelled of aftershave and a hint of the outdoors, the damp, earthy scent she recognized from the river.

"How do you know him?" Parker asked.

She looked around the bar, sizing up the men and the handful of women. Most of them looked like cops. They looked like her father and Toby and the retired detective. And Parker. They all had an air about them, their clipped, neat hair, their shoulders squared, their eyes attentive even in a relaxed setting of a bar. The job never left them. She wondered if that was one of the reasons why the divorce rate was so high. They didn't know how to relate to their families once they were home, as though they were constantly on guard, talking to loved ones as though they were interrogating them. Or at least that had been Becca's experience.

"I met him once a long time ago," she said. "He came to the house looking for my dad." She stopped, unsure how or if she should continue. The day the detective and his partner had pulled into her driveway had been the same day her father had chased her outside, the same day her father had brought a strange woman to their house, to their home, and twenty years later Becca still felt the sting of what he'd done.

"What did he want with your dad?" Parker asked.

She looked Parker in the eyes, searching for her friend, the one she'd trusted completely when she'd been a kid. He looked back at her, and for a second, she was lost in his stare, seeing the same old Parker and something more. Her heart beat a little faster. "I'm not sure," she said. "My father had kicked me out of the house." She looked at her hands in her lap.

Parker didn't say anything. He seemed to be waiting for her to continue. When she didn't, he tossed money onto the bar to cover the tab and more. "Let's get out of here," he said.

"Where should we go?" she asked.

"My place?"

168

Becca followed Parker in her Jeep, anticipation and nervousness knotting her stomach. She told herself repeatedly on the twenty-minute drive back to Portland, back to the river, she was being ridiculous, getting herself all worked up. But she hadn't been alone with another man, in another man's home, in the last five years. Fishing was one thing. This was something else. "Get a hold of yourself," she whispered and gripped the steering wheel. "It's just Parker."

She pulled in behind him and cut the lights. It was darker than pitch, and she stumbled trying to find the path to his front door.

"Hang on," he said, his voice coming from somewhere in front of her.

"I forgot how dark it gets underneath the trees around here." The condo where she and Matt lived was always lit, motion detectors turning on the second you stepped outside. But here along the river at the edge of the woods, you could put your hand in front of your face and not see it. Only when you stood along the riverbank could you look up at the night sky and see the light of the moon and stars. She had forgotten this, forgotten the sights, smells, and sounds of the place she'd once loved.

Parker flipped a switch from somewhere inside, turning on small lanterns that lit the walkway to the porch. Each step she took on the lit path felt almost magical, as though she were walking on her very own yellow brick road.

"I'm just going to change out of these clothes," he said, loosening the tie around his neck and what she thought of as his detective uniform. "Make yourself comfortable. I'll only be a second."

She looked around his place, surprised to find the cabin open and spacious and what she considered rustic chic. The hardwood floors, the leather furniture, the wood fixtures, all various shades of brown, but intertwined were pops of cherry red, a throw pillow, a small area rug. She touched the blanket tossed on the back of the couch, a patchwork that looked to be handmade. A stack of magazines teetered on the floor next to what looked to be Parker's favorite chair, the remote control resting on top of the armrest. She picked up a magazine, *Field & Stream*. She sifted through a couple more, *Fly Fisherman, Bassin'*. He was the boy she remembered from high school, and in a good way. She smiled, thinking about how much he enjoyed fishing. She put the magazines back the way she'd found them and wandered into the kitchen, running her hand over the wood-block table, pausing next to a large island with a granite countertop, taking in the stainless steel appliances.

Parker appeared from the back bedroom, wearing jeans and a rumpled T-shirt with the decal GONE FISHING. She almost laughed, immediately at ease now that he wasn't wearing the detective suit. She wasn't sure she'd ever get used to seeing him in a jacket and tie.

"Is this a gourmet kitchen?" she asked.

"I like to cook." He looked a little embarrassed about it.

"What do you cook?"

"Mostly whatever I catch in the river or what I pick up at the farmers market."

"Do they still have the open market on Wednesdays and Saturdays?" Twice a week Becca and her mother had driven to town to pick up fresh fruit and produce from the stands lined all along the street near the pedestrian bridge in the center of town. They'd made a morning of it, picking out strawberries and sweet corn and tomatoes. Sometimes they'd bumped into Becca's father. He'd be standing outside his patrol car talking with the locals and tourists. He'd make a big production out of seeing them, doting on her mother, putting his arm around Becca's shoulder as though he were a politician running for office, showcasing what a wonderful husband and father he was to his family. It had been an act. It had been bullshit.

"Nothing ever changes around here. You should know that," Parker said about the market. He gazed at her for a long moment before turning away. "Do you want a drink?" He pulled open the refrigerator door. "I don't keep alcohol in the house. But I have root beer."

He put ice in two glasses and poured from the can. They sat across from each other at the table with their drinks.

"Your place is really great," she said and meant it. Not only did the decor suit her taste, but to wake up every morning and step out the back door to the sun rising over the river, well, this was the dream house she'd always imagined herself in. It was perfect.

The mask he'd been wearing in the bar, the one he'd worn with the retired detective, had been completely removed from his face. "I'm happy here," he said in such a way as though he were asking if she was happy too.

Was she? No, she didn't think she was. The pristine condo and its secure walls had always made it hard for her to breathe. The gated community caused her throat to close.

"Why no alcohol?" she asked to redirect the conversation away from her happiness, or rather, unhappiness. "You used to drink beer, as I recall." She remembered the partying they'd done in high school. Not all of her memories of home were bad ones. Some of her best times had been with Parker fishing, partying, hanging out.

He turned the glass around in his hands. "I did a lot of partying when I was in college. I started waking up not remembering anything that happened the night before. I couldn't remember conversations I'd had or where I'd been." He paused. "And then one morning in my junior year, I woke up next to some girl I didn't recognize. I didn't know her name or how I ended up in her bed. She was a complete stranger to me. And I didn't like not knowing the person I'd spent the night with. It felt wrong. I didn't like who I was." He drank from his glass and set it down, keeping his eyes on the table in front of him. "So I stopped drinking, and I never looked back."

"One night with a stranger was enough to turn you around?" Becca had done some partying in college but not enough for her to wake up in bed with some strange guy. Mostly she'd focused her energy on her studies, her eye on veterinary school.

Parker smiled a little. "Well, there was a couple more nights of partying after that."

"And girls?"

"Them too."

"Oh," she said, disappointed in some way. Why did she care how many girls he'd been with? What did it matter now?

"But eventually, I stopped drinking, and the rest took care of itself. Apparently when I'm sober, I'm not as charming with the ladies as I am when I'm drunk." He continued. "But that didn't matter to me. Besides, I started to see a pattern. All the girls I'd been hooking up with had something in common."

She'd only ever been with Matt. She had no one else to compare him to. "What did they have in common?"

He drank the rest of the soda in his glass and set it on the table, staring at her with that intensity again that had made her uncomfortable. "They all resembled you," he said.

"Me?" She was confused at first, but in her confusion, she knew it was what she wanted to hear. She'd waited all those years in high school for him to see her as more than a friend. "What are you saying?" she asked to be clear, gripping the seat of her chair with both hands.

"I was missing you, and I was drinking. I guess I was searching for a substitute. But they weren't you. All I kept thinking was they weren't you."

She touched her forehead. Her hand was shaking. She didn't know what to say, or if she could even talk if she found the words. He didn't move. He kept staring at her, waiting for her to do something. He looked hopeful and vulnerable.

"I missed you too." She touched her neck. "I didn't realize how much until I saw you the other day." She furrowed her brow. What was she trying to say? Did she feel something more? She didn't know. She opened her mouth to say something, anything, but he cut her off.

"Did you know that I searched for you the summer you left? I looked for you everywhere. And then your dad told me you went to boarding school. He said you didn't want any contact with me and that I should stay away from you."

"I never told him that I didn't want any contact with you." Of course her father had manipulated them both. She should've known. "I never knew you came looking for me. He never told me." Her brow furrowed. If what Parker was saying was true, she needed to be honest with him too. "When I left, things at home weren't good, and things between us weren't the same. Everything felt different. I was confused about so much. I needed a clean break. I just . . ."

"Becca, listen, the thing between us, I was a stupid sixteen-year-old boy. I was afraid of my own feelings. And the other girls." He shrugged. "I guess they felt safe."

She nodded. They'd both been so young. It had happened so long ago. She didn't know what made her do it, but she reached across the table, took his hand. She saw the yearning in his eyes. And all she knew was right then, right there, she wanted to touch him. She wanted him to touch her. She wanted his body close. There was no other place she wanted to be. He must've read her mind, because he stood, pulled her out of the chair and into his arms. He was so tall she had to stand on tiptoes to reach around his neck. She pressed against him. He squeezed her tight as though he never wanted to let her go.

They held each other for a long time. Her body responded to his touch in ways she never would've guessed. If she leaned back even a little, she would kiss him, and if she kissed him, she didn't think she would be able to stop. Her body ached for more of him, for him to touch her in all the places that made her weak and out of breath. But there was Matt. He didn't know about Matt. And he didn't know about John being at the river, what she may or may not have seen, what it might mean to his case. It was the reason she'd searched for him in the first place. But she couldn't bring it up now. She didn't know how.

Her muscles constricted, and she felt tense suddenly. Parker must've sensed the change in her. He pulled away.

They separated. He looked a little embarrassed, apologetic. He was trembling.

"I . . . I," she stuttered. "I should go."

He ran his hand through his hair, nodded.

But she couldn't get her feet to move, and when she met his gaze, she found herself reaching for him again—she couldn't help it—and he pulled her into his arms. This time she kissed him long and hard. Before she could stop herself from going any further, not that she wanted to stop, they'd moved into the bedroom, fumbling with each other's clothes. She didn't have time to catch her breath, to think.

She'd forgotten who she was, where she came from, but in Parker's arms, in his bed, it all came rushing back. His skin, his touch, the smell of his sweat, the sweetness in his breath as though he'd been sipping honeysuckle that grew wild along the riverbank, it all reminded her of what was once good, what was once home. There wasn't any of the anger or the guilt or the apology of another woman between them. Becca wasn't trying to reclaim what was hers or stake a claim of any kind. It was just her and Parker and no one else.

But there were other things there too, darker things, slithering on the periphery of her mind, things she had promised to never talk about, things she'd kept hidden even from herself.

🦋

Becca sat up abruptly. *This was a mistake.* But how could a mistake feel so right? *No, this was wrong.* She was no better than Matt. Or her father.

"I have to go," she said.

"Now?" Parker leaned on his elbows. His chest bare, his abs sculpted. But it was his strong thighs between her legs that she was thinking about that made the heat on her neck rise as she pulled on her clothes as quickly as she could.

"I wasn't supposed to be gone this long." She made up the first excuse she could think of. "I have to get back to my dad." She kept talking while she zipped her jeans, clasped her bra, tugged her sweatshirt on. "I'm supposed to be helping Jackie."

"Okay," he said, a little put off. "Are you okay? I mean, are you okay with what happened?"

"Yeah," she said. "Totally. I'm fine." She pointed to the bedroom door. "Can we talk about this later? I really have to go."

"Sure," he said. "Yeah, okay."

She raced through his cabin, threw herself out the front door and into the dark night. She hurried along the enchanted walkway, as she had come to think of it now. It wasn't until she was in her Jeep and a few miles up the road that she pulled over to collect herself. What did she think she was doing? She looked over her shoulder.

Maybe she should turn around, fall back into Parker's arms, burrow deep in his warmth, a place where she could hide before the outside world inserted itself between them, tore them apart. But she had run out on him for reasons that had nothing to do with him and everything to do with her.

She rolled the windows down, in need of fresh air. The sound of rapids rushed by; she had to be close to Dead Man's Curve.

Tangled with the noise of the river was the rumbling of an engine growing louder and louder as it came closer and closer. Her breath caught as the single headlight of a motorcycle approached from behind. The biker slowed, the engine purring alongside the Jeep, the rider stopping long enough to look inside the driver's-side window. She couldn't make out his face in the dark, but she knew it was John. Was he following her? Spying on her? Or was this some kind of warning, because she knew something she shouldn't? He nodded ever so slightly, revving the engine, then speeding away. In the next second, he was gone.

She pulled from the curb and back onto the road, gripping the steering wheel until her knuckles were white.

CHAPTER TWENTY-SEVEN

John parked his father's chopper in the barn. He removed his helmet, but he stayed on the bike, not wanting to get off just yet. Ever since he'd gotten it up and running, all he'd wanted to do was ride it. It was as though he was channeling his father through the bike, hearing his father's advice, following his imaginary orders. John's own motorcycle sat idle on the side of the house.

He continued sitting on Russell's chopper in the barn in the dark. Nearby, an owl screeched into the night. The light from the moon crept through the opened double doors, casting shadows on the dirt floor. The autumn air was cool and crisp, but he was sweating underneath the leather cut, his thoughts on Becca.

He'd followed her first to the police station and then to Benny's Bar, where cops congregated off duty. He knew the bar, knew of the owner, Benny, but he'd never been inside. The Scions kept their distance from such places for obvious reasons. She hadn't been aware he was following her. She hadn't noticed him, not until he'd wanted her to notice, when he'd pulled alongside her Jeep. He'd meant it to serve as a warning. *I'm watching you*, he'd wanted to say. He'd been able to get a glimpse of her face from the dim lights of the dashboard. She'd looked scared, and after her actions tonight, she should've been.

If she was talking to the police, she left him no choice. He was going to have to take care of the situation. He didn't want to hurt her. He'd never wanted to hurt her. Everything inside of him screamed he was supposed to protect her. He'd felt this in his core, in his bones, ever since she'd been a little girl.

John bent at the waist, his head between the handlebars. He was having trouble breathing. He'd never survive in jail. He smacked his fist on the leather seat between his legs, the pain in his knuckles flaring from an old wound, the arthritis forming around the damaged joints where he'd broken his hand pounding his fist into the face of the guy that had tried to touch her, tried to pick her up in Sweeney's Bar when she'd been a teenager.

After he'd given her a ride home, he'd returned to the bar, a white-hot fury burning his insides. He'd found the guy with the skull rings sitting at the table, pawing another girl. He'd grabbed the collar of the guy's cut and lifted him out of his seat, tossing him to the floor. Rage had taken control of him, had coiled around the muscles in his back and arms. He hadn't been able to stop. He'd struck him over and over again, beating him until every bone in the guy's face had cracked. If Beth hadn't been there, if she hadn't placed her tender hand on John's shoulder, her voice cutting through the chaos in his mind, he'd have beaten the guy to death.

He rubbed his hand where the knuckles ached with the memory, where the rage moved below the surface of his skin, a constant flickering in his veins.

Russell's voice exploded in John's head. *You no longer have a choice*, it said. *It's time you take her out.*

CHAPTER TWENTY-EIGHT

After leaving Parker's cabin, Becca had returned to her father's house. She'd found Jackie in the kitchen, flustered, her father crying out upstairs. Becca had spent the rest of the night sitting with him, until the very early hours of the morning, trying to make him as comfortable as possible.

Now, she headed outside with Romy. The sun was bright, too harsh for her tired, bloodshot eyes. A cool breeze blew. She tossed a stick for Romy to chase.

She tried hard not to think about Parker, to push the thoughts away. But the events of last night played over and over again in her mind, as though they were stuck on rewind. If she were honest, she was scared to tell Parker the things she knew about John. Something inside of her held her tongue. She wasn't imagining it; something was there in her past. She hadn't realized it until John had pulled his motorcycle alongside her Jeep. The memory had surfaced, but it had been fleeting, an image that could only be seen out of the corner of her eye.

Becca picked up the stick, tossed it again for Romy. When Romy brought it back, Becca sat on the cold ground among the crabgrass and weeds, scratched behind the dog's ears, buried her face in the dog's fur. Eventually, Romy tired of the attention and trotted away to do her business.

Becca got up and walked to the Jeep to grab the plastic bags from the console. She glanced up at her father's bedroom window, remembering the time when Sheba had done something much worse than going to the bathroom in his yard.

🦋

Becca was playing in the driveway with colored chalk, making a hopscotch only she would ever use. She took care to make the hopscotch challenging but not too difficult, so she wouldn't become frustrated if the rock she'd tossed happened to miss a square. She hadn't been paying attention to Sheba. The dog had wandered into the backyard with her rawhide bone.

"Becca, goddamn it," her father hollered. "Get over here."

She dropped the chalk; the green dust covered her fingers and palm. She walked around the back of the house, head down.

"Look at this," her father said. His voice rose to a level of near hysteria. "Do you see what your dog did?" He pointed to a spot on the ground not far from his boots. The grass had been dug up, and nothing remained but a pile of dirt where Sheba had been digging.

She nodded her head once—a small movement, but one he acknowledged.

"This isn't the first time either, you know. I've been filling in these holes all over the yard. She's got to stop. Train her or something," he said, lowering his voice to a more reasonable decibel. "I'm going to fix this." He pointed to the dirt pile. "But it better not happen again. Do you hear?"

"Yes, sir."

"Now, go on. And get that dog out of here. She's got to learn she's not allowed to dig up my yard."

Becca worked with Sheba over the next few weeks, hiding Sheba's favorite toys in the ground at the edge of the woods near the base of an oak tree. Over time, Sheba learned to dig in that one spot, thrilled to see which toy she would discover. And she didn't dig up Becca's father's precious yard again.

Becca shook her head at the memory, wondering what in the world had made him so obsessed with his yard. "It's about image," her mother had told her. It had been during the spring of Becca's junior year in high school. "And it's about control. If he can keep his yard looking good, the sparkling image of happiness, then he believes everything else in his life is good and under control."

"You know that sounds crazy, right?" Becca had said.

Her mother had smiled a wicked smile. "It does sound crazy, doesn't it?"

It had been one year later, on the morning Becca had been packing, her senior year at the boarding school in Philadelphia ending, that she'd spied her mother's suitcases in the trunk of the car.

"I got an apartment right here in Philly," her mother had said. "Just someplace for me to stay for a little while."

"I don't understand." Becca had rented a room on campus where she'd enrolled in a summer class before college officially started in the fall.

"I'm leaving your dad," she'd said as a matter of fact, no emotion in her tone. "I finally reached a point where I had enough. A person can only take so much. And besides, you're all grown up now, starting college. You have your own life. There's no longer anything left for me there, not with you gone."

She hadn't had to ask why or what her mother had been waiting for. It had been clear she'd been waiting for Becca to grow up, to leave home for good and start her own life, so she could be free.

"What about Dad?" she'd asked, for the first time worrying about what might happen to him.

"He has his yard," her mother had said.

❦

Becca grabbed one of the plastic bags from the Jeep. She closed the door, walked around to the side of the house, picked up Romy's poop. By the time she returned to the garage in search of the garbage can, a car had pulled into the driveway. It wasn't just any car but a spotless black luxury sedan. She froze, unable to move, watching as Matt parked and got out of his BMW.

"Becca," he said in a breathless way.

She'd almost forgotten how beautiful he was—his shiny black hair, his perfect teeth, his eyes the color of the bluest sky, his perfectly sculpted shoulders and chest. Romy darted from the backyard, barking and jumping around Matt's feet.

"Hello, girl," he said, bending down and petting the dog. "Did you miss me? I missed you." When his reunion with Romy was over, he stood and stared at Becca. He slowly made his way over to her.

She allowed him to envelop her. He held her close, tight, the smell of his cologne familiar and oh, so good. And still she kept her arms by her sides, the bag full of dog poop in her hand.

"I missed you so much," he said.

They separated.

She looked into his blue eyes. She could lose herself in those eyes. "How did you find me?" She was sure she hadn't mentioned her father's address.

"It wasn't that hard. There's only one Clint Kingsley in Portland." He stuffed his hands inside the pockets of his ironed jeans. "I didn't realize he lived so close. It only took me fifteen minutes to get here."

"How's Lucky?" she asked. "You're taking good care of her, right?"

For a moment he had a blank expression on his face as though he had no idea who she was talking about. "Oh, yeah," he said finally.

"Matt," she said, alarmed. "You are feeding her, aren't you? And changing her litter?"

"Of course."

She didn't know if she believed him.

"I am," he said more convincingly.

"Becca," Jackie called from inside the garage.

"Out here," she said.

"I thought I heard a car pull up." Jackie looked at Matt.

Becca introduced them. When she didn't try to explain to Jackie who Matt was or how she knew him, Matt jumped in.

"Becca and I live together." He faltered. "We're together. She didn't mention me?" He gave Becca a strange look.

"Yes, of course she did. Please come in," Jackie said and glanced at Becca, giving her a look that said, *Why didn't you tell me?* She took Matt's arm and led him inside the house.

Reluctantly, Becca followed behind, tossing the bag of shit she was holding into the garbage can. Romy raced past, almost knocking her over, rushing to get through the door first, taking her place on the floor in the kitchen by Matt's side.

"What can I get you? Coffee? Tea?" Jackie asked.

"Coffee would be great," Matt said, smiling at Becca as she sat across from him at the table.

Jackie busied herself with the coffeemaker, looking over her shoulder first at Becca and then at Matt, pausing to stare at him a beat too long. When Matt bent down to scratch behind Romy's ear, Jackie fanned herself and mouthed to Becca, *He's gorgeous.*

Becca shrugged as if to say, *I know.*

The coffee brewed, and Jackie leaned against the counter, crossing her arms. An awkward silence followed. It wasn't until Becca's father started coughing that Jackie excused herself and left them alone.

"How's he doing?" Matt asked of her father.

"Not good," she said. "What are you doing here? I said I'd be in touch. I needed time."

"I know you did. But I couldn't stay away. I wanted to be here for you. I wanted to help you through this."

"I know, and I do appreciate it, but . . ."

Before she could finish, Matt got up, started pacing. It was a habit he had whenever he was preparing for an argument, to plead his case. "No buts, Bec. Let's not fight. I hate it when we fight. Besides, I'm here now." He stopped and stood in front of her. "I've been thinking about us a lot lately. We've been together a long time. And it's only right for me to be here with you when you're going through something like this."

"Matt," she started to say, but Jackie walked back into the kitchen. Then someone behind Matt cleared his throat. Matt swung around. Becca looked up. Parker stood in the doorway. He was wearing his detective suit. Romy greeted Parker by sniffing his shoes, licking his hand at his side.

"You must be Parker," Jackie said and shot Becca a look. "He called this morning while you were outside. He has some questions for Clint."

"Parker." Becca's voice was strained. Her mind jumped first to an image of him lying naked in his bed, then switched to John standing by the river, how he'd pulled his motorcycle alongside of her last night only minutes after she'd left Parker's place. And now Parker was here to ask her father questions.

Matt stepped forward, arm outstretched. "Hi. I'm Matt."

The two shook hands, sized each other up.

"Becca's boyfriend," Matt added, winked at her.

Parker nodded, turned to Jackie. "Can you tell Clint that I'm here?" he asked and made a point of putting his hand on his hip, pulling his jacket back, revealing his sidearm. There'd been a second the detective mask on Parker's face had dropped, a second for Becca to see the surprise register in his eyes when Matt had said he was her boyfriend. But it was more than just surprise. Underneath the stoicism, she saw how hurt he was, how angry and embarrassed he felt.

"Follow me," Jackie said to Parker.

Parker nodded again at Matt, ignored Becca, and followed Jackie upstairs.

Becca stood, wanting to chase after him, to say she was sorry and she had every intention of telling him about Matt but there never seemed to be a right time. But Matt caught her by the elbow.

"What's going on?" He slipped his arm around her waist. "Do you know that guy?"

"Yes," she said, wondering how she could ever explain it to him, where she would even start. "He's an old friend."

"Just an old friend, huh? Are you sure he knows that?"

"Yes." *No.* She hesitated, thinking of the right words. "Matt, listen, please. There's something . . . I'm not . . . I mean . . . I can't."

"Shh." He put his finger on her lips. "It's okay. I know you weren't expecting me to show up at your dad's house. But I had to come, Bec. You leaving and me not knowing when you were coming back, well, it opened my eyes. It showed me how much I need you in my life, how much I want you in my life."

"But," she said, and he put his finger back on her lips.

He continued. "Let me stay and help you through this. Please," he said and lifted her chin so she would look at him. "That's all I'm asking."

No, she wanted to say, *that's not all you're asking. You're asking for so much more. You're asking me to look the other way, to forget about why I left for my father's house in the first place, to forget you never came home that night because you were with another woman.*

"There's something we have to talk about," she said. "There's something you need to know." She had to tell him the truth about Parker. It was only fair.

But Jackie returned again, interrupting them a second time. "They wanted to be alone to talk," she said of Parker and Becca's father. Then she pulled a mug from the cabinet. "Do you take your coffee with cream and sugar?" she asked Matt.

"Black is fine," Matt said, eying Becca.

Everything was moving too fast, spinning around her like a whirlpool, a river current threatening to pull her under. And in the background, behind Jackie's chatter and Matt's words, were the murmur of her father's and Parker's voices and the rumble of a motorcycle racing by.

CHAPTER TWENTY-NINE

Parker stood at the foot of the bed, his face neutral, void of the burning anger in his stomach, the ache in his heart. Clint was struggling to pull himself up against the pillows that were meant to support his back even though the hospital bed was raised so he could sit and confront his visitor. Parker watched, unsure whether he should help, barely recognizing the man in front of him. He hadn't seen Clint in the last ten years, not since the last time he'd knocked on his door looking for Becca. What a fool he'd been then. What a fool he was now.

When Parker had been a kid, the fact that Clint had not only been chief of police but also Becca's father had been more than intimidating. Clint had had a formidable presence, standing at six feet three and weighing 215 pounds. Parker would watch Clint walk through doorways just to see if his shoulders would fit through the open space or whether he'd get stuck, wedged in the door's frame.

Now, Clint was nothing but bones covered in dull, translucent skin, a shell of the man he'd once been. He gave up his struggle to sit up and slumped back on the pillows. His eyes were glassy. Pain hung on his face like a bad picture. He grimaced and waved his hand at Parker, signaling him to speak.

"I was hoping you could help me on a case." Parker took a small step closer to the bed, ignoring the scratchy lump caught in his throat.

"I'm not sure if you heard about a body we pulled from the river a couple of days ago."

Clint stared at him.

"There are a lot of similarities in this case to an older case you had handled originally."

Clint continued staring hard and long at Parker. He could see in Clint's eyes that he understood what Parker was telling him.

"I thought you were here for my daughter." Clint talked through labored breaths, every word filled with pain and effort.

"No, sir," he said. "You've got the wrong guy."

Clint looked confused. Perhaps he wasn't aware of the pretty boy downstairs.

Parker tried to stand a little taller after feeling his shoulders slouch. "I'd like for you to tell me what you remember about the river body case." He stopped when Clint waved his hand at him again, this time telling him to go away.

Parker held his ground. "It's important to my case."

"Becca." Clint's voice cracked.

"Sir, with all due respect, my being here has nothing to do with your daughter. This is about the river body case."

Clint's crooked fingers balled into a fist. He started to cough. His entire body shook from the force of it. When he stopped, he looked Parker straight in the eye. He was very clear when he said, "I have nothing to say to you."

"I don't understand."

Clint waved his bent fingers at him for a third time, dismissing him again as another round of coughing rattled his insides.

Jackie rushed into the room, shooting Parker a look that asked what he'd said to Clint to upset him so much.

Parker didn't know what he was supposed to do, but it was clear Clint wasn't going to answer any of his questions. "If you change your mind," he said, "you know how to reach me."

He strode out of the bedroom, sailed down the stairs and out the front door, avoiding the kitchen and Becca. He passed by the pretty boy's BMW. It took all he had not to pound his fist on the hood, shoot out the tires. He hopped into his patrol car and slammed the driver's-side door. Becca came rushing out of the house, calling his name. He threw the car in reverse and backed out of the driveway, tires squealing as he raced down the road. He'd allowed her to distract him from doing his job, and for what? She had a boyfriend, apparently. Parker felt as though he'd been played. And then her father's refusal to talk with him had made him feel all the more humiliated.

Parker continued driving at a speed well over the speed limit. Who was going to stop him? Toby? Let him try. Besides, it would save him a trip. He was on his way to see the new chief anyway. After all, Toby had been the captain on the first river body case. Maybe he knew something about what Clint was hiding. And Clint was hiding something. Parker had sensed it when he'd been talking to him. He'd felt it in his gut the moment he'd mentioned the body they'd pulled from the river. He was sure he'd seen something in Clint's eyes, a fear that had had nothing to do with his illness. It had been there in the room with them, hanging in the air with the scent of death. Clint had been afraid, but what had he been afraid of? Sometimes it wasn't what the person said but rather what they didn't that told you more than their words ever could.

He continued to Delaware Drive, when his phone went off. He pulled over to take a call from Rick. And why not? He wasn't getting much help from anyone else.

"I found something that might be of interest to you," Rick said.

"I'm listening." Parker watched a couple walking hand in hand, making their way toward the pedestrian bridge. He looked away.

"The victim had a girlfriend, Candy. I found her online on one of them social media sites. Man, people blab about everything these days. Why can't they keep their mouths shut? But hey, who am I to complain? It makes our job that much easier. Anyway, seems she has a connection to some people in your town."

"Oh yeah," Parker said, knowing who Candy was. Did Rick think because Parker was a rookie he didn't know how to do his job? Maybe. Maybe that was the real reason he'd been given the river body case in the first place, and it had nothing to do with his connection to the town. Let the rookie have it, and maybe he'd mess it up, because no one wanted the case solved anyway. No one wanted to disrupt the symbiotic relationship between the motorcycle gang and the entire Slate Belt area.

Rick continued. "She was posting about how much she missed her boyfriend, blah, blah, blah. But she mentioned her aunt who had passed a few years ago of cancer, a Beth Jackson, married to a John Jackson. Ring a bell?"

When Parker didn't respond, he said, "I did some more digging, a few more clicks. Guess where John Jackson lives?" He didn't wait for a reply this time and kept talking. "He's still at his old man's house about a mile down the road from our buddy Clint."

Parker closed his eyes. He knew all of this, although he hadn't known Russell had been Becca's neighbor when they'd been kids. That was the strange part about their town. The people were so spread out that it was impossible to know who your best friend's neighbors might be.

"So," Rick said. There was a beat or two before he added, "You knew, didn't you?"

"I have to go," he said. "Thanks for the help."

Parker pulled into the lot of Portland's police department. He cut the engine and got out of the car, spying the chief's cruiser as he walked into the squat brick building. The place was a mishmash of colors, mostly beige and cream. It smelled like coffee.

Jenna, the only secretary in the department, sat behind a small desk behind the counter. She hadn't changed. She still wore her hair long and straight and parted to the side. But her black frames were new, giving her a no-nonsense look, a different kind of look than when she'd walked the halls in high school.

"Is the chief here?" Parker asked.

"Hey, Parker. He's in his office. Go on back."

He rapped his knuckles on her desk. "Thanks, Jenna."

Any other day he would've knocked before entering the chief's office even though the door was wide open. Given his foul mood, he walked in without bothering.

"What brings you by, Detective?" Toby asked, closing the file at his desk.

"I just came from Clint's," he said.

Toby sat back in the chair. Underneath his uniform was a body he'd allowed to go soft with age, plump, a sign he was comfortable in this town with his job and position. He ran a hand down his face, his stubby fingers stopping at his chin. "He's in bad shape," he said.

"Yes."

Toby nodded. "What can I do for you?" he asked.

"What do you know about the first river body case?"

"It's been a long time. I can't say I remember much. Nothing is jumping out at me anyways. As I recall, it was taken from us pretty quickly by some of your guys." He pointed at Parker's suit, his uniform. "Why?"

Parker sat in one of the chairs in front of Toby's desk without being asked. "We found the rifle." He'd gotten the call earlier that morning.

His team had dragged the river for nearly twenty-four hours before finding it. If only they'd found the knife too.

"Who'd you trace it to?"

"It looks to be clean."

"Prints?"

"We're working on it."

Toby threw his hands up. "Well, I guess you don't have much then, do you?"

"What does Clint know about the first case?" he asked. "What's his real connection to the Scions? There's more to it than him just being Russell's stepbrother."

"Now, hold on, Son," Toby said. Parker hadn't been called *son* since he was a boy running plays on the football field and fishing in the river with his dad. "I think you're jumping to conclusions you don't want to jump to. I've known Clint a long time, and there isn't any way he did something illegal. He was a good cop. He kept that stepbrother of his in line. And speaking of the Scions, I think I have something you might want to take a look at." He pushed the file on his desk toward Parker.

Parker opened it. It was an arrest report listing the names of eleven club members, including John Jackson, who had all been arrested for disturbing the peace.

"You see the date right there." Toby tapped the report where the date was typed in. "These fellas spent the night in jail. They weren't released until noon the next day. So, you see, they were in jail when your victim was shot and whatnot."

"Isn't that convenient." Parker looked up from the file. "It looks like this name was added on as an afterthought." He pointed to John Jackson's name, which had been typed underneath the other names.

"Watch yourself, Son." Toby shifted in his chair, lifting his bulk and settling it back down again. "You don't want to go around accusing the wrong people."

"Why don't you level with me," Parker said. "What exactly is going on here?"

Toby grabbed the report from Parker's hands. "Damned if I know," he said. "My advice to you is to take this seriously"—he shook the report in Parker's face—"and start looking for another angle. Because if you don't and you're looking for trouble, well, that's exactly what you're going to get." He dropped the file back onto the desk.

"That's it?" Parker asked. "That's all you're going to give me?"

"That's it."

"Right. Well, thanks for nothing," Parker said and stood. "It's been a pleasure."

"Son," Toby said, "I don't suppose there's a chance you're going to take my advice and leave this one alone."

"I can't do that, Chief," he said and snatched the file on his way out the door.

CHAPTER THIRTY

Becca sat in the chair next to her father's bed. Her back was sore, and her neck was stiff from craning it forward, staring, waiting for him to open his eyes. *Wake up*, she pleaded silently. *Why did Parker want to talk with you?*

The last time she'd checked, Matt had been in the backyard, pacing back and forth, stomping the crabgrass and weeds. He'd been on his cell phone with a client, a call he had to take, he'd explained to both her and Jackie over an hour ago.

Becca rubbed the back of her neck and stood to look out the window again. She arched her spine and twisted from side to side. Matt had stopped pacing. He was bent over, scratching Romy behind her ears. Normally, the sight of the two of them together would've filled Becca with . . . what? Affection? Yes, she would say it was affection she was feeling, fondness. Whenever anyone showed kindness to an animal, her heart lifted. But this was Matt, the man she had lived with for the better part of five years; the emotion she should be feeling was love.

Romy lay down, hoping to get her belly scratched, but Matt ignored her at this point, distracted by his phone call.

"Becca," her father said.

She spun around and returned to his bedside. "I'm here," she said.

He touched his throat. She picked up the Styrofoam cup filled with water, angled the straw to his lips. He wouldn't drink. She was struggling to accept he was getting weaker with each passing hour, so much weaker than when she'd first arrived a few short days ago. She was keenly aware she was running out of time.

"We need to talk," she said, looking down at the Styrofoam cup in her hand. "It's important. It can't wait."

He blinked. She wasn't sure he understood, but she pressed on.

"There are things I'm starting to remember. Things I don't think you want me to remember." She paused. She wasn't being clear. She could be talking about any number of things she wished she could forget, not just the things he wanted her to forget. *I knew about the other women. Mom and I both knew.* She wanted to shake him. *How could you do that to us? To me?*

Now that she was older, she understood the cracks in her parents' marriage, the holes, weren't about her. And maybe they weren't about her mother either. There were flaws inside of her father, weaknesses, and she and her mother just happened to be the collateral damage. But somehow, she couldn't say these things to him. Sometimes the pain was still too raw. Although she was beginning to understand how infidelities happened, how under the right circumstances, it could be almost impossible to stop them.

She took a deep breath and continued. "There was something that happened when I was a little kid." She'd blocked it from her mind, or rather it had been eclipsed by another tragedy that had occurred a few short days later when her father had brought the other woman into their home.

"Do you know what I'm talking about?" she asked.

His eyes were no longer focused on her, his gaze vacant.

"I think it might have something to do with the body they pulled from the river. I know it doesn't make sense, but . . ." *I might know something about it, Dad. I'm not sure. I think I might be involved. Help me to remember.* The memory was there, and it was getting closer, but each time she reached for it, clinging to the threads of a frayed childhood, the images faded, becoming blurrier, until they slipped away.

His head rolled to the side.

"Dad." She touched his shoulder, then put her hand in front of his mouth to check he was breathing. She pressed her middle and index fingers to his carotid artery. She felt a pulse. Thank goodness. She sat back in the chair. It had taken all the courage she could muster to bring up her childhood, where the dark corners of the past lurked.

Where all she had to do was look.

Becca's father's eyes had closed and stayed that way. Outside, a lawn mower started. She went back to the window and found Matt riding her father's John Deere. She didn't even know he knew how to drive a riding mower. It was so out of character that she was stunned into watching him complete the neat little rows one after the other, the bag collecting the cuttings and the fallen autumn leaves. If she squinted, blurred her vision a little, it could've been her father sitting in the yellow bucket seat. They were more alike, her father and Matt, than she'd ever wanted to believe. How could she not have noticed this before? She backed away from the window, found herself rushing out of the room.

Jackie was in the kitchen on the phone. There was a stack of medical bills in front of her. She smiled when she saw Becca and motioned to the backyard, where Matt was cutting the grass. She gave Becca the thumbs-up and continued talking to whoever was on the other end of the line.

Becca slipped past her, not knowing where she could go to get away from everyone in the house, a place she could go to be alone, sort through the mess in her mind. She paused next to the basement door, deciding it was as good a place as any, and quietly opened it. She hit the light at the top of the steps, looked down the narrow staircase.

When she'd been a child, the basement had been off-limits. It had been where her father had escaped on the rare nights he'd been home, the place he'd gone to get away from Becca and her mother. She'd been curious about what had kept him away from them, what he'd been doing in the damp cold below. And she hadn't forgotten the scolding she'd taken for the one time she had ventured down to his cave, as he'd referred to it, how he'd grabbed her arms, fearing she'd cut herself on his fishing lures or accidently ingested poison.

What she'd found had been two tackle boxes overflowing with hooks and lures along with dozens and dozens of containers of all different sizes containing pesticides for killing weeds, insects, a variety of plant diseases. They'd been stacked along the floor and lined up along the shelves against the wall. She may have been young, but she'd been old enough to know not to touch the sharp points of a hook or open containers carrying chemicals, whether the image of Mr. Yuk's face had been stuck to them or not.

Besides, she'd been more interested in the box of magazines she'd spied underneath her father's workbench. She'd dragged the box out and removed a magazine from the pile only to find a picture of a topless woman. She'd looked over her shoulder, straining to listen for any sounds coming from upstairs. When she hadn't heard anything, she'd opened the magazine to the centerfold of a woman with her legs spread, displaying her most private part.

Becca had thrown the magazine and kicked the box back under the desk, wiping her hands on her jeans—but only after she'd paged through the entire issue, seeing the women's curves, comparing her own body to the women's on the smooth, glossy pages and feeling desperately inadequate. She'd wished she could've stopped herself from looking, mostly because it had felt wrong to look, and she'd been embarrassed not only for herself but for the naked women too. But she'd looked. She'd been young and curious about her body, about sex.

What she hadn't been able to articulate at the time was how it had made her feel cheap and worthless. And wrapped with all the other emotions she'd felt toward her father, she'd had to contend with these feelings too.

Now, she made her way down the steep stairs for the second time in her life. The air was damp and filled with the scent of mold and earth and something else she remembered from her childhood, the scent of her father, a mixture of the outdoors, the soap he'd used, tinged with the smoke from his rolled cigarettes, the way his skin had smelled when he'd returned home after one of his shifts.

She continued to the bottom step and hesitated, her hand covering her mouth to keep from gasping. Everywhere she looked, in every conceivable space, there were containers and more containers, bags and tubes and pumps. All of which contained chemicals, some kind of poison or another, all meant for lawn care.

Had he really thought he could've kept them together with a perfect yard like her mother had said? The idea was so absurd, pathetic even. *You did this to yourself, Dad.* Although she was beginning to wonder if it had really been of his own making, or rather if it had been the result of a man who had been so burdened with guilt, plagued with remorse from what he'd done.

She wove around several of the large plastic buckets, finding a path to the workbench at the far end of the room. She wasn't sure what her intentions were as she started rummaging through his tools and fishing lures, removing cobwebs from the desk. The dust and dirt made her sneeze. She didn't find anything of interest on top of the workbench or inside any of the drawers other than a pile of the rolling papers for his cigarettes, the ones that had led to his cancer. She supposed what she really was after was whether he'd gotten rid of the box of magazines.

Slowly, she pushed the metal stool aside. The cardboard box was in the same spot on the floor underneath the bench. She yanked it out, opened it up. The same magazine was on top, but now it was faded and yellow. She bet if she dug through the stack, she'd find some issues that could be worth money, collector's editions. She pushed them aside. At least he hadn't added to his collection.

In the corner next to the table leg, she saw another box, one she hadn't noticed before. It had a lock. She got down on her hands and knees, pulled it out. A spider darted across the floor. She jumped, nearly banging her head.

She took a deep breath and tried again, grabbing the lockbox and putting it on top of the desk. The key was in the lock. All she had to do was turn it. Whatever was inside might not be important. Otherwise, why would her father leave the key in the lock? But she'd come this far, so she might as well check. She paused. This was a violation of his privacy, a blatant violation. She turned the key.

Inside, she found her father's copy of the divorce agreement, his birth certificate, and buried farther down was her parents' marriage certificate. There was the title to his truck and the deed to the house. The last item she pulled from the bottom of the box was a manila folder. Her palms were clammy. Upstairs, she could hear Jackie talking on the phone amid the hum of the lawn mower outside. She opened the folder and found a single sheet of paper with the Portland Police Department's letterhead.

She searched behind her for the metal stool she'd pushed away and plopped down on it. The date at the top of the page was October 14, 1994. It was written in her father's sloppy handwriting. It appeared he'd interviewed someone and jotted everything down so he wouldn't forget. The one sentence that stood out, the one her father had put an asterisk by: "The victim was last seen by the witness wearing a blue hooded sweatshirt and jeans." The witness's name was blacked out. Scrawled next to it was another note. "Witness does not want to be identified." There were other notes on the page in the same sloppy handwriting, but Becca had read all she needed to. Her body quaked. The tremors reached as far as her core.

The person her father had interviewed hadn't wanted to be identified, and maybe that had been the reason why her father had buried the interview. But Becca believed there had been another reason, a more threatening concern that had been much closer to home. The shadows that had been lurking, swirling around in the dark corners of her memory, became crisper, clearer, in the form of a blood-stained blue hooded sweatshirt in a barn at the killer's feet.

"Becca," Matt called from the top of the basement stairs.

She jumped. Her hand flew to her chest where her heart raced. "I'll be up in a minute." She folded the sheet of paper with her father's sloppy handwriting into a small square and shoved it into the back pocket of her jeans.

Matt started down the steps.

"I'm coming. I'll be right there." She stuffed the other papers, marriage certificate and divorce papers, truck title and house deed, back into the lockbox and pushed it under the desk, making sure to put the box of girly magazines in front of it. She stood and spun around as Matt reached the bottom step.

"Holy shit," he said, looking around at the inventory of lawn-care chemicals and supplies. "Your dad wasn't messing around."

"He took his grass very seriously," she said and wound her way to the steps, stopped in front of him.

"Did something happen?" he asked. "You look upset."

"No, it's . . . I'm fine. It was a spider. It startled me."

"Do you want me to kill it?" He looked over her shoulder.

"No, it's fine," she said. She had to get the focus away from her, put it on him. "I saw you on the mower. You didn't have to do that."

"I wanted to be helpful." He smiled his perfect smile. "Although I did have an ulterior motive." He pushed her short hair across her forehead. "I thought if I could make myself useful, you'd want me to stick around. But it appears my good intentions have been wasted. I got another call from the office." He hesitated, and she noticed he couldn't meet her eye. "It doesn't matter, except that my client isn't happy, and I have to go."

"Oh." It was all she could think to say. He had to go, and she had one less thing to deal with.

He took her hands in his. "I'm sorry. I really wanted to stay, but I have to handle this. Promise me you'll come home soon."

"Hey, you two." Jackie was standing at the top of the stairs with the phone still in her hand. "Could you come up here?"

There was something in Jackie's voice that had Becca racing up the steps.

❦

Jackie held the phone to her chest, covering the receiver, when Becca and Matt came up from the basement. She said to Becca, "Could you check on your dad? He's been awfully quiet up there, and I'm worried. I'm finally making some headway with the insurance company, and I don't want to have to hang up on them now."

Becca motioned to the pile of medical bills. "Is there a problem?"

Jackie shook her head, and at the same time she said, "Yes, I'm still here," to whoever was on the other end of the phone. She motioned for Becca to head upstairs to her father's bedroom.

Becca walked out of the kitchen. Matt followed her.

"Do you need my help?" he asked.

"No, I can handle it."

"But shouldn't I come with you? Don't you think it's about time I meet him?"

"Not now," she said.

"Then when? It's not like we have a whole lot of time here."

"That was insensitive."

"I didn't mean it to be."

"Look, I have to get upstairs to my dad. Can we talk about this later? And besides, I thought you had to leave?"

"I do have to go. I've got a car service coming to my place in an hour. Our place," he corrected.

Right, our place, she thought. How strange it sounded, but she couldn't think about that now. He leaned in to kiss her. She turned her head, and his lips landed on her cheek instead. He looked surprised, but he turned to go without saying a word about it.

Becca made her way to her father's bedroom, touching the folded sheet of paper in her back pocket before opening the door.

He wasn't moving, but it wouldn't be so unusual if he were sleeping. She approached his bed one small step at a time. *Don't leave me now*, she said silently. He opened his eyes when she reached his side. She breathed a sigh of relief.

"I'm checking in on you." She pulled a blanket up around his shoulders. "Do you need anything?"

He grimaced and writhed. It must be time for his pain medication. She wasn't sure how long it had been since Jackie had given him anything.

"I'll check if it's time for your meds," she said and turned to go but stopped. She pulled the folded sheet of paper from her pocket. She had to ask him about it. Matt was right about one thing: she was running out of time. She unfolded the paper and held it up for her father to see. "I found this."

His eyes opened wide.

"I know what it is," she said. "I think I know why you didn't want me to say anything."

He twisted and turned, pulling at the blanket and sheets, agitated and wincing in pain.

"Okay," she said. "I'm sorry." *Please.* "We'll talk later. I'll go get Jackie. I'll get your meds." She folded the sheet of paper and shoved it back into her pocket as she hurried out of the room. She paused in the hallway, her hand at her throat. She hadn't meant to upset him. But how was she supposed to find out the truth?

Becca rushed into the kitchen as Jackie hung up the phone. "What's wrong?" Jackie asked.

"He's in a lot of pain."

A loud thump came from upstairs. Both Jackie and Becca stared at each other before running for the stairs. Becca was the first to reach her father's room, finding him on the floor at the foot of the bed. Jackie ran in behind her and gasped.

They crouched on either side of him.

"How in the world did that happen?" Jackie asked. The hospital bed's rails were up.

They tried lifting him to his feet. He made a moaning sound.

"Can you stand?" Jackie asked and then mumbled, "That was a stupid question." To Becca she said, "Put the rail down. Then grab his legs. We're going to have to lift him."

Becca did as she was told and put the bed rail down before lifting his legs while Jackie slipped her hands underneath his arms. He was heavy, considering he was all bones. They were lifting dead weight, Becca thought, then pushed it out of her mind.

"Easy. Easy." Perspiration covered Jackie's upper lip.

Becca's father continued moaning, a deep, guttural sound that had a frightening effect on both women. They got him onto the bed a little crooked, but he was on far enough that Becca could put the rail back up. Jackie wiped her upper lip with the back of her arm.

Becca's father curled into a fetal position. He looked small and childlike. His body position seemed to say he was ashamed for turning into this frail, dying man. He continued to moan as Jackie administered the morphine.

Becca touched his shoulder as a way to comfort him because she didn't know what else to do.

Both Becca and Jackie stood by his bed, listening to his moans weaken as the medication massaged the pain. After some time had passed, the terrible sound he'd been making stopped, and her father slipped into a drug-induced sleep.

"I need a drink," Jackie said. "How about you?"

Once they were in the kitchen, Jackie poured each of them a straight shot of whiskey. They drank it down. The alcohol burned Becca's throat, heating her insides and searing her stomach. She set the glass on the countertop.

"What the hell was that about anyway?" Jackie poured herself another shot, tipped the bottle toward Becca's glass.

Becca held up her hand to stop her. "I'm good." She didn't mention to Jackie what she believed had made her father get out of bed. It was the sheet of paper Becca had shown him. He was coming after the sheet of paper.

Becca grabbed the whiskey bottle. "On second thought," she said, "I think I will have another."

CHAPTER THIRTY-ONE

Jackie had been up and down throughout the night, trying to stay on top of the pain, giving Becca's father morphine every few hours. Becca would wake, shuffle down the hall in her bare feet, ask if there was anything she could do.

"Go back to bed," Jackie would say each time. "One of us should get some sleep. Tomorrow is going to be a long day."

The last time Becca heard Jackie get up was four o'clock. Becca closed her bedroom door, unable to fall back asleep. She hadn't been able to talk with her father again about the sheet of paper she'd found in his lockbox, not after she'd believed it had been the reason he'd fallen out of bed in the first place. Now, she pulled her laptop out and searched the local newspapers online. There were two articles about the recent body they'd found in the river. The first article offered little information. It didn't even mention Paul, the owner of the antique store who had found the body originally. Becca remembered the television broadcast, how Paul had tried to shield his face and his grandson from the camera. People were afraid. No one had wanted to come forward with information. No one had wanted to get involved.

The second article she read was more about the victim. She looked at the grainy mug shot. His eyes were small, and his jaw was big and square. He looked like something out of a cartoon. She continued reading about his previous run-ins with the law. The article was slanted, in her opinion, taking the focus away from the killer and shifting the blame to the victim. She had no doubt this was what the local reporter had intended, helping the townspeople in Portland sleep a little easier at night.

But she wasn't able to shake the fact that the victim had been somebody's son. He'd had a mother and father, maybe a brother or sister, maybe even a wife and kids. Somewhere someone was missing him, mourning his death.

Becca shut off the power and closed the laptop. A weight as heavy as an anchor sat on her chest, the kind of steel anchor that Parker had used to toss over the side of the boat to keep them from drifting. Only now, instead of being in the boat, she was sinking to the river bottom like a mudhook.

❦

The sun was coming up when Becca peeked into her father's room. She checked the rise and fall of his chest. His breathing was ragged. But he was breathing, she reminded herself. He was breathing. Jackie was still in bed, finally able to get some rest after the long night.

Since both her father and Jackie were sleeping, Becca decided now was a good time to leave the house and find Parker. She had to at least try to explain Matt to him. But what about John? If she told Parker about John, about what she'd seen, would he think she'd deliberately kept something else from him? Would he ever trust her again? How could she tell him she was scared, when there was still so much she didn't understand?

She followed Route 611 and River Road to Parker's cabin. Romy stuck her head out the open window, tongue hanging out and tail wagging, breathing in the fresh air, excited to be taking a road trip, although it was a short one. Becca took her time on the drive, unsure what she would say to Parker once she got there.

"What am I going to do, Romy?" She reached over to scratch the dog's back. Romy swung her head inside the Jeep, licked Becca's arm, before sticking her head back out the window.

Becca turned into Parker's driveway. His car was gone, but she got out anyway. Romy sniffed the ground all along the path to Parker's front door. Becca knocked and listened for any sound coming from inside, but all she heard was the occasional bird and the slow-moving river. She was hesitant to leave. Instead, she walked around back and headed down the steps to the dock. Romy raced in front of her, no doubt wanting to jump into the calm water below. Becca told her to stay.

"You can swim another day," she said and remembered Parker had mentioned going to the farmers market in town every Wednesday and Saturday. She might be able to find him there. She folded her arms against the chill coming off the water. The sun was up, but the air was cool—a perfect autumn day. She wished she could just stay there forever, forget her troubles, for the world to go away.

She took a deep breath, then turned toward the stairs.

Delaware Drive was a bustle of activity. Tents lined the sidewalk, displaying all the usual suspects of autumn's harvest. There were baskets of apples from the local orchard. A woman was handing out free samples of apple cider. Pumpkins and gourds were set on top of haystacks. Cornstalks were tied to signposts. A family of tourists dressed in jeans and white shirts made their way to the pedestrian bridge to have their picture taken with the river and mountains.

Becca pulled her Jeep in the first parking spot she could find in front of an old abandoned railroad car sitting alongside the tracks. She clipped the leash to Romy's collar. Fallen leaves blew across the street along with pieces of straw. Everything about the market was exactly how Becca remembered it, and as she walked through the crowd, she stopped every few seconds to look around, to take it all in.

Two Harley-Davidson motorcycles were parked not far from the bridge. More motorcycles were parked farther down the street, closer to the alley that led to Sweeney's. A couple of Scions stopped at the apple stand. One of the men, the one with a skull-and-devil's-horns tattoo on his forearm, put a jug of apple cider on the sidewalk at his feet. The guy who sold him the cider said something. The Scion laughed. "I got that bear good," he said and raised his arms as though he were holding a rifle. "Boom." He lowered his arms, picked up the cider. "It won't be eating anyone's trash anymore, that's for sure."

A small boy tugged on Becca's shirt sleeve. "Can I pet your dog?"

"Of course you can," she said, a little distracted, searching the crowd for Parker. "She's superfriendly."

Romy licked the boy's hand and face. The boy's mother came over and asked Becca about Romy, saying they were thinking about getting a dog. Becca talked to the woman and her son for a few minutes, happy to answer their questions. While they were talking, she became aware of how much she missed the clinic and her job, how much easier her life always seemed to be when she was surrounded by animals.

When the woman and her son had moved on, Becca continued walking up the street. She made sure to keep a safe distance between herself and the Scions. They'd since moved to the soup stand, stopping to talk with the people waiting in line for pumpkin soup. It was as though they'd stepped out to mingle, a public relations effort to remind the townspeople they were there but they weren't a threat, at least not to them.

Farther up the street, Parker was standing in front of a wagon full of pumpkins. He held a large oval pumpkin in his hands, turning it over as though he was inspecting it for flaws. Becca weaved through the crowd, Romy at her side.

"Hey," she said, allowing enough slack in Romy's leash to let her sniff Parker's jeans. The dog nudged his leg with her nose for attention.

He glanced at Becca, keeping the pumpkin raised, then continued turning it around in his hands. "I'll take this one," he said to the attendant. "But hang on, I'm not done." He put the pumpkin off to the side and petted Romy for a moment. Then he picked up another pumpkin, this one short and fat and round.

"You can't ignore me forever."

"Yes, I can," he said, looking at the attendant. "I'll take this one too." He set it down and walked around the wagon.

She followed him. "I would've told you about Matt earlier."

He turned toward her. "Then why didn't you?" He crossed his arms in a defensive stance, squaring his shoulders and puffing out his chest. He used to stand in the same position along the sidelines of the football field. It was his game stance, his attempt at showing the other team how tough he was. She wasn't sure it had ever worked.

"It never seemed like the right time."

"You could've said something the other night." He grabbed another pumpkin, harder than he should have, and knocked over several smaller pumpkins. "You let me go on and on, spilling my guts to you. Why didn't you stop me and tell me then? Why did you let it go as far as it did? You made a fool out of me."

"I didn't mean to," she said. She was frustrated. Nothing was coming out right, at least not the way she'd intended. "You're not a fool." She reached for him, but he pulled his arm away.

He strode to the attendant with another fat pumpkin. "How much for these three?" he asked and pulled cash from the wallet he carried in the back pocket of his jeans. He paid for the pumpkins and picked all three up in his arms with ease. He brushed past her. She grabbed his bicep.

"Matt cheated on me," she blurted. "And I think he's been cheating on me all along." She hadn't expected to admit this to him, but she was surprised at how good it felt to say the words out loud, to put it out there and not carry it inside any longer.

Parker frowned, and his eyebrows pulled together in a knot. "Is that why you slept with me? To even the score?"

"No," she said. "How could you think that?"

He stared at her. She could see the anger in his eyes, heard it in his words, but she could also see how much he was hurting.

"It's the real reason why I came home," she said. "It wasn't to see my dad, although that was part of it. I know how horrible it sounds, but it's the truth. And in a twisted, mixed-up way, no matter what my original intentions were, I'm glad I came home before . . . before it became too late." All these years the child inside of her had been so angry at her father for sending her away, for his betrayal that had cut her so deeply. And then after she'd left, after college and veterinary school, she'd ended up right back where she'd started, living with Matt, a man who had been just like him.

"You still should've told me." He shrugged her off, strode away.

"Parker, wait," she yelled and happened to look across the street, spotting John on his motorcycle, *watching her*. For a moment she couldn't move, her feet cemented to the sidewalk. She was afraid, and yet there was something deep inside her bones telling her not to be. He'd never had a reason to harm her before. But then he turned his head in the direction of where Parker was loading the pumpkins in the back of his car. It was when he returned his gaze to her that she knew whatever had been between them, their relationship to one another, their unspoken pact, had changed.

She tried to call for Parker again, but John's glare was like a razor in her windpipe, making it hard for her to speak. She tugged on Romy's leash. They wove through the crowd, darting in and out of the hordes of people surrounding the stands. She didn't have to look back over her shoulder to know John was watching her. She felt his eyes on her back, a familiar feeling and yet unfamiliar, one that had never felt so terrifying until today.

She reached Parker's vehicle too late. He was already pulling into traffic, driving at a slow speed through the market.

Dammit, Parker. Her heart pattered in a million different beats.

❦

Becca drove as fast as she could through the busy town, edging down River Road. The chill on her spine had nothing to do with the breeze blowing through the open windows. She caught up to Parker, followed him to his cabin. He turned into his driveway. She pulled in behind him and climbed out of the Jeep with Romy.

"I can't believe you followed me," he said and slammed the driver's-side door.

Romy jumped around him. Parker bent down to pet her. The dog rubbed against his legs, licked his hands. When Romy was satisfied, she trotted away to sniff the ground.

"There's something else you should know." She took a deep breath. The air tasted like autumn—dead leaves, dirt, a trace of winter. "I saw someone by the river the day before the body turned up," she said, trying to be brave, although she was feeling anything but. She hesitated, unsure whether she could say John's name out loud. Fear was a paralyzing emotion, and telling even a small piece of what she'd seen strangled her throat.

Her phone went off. She recognized her old number from her father's house. It was as though he knew what she was doing, and he was trying to stop her.

Parker stepped closer. He was asking her questions, but she wasn't paying attention to him, putting her finger up, signaling him to wait.

"Hello," she said, pressing the phone to her ear.

"You need to come home," Jackie said, sounding more than just tired. There was a hint of something else in her voice, something that sounded very much like finality.

"I'm on my way." She hung up. "I have to go. It's my dad."

"But . . ." Parker said.

She cut him off and called for Romy to come. The dog hopped back into the Jeep. Becca jumped in on the driver's side. Maybe she was using Jackie's call as an excuse to get away, but it was also more than that. It had to do with her father, what she'd promised him, what he'd done for her.

"What did you see?" Parker asked.

She started the engine.

"Was it a man? A Scion? Would you be able to identify him in a lineup?" Parker asked as she put the Jeep in reverse, started backing out of the driveway.

She nodded yes to all of it. She thought about the tone of Jackie's voice on the other end of the phone, knowing why she'd been summoned. *Please wait for me, Dad. I'm coming.*

CHAPTER THIRTY-TWO

As soon as Becca left, Parker rushed into the cabin for his gun. It was time he had a little chat with this John Jackson.

He was minutes behind Becca. He slowed as he approached her father's house, pulled over. She was getting out of her Jeep. He was reacting on pure adrenaline, gut instinct that she was the witness he needed to prove that the police report Toby had given him claiming John had spent the night in jail was crap. He didn't allow his thoughts to go beyond that, refusing to think about what she'd admitted about her pretty boyfriend. There would be time for that later.

"Hey," he called to her.

She shook her head, waved him away as she raced inside the house.

He smacked the steering wheel. Why had she waited so long to tell him what she'd seen by the river? What else was she hiding? He stared at the house, contemplated going in after her. But then he thought about the look on her face when she'd gotten the phone call to come home. He couldn't just barge in, make demands when it appeared her father was close to the end.

He pulled back onto the road, and in another mile, he reached the farmhouse and parked on the gravel driveway. He hesitated after putting the car in park. He should've had another detective riding along with him. He should've called Bill. But if his sergeant found out that Parker was personally involved with a potential witness, he'd take him off the case. And Parker couldn't allow that to happen. Call it pride or whatever, but he wanted to be the guy who put a Scion behind bars. The kid in him yearned for the satisfaction of finally being able to tell his father that he'd gotten one of them. It had been the real reason Parker had become a cop in the first place, had transferred to the field station with the hope that one day he'd be able to remove the fear of the Scions from his father's face.

He got out of the car. There was a single motorcycle parked outside the barn, but otherwise the place looked deserted.

Parker knocked on the screen door and peeked in. He didn't hear any movement inside. From his position on the porch, he could see into the living room, the worn plaid furniture, an old TV. The place looked tidy, nothing out of the ordinary.

He knocked again, harder this time. When he didn't get an answer, he made his way to the barn, pausing next to the motorcycle. The engine felt cool. The keys weren't in the ignition. The large barn doors were thrown open. He stood off to the side, looked in. Several hay bales were stacked along the far wall. To his right sat an old wooden stool, and in front of it, a workbench. A greasy towel rested on top. Tire tracks from one or more motorcycles covered the dirt floor along with boot prints. He spied a rifle leaning against the inside door to his left. His pulse spiked. *Easy.* Its barrel was small, probably a .22, and they were as common as kitchen spoons in these parts. Besides, they'd found the .30-06 that had been used in the crime. There was no sign of a hunting knife lying out in the open. He didn't see anything that would allow him to get a search warrant to search the property. A breeze rustled the leaves.

Walking around the side of the building, he came upon a fire pit, smelled the scent of burning leaves. He got closer, looked at the ashes, the blackened stone. A bird took off from one of the nearby trees. He jumped. *Shit.* His heart thrashed against his sternum.

He continued around the barn, alert to every sound, every movement, the groundhog peeking through the tall grass, the squirrels darting between the trees, the cackling crows overhead. But other than the animals and birds, he was alone, and wherever John Jackson was, it wasn't here.

❦

Parker had forgotten about the pumpkins in the trunk of the car. He was pacing in his living room, planning to return to John's farmhouse once he'd had a chance to talk with Becca again. He was still mulling over what she'd seen at the river. He'd tried *not* to think about her confession about her boyfriend this entire time. But now that he was home, there it was. Her *cheating* boyfriend. He ran his hands through his hair and down his face, wondering what the hell he was supposed to make of *that*. He still couldn't wrap his mind around it. But she couldn't possibly stay with the guy, not after what she'd admitted about him. Could she? Was she so in love with the jerk she'd simply overlook his betrayal? Was it true girls picked men like their fathers?

He dropped onto his favorite chair, knocking into the stack of fishing magazines piled on the floor by his feet. Several of them toppled over onto the area rug. He didn't bother picking them up. The truth was, he didn't know what Becca would do. The Becca he thought he knew would never have put up with that kind of bullshit.

He tried calling her. Twice. He had more questions for her obviously, but he also wanted to know if her father was okay, how he was holding up. He left two messages with Jackie. All he could do now was wait for Becca to call him back.

His cell phone went off. He recognized the number from the lab.

"Working overtime again?" he asked.

"You know me. I can't stay away from this place," Mara said. "We've got a partial print."

He pictured her bushy hair, her white lab coat, her sitting in front of a microscope looking at the killer's fingerprint. The image reminded him of every crime show he'd ever seen on TV. In fact, he'd only ever been inside the forensic lab a handful of times since his promotion.

She continued. "There were a couple of rounds in the clip. I lifted a partial print off one of the casings. My guess is that the magazine must've protected the print from the friction of the water current. It's not the best, mind you, but I'd say we got lucky finding this one at all."

"Did you run it through the system?" He hated how he sounded, fresh, new, hopeful, and as excited as she was. He imagined the seasoned investigators in his troop would take the call in stride and not get too worked up over a partial print.

"Not yet. I wanted to call you first," she said. What they didn't tell you in the TV crime shows was how tedious a forensic scientist's job really was. They could go days, weeks, months running tests, examining evidence, and still not come up with anything conclusive. Not to mention being shut in a laboratory all day and sometimes all night. And in Mara's case, sometimes all weekend too.

"Thank you, Mara. You're the best."

"Aw, shucks, go on. No, seriously, go on."

He laughed. Mara was smart and young and, like Parker, a newbie in her field, but already she'd made a name for herself, bringing knowledge of the latest technology from one of the best schools in forensic science. She was also engaged, not that Parker was interested. "Find me a match," he said.

"I'm on it," she said and hung up the phone.

Parker pulled himself out of the chair and went into the kitchen. The original river body case was in a box on top of the table along with his notes and the files from his own recent case. He settled into a chair and flipped open a manila folder. He started pulling out reports, the medical examiner's report, Candy's statement, the tampered-with police report from Toby on the Scions. Lastly, he pulled a photo of the victim's body. He spread everything out on the table, trying to put the pieces together in his mind, forming a timeline of the events that had led up to the crime.

He stood and paced the room. There was stubble on his chin from not having shaved since the day before, or maybe it had been the day before that. He scratched it absently. He continued pacing, only stopping to use the bathroom. More than once he considered packing it up and driving over to headquarters. It would be easier there, where he had access to bulletin boards, where he could hang the evidence he'd collected and re-create a better visual of the sequence of events. Also, it would help if he had another set of eyes on it, maybe two more sets. He was sure Bill and the other detectives expected him to come to them. They would give him shit, but they would help without hesitation. Parker liked the camaraderie, the trust the men in his troop developed that said, *I've got your back.* All he had to do was ask.

And yet, he couldn't go to them. He was alone. The case was his because it was his hometown, the crime having taken place in his backyard. And now with Becca's involvement, it had become even more personal. He thought about his father. And then he thought about Rick, how he couldn't seem to move past the original case. Parker wondered if he would end up like Rick had, living his life haunted by the river bodies.

He opened the box containing the files on the original case and began sorting through them, pulling out the reports and statements and laying them on the table next to the others. He laid the photograph of the first victim next to the other one. What did these two men have in common? Both victims died of a single gunshot wound to the chest, both shots fired from a .30-06 rifle. Both were stripped of their clothes, gutted, and their bodies dumped into the Delaware River, only to turn up twenty-four hours later. The crime scenes were twenty yards apart. And both victims had rap sheets and were known to have connections with motorcycle gangs, indirect connections with the Scions. The motive for the killings looked to be gang related, but nothing jumped out at the crime team handling the OMGs (outlaw motorcycle gangs). The rifle used in the latest shooting had been the only weapon found.

The suspect in the first case, Russell Jackson, had been a hunter. His son, John, was a hunter. Both men would know how to field dress. Russell had been the enforcer in the club. Now, John was the enforcer. Was John just following in his old man's footsteps, imitating his old man's crime? After all, there'd been two different kinds of knives used in the field dressings. One was a five-and-a-half-inch large-blade knife, and the one in the most recent case a hunting knife with a gut hook. He'd been looking at each case as though they were together but separate, each having a different suspect.

Parker thought about his own father again, remembered a conversation he'd had with him after Russell had shown up at the house, the back of Russell's arm slit open from a knife wound, his knuckles busted on both hands.

"He fought in Vietnam. Did you know that?" his father had asked.

Parker had shaken his head.

"He was trained to be violent. I'm not sure that can be turned off so easily, not without help anyway."

His father's words struck him now, the psychology of it, how violence was thought to be a learned behavior.

Russell had been a violent man. And John had been raised by him.

But still, something about it wasn't right. He picked up the photos of the victims again, studied them. He reread the medical examiner's reports. He stood, paced around the kitchen table. Something nagged at him in the back of his mind.

The more he thought about it, the more he was convinced the gutting wasn't just a pure act of violence carried out by two separate individuals. It was too personal. It had meant something to the killer. Otherwise, why not just walk away once the victim had been shot? Perhaps the killer was satisfying some kind of perverse compulsion or need? Or maybe it was a scare tactic to keep the other members of the club in line?

Whatever it was, this guy had put his own personal stamp on his victims; his signature, so to speak, like Rick had said; his private MO.

CHAPTER THIRTY-THREE

John was running, ducking under low-lying branches, weaving through oak and maple and hickory trees. Sweat soaked his back underneath the layers of camouflage. He gripped the rifle in his moist hand, moving as sure-footedly as any forest animal. He wasn't supposed to have been the driver on this hunt, but at the last minute his father, Russell, had needed him. The *club* had needed him. Hap, the presiding member of the Scions even then, had agreed John was the fastest in the woods. He was the one most suited for the job, especially if he was going to take over Russell's position one day.

Russell had debated with Hap whether to involve John, but he was twenty-five years old and by no means a boy. He was a man, and it was time he earned his full-member patch.

John continued running, cutting left and right, stomping the soft earth with his boots. He loved being in the woods, running, tracking, hunting. The mountains and the river were the two places John called home. He'd often sleep outside underneath the stars next to the fire pit behind their barn. Sleeping in a room, in a bed, a roof over his head, had suffocated him as a boy. By the time he'd been twelve years old, he'd been sleeping outside more than in. Around the same time, Russell had handed him a rifle. He'd said, "If you're going to sleep with the animals, you'd better learn how to protect yourself."

And John had. He'd slept with a rifle by his side, picking it up once when a lone wolf had startled him awake. He'd fired a warning shot, chasing the wolf back up the mountain.

He pushed on. Dew soaked the bottom of his pants. He told himself this was just another hunt. He was chasing a deer. He crested a hill and came to an abrupt stop. It was only then that he heard the river's rapids, or maybe it was the blood rushing in his ears. His chest moved up and down, his breathing heavy. Russell was waiting off to John's right. And the target John had been chasing, the traitor in the club's eyes, had stopped in the middle of a small clearing in the center of their trap.

The traitor pulled out a knife, turned in a full circle before he spied Russell pointing a rifle at his chest.

John sucked in a sharp breath, waited for the gunshot. He waited. And waited. The silence was deafening. Why was it taking so long? *Pull the trigger, Dad.* He wanted it over with. He wanted to go home. And then his father lowered the gun. Had he changed his mind? Had he realized this was a mistake? Was he flashing back to the war like he sometimes did, shell-shocked?

Panic swelled inside John's rib cage. He didn't move, still waiting, knowing as each second passed that something was wrong. The traitor pointed the knife at John's father, took a step toward him. Russell raised the rifle again, and this time John saw his father pull the trigger, but nothing happened. The gun didn't fire.

A slow smile spread across the traitor's face. He waved the knife in front of him as though he were saying to Russell, *I got you now.* He took two more steps toward John's father.

Oh, shit. John hesitated, unsure what to do. *Dad?* Then John raised his own rifle and peered through the scope, lining up a shot. His hands were steady, but his knees were shaking. His guts churned, his stomach protesting, growling as though he were hungry. *I can do this*, he thought. *I have to do this.*

His father stood motionless, staring at the man with the knife as if he was daring him to come closer.

John looked away from the scope. Russell glanced in John's direction, and he swore he saw his father give a slight nod of his head. In the next second, no longer thinking about what he was about to do but what he was expected to do, John peered through the scope again and lined up his shot. He pulled the trigger. The traitor went down in a heap. The knife dropped to the ground by his side.

It wasn't until John lowered the rifle that he started to shake all over and not just in his knees. His entire body rocked with tremors. His vision blurred. *What happened?* He felt confused. His head was fuzzy. He wasn't aware of time passing. He wasn't aware of anything but the trembling. And then a hand resting on his shoulder.

"John," his father said. "You still with us, Son? Come on, now. Pull yourself together."

John shook his head, trying to clear his eyes. He knocked his father's hand off his shoulder and marched to where the traitor had gone down. But what he saw on the ground wasn't a man but a deer. It was only a deer. He'd shot a deer. Something like relief washed over him, and he knelt beside his kill. He found the knife on the ground and began to field dress the animal. His father was standing over him, cursing him.

"What the hell are you doing? He's dead, Son. There's no need to do that." He put his hand on John's shoulder again.

"Get off me," John snapped.

"Son," his father said, his voice low and reassuring. "It's going to be okay. You did the right thing. For the club. For me."

John blocked out his father's words. He concentrated on the job at hand. When he'd finished, his father pushed him out of the way.

Hap was there. When had he gotten there? John didn't remember Hap coming with them. He heard his father say something about John and shock.

He watched as his father and Hap dragged the deer down the bank to the river. *Yes, that was good. Put him in the river.* John wasn't in the mood for venison anyway.

CHAPTER THIRTY-FOUR

Parker linked his fingers behind his head, stretched his back, continued pacing. Papers were strewn about the kitchen, covering the countertop, the stove, the table and chairs. He'd reread every slip of paper in both files, studied the photos of the victims, and scrutinized the details in the wound analysis reports, looking for similarities between the two field dressings. He was going on a hunch that field dressings could be as unique as a person's handwriting. There could be some identifying factor like the slant of a letter, the pressure of the scrawl, the slice of the blade. If he could prove both wounds had been inflicted by the same person, he'd be that much closer to making an arrest.

What Parker needed to do was put the files back together and have an expert at the lab take a closer look at the evidence, specifically the knife wounds. But right now, he wanted a little more time with his thoughts. He didn't want to disrupt the organized mess in his kitchen, but he was starting to get hungry.

He picked up his phone, checked for messages. Nothing.

He opened the refrigerator and pulled out lettuce, tomatoes, celery, an onion. He'd heat up the leftover fish he'd had the night before and make a fish taco. When he'd finished preparing his meal, he carried it on a plate and ate in the living room. He didn't want to drop any food on the scattered papers at the kitchen table, nor did he want to disrupt the visual he'd created with the pieces of the puzzle to the case. It wasn't until he finished eating that he remembered the pumpkins in the trunk of his car.

He brought the pumpkins inside, laying old newspapers on the coffee table, placing the pumpkins on top. Every year since he could remember, he'd carved pumpkins to put on his front porch for Halloween. He'd done it with his parents when he'd been younger, and he'd kept the tradition going through the years. Back then, Becca had joined him. She'd made fun, silly-faced jack-o'-lanterns, where Parker had preferred a scarier look.

"It's Halloween," he'd said after seeing the big toothy smile on her pumpkin. "It's supposed to look scary." He'd turned his pumpkin for her to see his work, the angry eyes slanting inward, the crooked nose, the evil grin.

"I didn't know we were carving self-portraits."

"Ha ha." He'd tossed a handful of slime and seeds at her. She'd tossed it right back, and by the time they'd finished, they'd both been covered in pumpkin brains.

He pushed the thought away after hearing his phone go off. He wiped his hands on his jeans and picked it up. It was a text message from Mara about the partial print. Still searching.

He put the phone down and picked up the knife. As he slid the blade into the skin of the pumpkin, cutting around the stem, creating a lid, he wondered what the killer had been thinking when he'd taken the knife to his victims. Why would he field dress them after they'd been shot dead? What was the purpose? Maybe the answer was simple—to send a message. But for whom?

Parker set the pumpkin lid aside and stuck his hand into the fruit, grabbing fistfuls of strands and seeds, removing the guts.

CHAPTER THIRTY-FIVE

Ten-year-old Becca loved nothing more than riding her bike. Jumping rope came in a close second. But riding her bike, well, that felt like freedom—the wind in her face, the sun on her back, the means to flee from home.

It wasn't unusual for her to hop on her bike and ride off without telling her parents where she was going, especially if she'd been left in her father's care. She'd overheard him tell her mother once, "Children should be seen, not heard. And sometimes they shouldn't even be seen." He hadn't sounded angry or even cruel when he'd said this but more reflective, as though he'd had his own private reasons for believing it to be true.

When her mother left for the nursing home where she volunteered and her father was put in charge, Becca did what she always did: she got on her bike and fled, racing down the driveway and onto the street.

She pedaled past cornfields that flanked the road. She coasted downhill, tapping the brake to control her speed. She was approaching Russell's farmhouse at a rapid pace. Old man Russell was big and burly, with leathery skin and dirty hair, and she was frightened of him, but it wasn't his size or his looks that scared her. There was a feeling she'd get whenever she came in contact with him, a sense he didn't like her.

Maybe it had something to do with her father. The two men couldn't be in the same room without going at each other.

On any given day, a row of motorcycles lined Russell's driveway, the same bikes that roared up and down their otherwise-quiet country road, sometimes at all hours of the night. Her father complained about the noise and the men and Russell, but he never did anything about any of them. And he could've, given his position in town.

The autumn air was crisp in her face. Her knuckles were white, her fingers cold. She was close to the bottom of the hill where Russell's farmhouse squatted to her left. His old barn leaned next to it. Her plan was to pedal fast, pick up speed, and race by without being seen. The closer she got to his farm, the harder her legs pumped. Her heart rate accelerated.

She was almost past his place, free and clear, when she heard the sound of a dog yelping. The cries were coming from somewhere inside the barn. She hit the brake. The back tire skidded sideways, nearly tossing her to the ground. She regained her balance and listened, straining to hear over her panicked breathing.

Sheba, her six-month-old puppy, had gotten out earlier that day, and Becca hadn't seen her since. She'd searched the woods and fields around her house all morning, calling for her, fearing the worst. There were hawks that circled the cornfields looking for small prey. And Sheba was small, a mutt of unknown breeds. Becca's mother had picked her up at the SPCA for Becca's birthday that spring. Her father had been angry.

"I don't want that mutt shitting in my yard," he'd hollered. He spent the weekends, the ones he wasn't working, riding his John Deere lawn mower, fertilizing, mowing, tending to their yard with a passion that baffled Becca. To her, it was just grass.

"I'll clean it up," her mother had said. "You won't even notice the dog's here." She had turned, mumbled under her breath, "Just like you don't notice anyone else in this family."

The dog yelped again. The sound was definitely coming from inside the barn. Becca got off her bike and pushed it off the road, laying it down in the yard. She looked over her shoulder. She didn't see any motorcycles in the driveway. The house looked dark and empty. She prayed Russell wasn't home.

"Sheba," she said in a quiet voice. There was another bark, but this one sounded like it came from a much bigger, meaner dog. Panic crept further up Becca's throat as she inched closer to the building. The barn doors were flung open. She stood off to the side and peeked in.

In the far corner by the piles of hay, a Doberman pinscher bared its teeth. White foam dripped from its jowls. Becca glimpsed the plump black belly of a smaller animal, recognizing the spot of white fur on its paw. Becca's chin trembled. She fought back tears.

She noticed John sitting on an old wooden stool. His head was down. His shoulders slumped. On the ground at his feet was a pile of clothes, dirty jeans and a red-stained blue hooded sweatshirt. The Doberman growled. It didn't seem as though John was aware of the dogs or the attack that was taking place around him.

Becca summoned all the courage she could, which wasn't much, and squeaked out her puppy's name again. "Sheba."

It was loud enough for John to look up. He saw her standing outside the barn door, but she didn't think he really saw her. His eyes were empty, as though he were somewhere else. His face was pale. More of that peach fuzz covered his chin. He was a man now. And he looked scared, more frightened than Becca herself.

The Doberman continued growling, snapping, trying to reach Sheba. The puppy managed to crawl in between two hay bales, just out of reach of the mean dog's bite.

John stood and looked down at his hand, where a bloody knife dangled from his fingers. It wasn't a hunting knife. It didn't have the gut hook at the tip. Becca knew this because her father was a hunter. Most of the men in the small town were hunters, and some of the women were too. She lived in a community where the school closed its doors the first two days of hunting season every year after Thanksgiving. Otherwise, they'd have to mark more than half of the boys and even some of the girls absent. Becca's father made her wear bright-colored clothes whenever she wandered into the woods during this time. "You have to make sure the hunters can see you so you don't get shot," he'd said.

And hunting season hadn't started yet. It wouldn't start for another month, and Becca was wearing jeans and an old gray sweatshirt, not the bright-orange jacket that was too big for her small frame and hung to her knees.

John's movements were slow yet jerky. He moved like someone who was "on the drugs," as Becca's father would say. Her father had not only warned her about hunters in the woods but also about drugs and alcohol and the dangers of all three separately and combined. He'd seen it all as chief of police. And John was acting like how her father had described—slow, erratic, confused. Dangerous. Someone *on the drugs*.

The Doberman lunged. Sheba yelped and scurried farther back inside the hay bales. Becca inhaled sharply, swallowing the scream that had worked its way from her chest to her mouth, gulping it back down her throat. John whipped around and stared at the dogs for the first time, registering the commotion in the corner of the barn.

"Rubes," he called and yanked on the Doberman's spiked collar, pulling the dog away from the puppy, commanding the dog to stay. To Becca's amazement the dog obeyed. John scooped Becca's puppy from between the hay bales, cradled her in his arm.

"Is this your dog?" he asked, more alert but somehow still off.

"Yes." She stepped on wobbly legs into the barn, glanced at the bloody knife still in his hand, the red-stained sweatshirt in a heap on the ground, the snarling Doberman.

"Did your mom get her for you?"

"Yes," Becca said, taking another step closer. "She got her for me for my birthday when the barn cat died. You remember giving me the barn cat?"

He nodded. "I bet your dad isn't happy about a dog."

"No, he isn't," she said, inching closer still, until she was an arm's reach away. "He likes the puppy even less than he liked the cat." Carefully, she took the knife from his hand and her puppy from his arm. He seemed not to notice nor care.

"Good thing she had that collar on." He pointed to the pink collar around Sheba's neck. "Or I might've let old Rubes here have her for lunch."

Rubes glared at Becca and the puppy, waiting for the attack command that wasn't coming.

Becca looked from the mean dog to the front of John's shirt and the leather vest he wore with the Scion patch. Both were smattered in blood.

She swallowed hard and took a step back, carrying Sheba in her arms. The puppy's roly-poly belly went out and in with each breath. She was alive, but Becca had no way of knowing if she was injured. "Is that blood from my dog?" she asked.

John looked at his hands, which Becca noticed were also bloody; then he looked at his shirt and vest. Rubes lowered his head, teeth bared, but stayed where he was.

"No," he said about the blood. "I was . . . it's just . . . it was a deer. I was field dressing a deer."

"I've never seen that much blood from a field dressing before."

He pulled at his fingers and wiped his palms together. "Yeah, well, this one got messy," he said about the dressing.

"Maybe it's because you used the wrong knife. You shouldn't be killing deer when it's not hunting season anyway," she said in a low voice. Becca loved animals, and although she liked the taste of venison, she didn't like the idea of hunting for sport.

"It happened, that's all." He looked at her as though he were seeing her clearly for the first time since she'd stepped into the barn.

He continued. "It was a mistake. I didn't mean to do it. But you can't tell anyone, okay?"

"I won't tell," she said, because she believed him. There was something in his eyes other than fear. She saw kindness.

"Listen," he said and looked around. "You better get out of here. If your dad finds out you're here, you're going to be in a whole lot of trouble." Rubes was no longer sitting. The dog was standing, glaring at Becca and her puppy.

"I can't outrun your dog." She nodded at Rubes. Sheba lifted her head, then laid it back against Becca's arm. The puppy was exhausted and maybe even bruised from where Rubes had gotten hold of her.

"Rubes won't go anywhere." He held on to the dog's collar. "Now go on," he said. "And don't tell anyone what you think you saw."

Becca left the barn carrying Sheba in her arms, pushing her bike toward home. She wouldn't tell anyone anything. Not about the knife, the blood, or the dog, Rubes. She should've been scared. Everything her father had warned her about had been right there in front of her, staring her in the face, a poster of what a bad person looked like, a representation of the evils of the world. Yet, somehow, she'd known John wouldn't hurt her. He was sorry for whatever he'd done. She knew that too. But most of all, she believed there was good in him.

After all, he'd saved her puppy.

CHAPTER THIRTY-SIX

John stayed tucked inside the hemlock, the rifle raised, straining to hear every word his old man was saying to Clint.

"Your little girl saw something she shouldn't have," Russell said.

Clint had been walking away, back toward the John Deere mower he'd left sitting in the yard, but he'd turned back around. The two men stared at each other.

"What did she see?" Clint asked.

"Enough to be a problem."

Clint was quiet for a long time. He stepped closer to Russell. "What are you asking me to do?"

"I need you to make sure she keeps her mouth shut."

"She's a child."

"Then you should have a lot of influence over her. Explain to her that she's never to tell anyone about the incident in the barn with my son."

Clint's eyes narrowed. "What incident in the barn with your son?"

"She didn't tell you?" Russell laughed. "Well, maybe she's forgotten all about it. You better hope so."

"Are you threatening my kid?"

"If that's how you want to take it, then yes. But I think you'll see that what I'm doing is protecting my son, as I suspect you'll want to protect your daughter."

The two men continued glaring each other.

John's breath came in short bursts. His heart pounded, but he didn't move. He stayed hidden in the pines, hoping Clint would take Russell seriously, would agree to Russell's terms.

"This incident has nothing to do with you or her or this town. It can all go away if you do what I'm asking," Russell said and picked up his rifle, the barrel pointed to the ground. "It's up to you how this ends."

Clint still didn't say anything.

"Do we have a deal, Brother?"

"Don't call me Brother."

"Do we have a deal, *Chief*?"

There was a long stretch of silence before Clint answered. He seemed to be taking his time, thinking over his options, although in John's opinion, he didn't have any. Maybe Clint had come to the same conclusion, because he said, "Okay. I'll make sure she forgets everything you think she saw. She won't talk to anybody about it. You have my word." He turned and strode through the yard, back to his lawn mower. He climbed into the seat and returned to cutting neat little rows in the grass.

Russell walked back through the woods, passing the hemlock where John was hiding, shaking, sweating.

"You can put the rifle down now, John," Russell said. "It's time to go home."

❧

John had watched Becca and her dog dart through the crowd in a hurry to follow the detective. He'd recognized the detective from the television news broadcast back when the young buck's body had been discovered,

234

the same cop she'd gone to visit at Benny's Bar and at the cabin along the river. Of course, John had known the detective prior to his joining the state police. He'd known him back when he'd been a teenager, constantly hanging around her, joined at her hip. But once Clint had shipped her off to boarding school and then later college, John hadn't known whether the two had stayed in touch, or at least not until a few days ago.

This concerned him.

He parked his father's chopper on the side of the road near the wagon full of pumpkins where Becca and the detective had been talking. It wasn't a parking space, but no one was going to say anything about it. Toby was two blocks away, mingling with the crowd. He was wearing his uniform, but it wasn't likely he'd be writing parking tickets today. The idea was to welcome tourists to the market and help local businesses thrive. Handing out parking tickets at such an event wouldn't help the community in their efforts to make a buck.

Farther down the street at the edge of the crowd, several of the club members had gathered. Their motorcycles were parked along the street in a row. The guys were hanging around the bikes, trying not to look bored, while their old ladies shopped at the stands. They were all playing their part, their women purchasing fruit and vegetables, chatting with the wives of the locals, announcing their place in the community, making their presence known. They were congenial, respectful, as though they were telling the town to pay no attention to the body law enforcement had pulled from the river.

John spotted Chitter and the prospect standing in front of the soup stand. Chitter was carrying a jug of apple cider. John approached them slowly, weaving his way down the sidewalk. Chitter greeted him with a nod. The lady in the stand handed John a free sample of what smelled like an awful lot of cinnamon in some kind of pumpkin soup.

"Thank you, ma'am." He motioned for Chitter to follow him.

The prospect tagged along but lagged behind the two full-patch members, giving them space to talk.

"What's up?" Chitter asked, looked at the people around them while shoveling the plastic spoon full of soup into his mouth.

"I have a situation," John said, nodding to a woman who walked by pushing a baby stroller.

"Okay." Chitter squinted his eyes. "Do we need a sit-down?"

"Not for this." John tasted the soup, coughed. He hated cinnamon. "I'll need another rifle. Clean." He kept his voice low.

"Doing a little hunting?"

"Something like that."

"Did you clear it with Hap?"

"Not yet, but I will." His shirt was wet and stuck to his back. He could smell his own body odor underneath the leather cut. *Nerves, for Christ's sake.* "How soon can you get it to me?"

"How soon do you need it?"

"Yesterday," he said.

"I'll have it to you this afternoon."

John nodded and walked away, the sweat dripping down the sides of his face. He tossed the sample of pumpkin soup into the overflowing trash can on the way to his father's chopper. He got on the bike and rode through town as though he were Moses and the people the sea, parting the crowd with the sound of the motorcycle's engine, the patch on his leather cut identifying his allegiance, who he was, a Scion, the enforcer.

What John didn't know was that seconds after he'd left the market, Rick Smith stepped from behind one of the displays. He pulled on a pair of nitrile gloves and plucked the discarded cup and spoon from the top of the pile of trash. To Rick's good fortune, all of the soup had not only leaked out but also hadn't stained the sides, leaving any fingerprints intact. Rick dropped the evidence into a plastic bag. Then he removed the nitrile gloves and tossed them into the trash, whistling as he made his way down the street.

◆

John parked his father's chopper in the garage, his hand clutching the smooth leather seat for support. His heart sped up, then slowed down, then sped up again. The dirt floor tilted beneath his boots. He stepped away from the bike. If he was going down, he didn't want to take the bike down with him. He wouldn't damage his father's chopper over some kind of anxiety attack, if that was what this was. Plus, he was sure the insurance on his father's bike had lapsed after his death. John carried the same insurance on his motorcycle as the other club members carried on their bikes too. It wasn't something they talked about openly, but just because they were on the fringe of the law more often than not didn't mean they were stupid. They paid for insurance like everyone else.

John made it as far as the workbench, picked up the towel he'd used to wipe the grease from his hands, and mopped his face. He groped around, searching for someplace to sit, finding the old wooden stool, the one he'd been sitting on when Becca had been just a little girl and had walked in on him in the barn. He plopped down on the hard seat. His heart did the racing, slowing thing again. He attributed it to stress and, if he was honest, nervousness. He waited, hunched over, while his heartbeat sought its normal rhythm. When he felt calm, stable, he grabbed the .22 he kept in the barn and headed into the woods.

The autumn leaves blanketed the ground, crackling underneath his heavy boots. Dried sweat clung to his skin, sending shivers up and down his arms and legs. He welcomed the cool mountain air into his lungs. A light breeze carried the scent of the river, earthy and clean. The sights and sounds and smells settled inside of him, calming him.

He could never give this up, he thought, trekking through the woods, breathing the open air.

After thirty minutes of walking, he climbed into a deer stand he'd built with his old man in a hundred-year-old maple tree. He laid the rifle across his lap, his thoughts on Beth and how much he wished she were there beside him. She used to shiver in the cold early mornings on the days she'd joined him, waiting for a deer or rabbit to happen by. He'd lay his rifle to the side, with no intention of using it unless he had to. He hadn't killed the animals in front of Beth. She hadn't had the stomach for it. And yet she'd never complained about digging in once the meat had been cooked and served on a plate.

When she'd been in the woods with him, they would watch the birds and squirrels and rabbits. They would listen to the sounds of the wildlife surrounding them. Sometimes, if they were real quiet and the animals had stilled, they could hear the whisper of the river. Beth would press her body against his for warmth, and in return, he'd wrap his arms around her, pulling her close. During her final days, when she'd been too weak to walk, the cancer having taken all of her strength, John had carried her, sitting her on the ground at the base of the trunk of what he would forever think of as their tree.

He closed his eyes. He could almost feel her body next to his, smell the soap on her skin, the touch of her strawberry hair brushing his cheek. What he remembered now, sitting in the deer stand alone, was the first time Beth had seen a doe pass underneath the old maple tree. She'd squeezed his arm, her breath quick and short, her eyes wide. "She's so big," she'd said. "And so beautiful."

The doe had stopped and listened, hearing the whisper of Beth's voice, picking up their scent. It had darted through the trees, graceful and swift, disappearing behind the hemlocks.

"How could you kill such a beautiful creature?" she'd asked.

He'd looked her in the eyes. "I only kill what I need to survive."

"Does that include the club's survival, John? Would you kill for them if they asked you to?"

"I would do whatever I have to do to protect my family," he'd said.

She'd kissed him then softly, tenderly, whispering into his mouth as she did, "You're a good man."

Beth had never asked him the question again.

🦋

A large rabbit hopped from underneath a hemlock. John raised the rifle. It took two more hops before landing in a perfect spot for John to take his shot. The gun fired with a bang. The rabbit leaped into the air, took several more hops out of pure adrenaline, and dropped to its side.

He slung the rifle over his shoulder by its strap and climbed down the tree, landing with a grunt, his hips protesting the jarring motion. Kneeling next to the rabbit, he pulled a hunting knife from its sheath and began the ritual of a field dressing. It was quick work. The rabbit was large for its kind but small by comparison to a deer—*Or a man*, his old man's voice said somewhere in the back of his mind. He tossed the guts to the side for the wolves. All the while he pretended his stomach wasn't twisting and turning. He was sweating again. He swallowed the saliva in the back of his throat.

By the time he walked out of the woods, rifle slung over his shoulder, the rabbit hanging by its feet in his hand, the calm he'd felt tucked safely inside the tree had been eradicated. Sweat poured from his hairline. The front and back of his shirt were soaked, his legs unsteady as he made his way to the rusty pickup truck parked alongside the barn. The prospect was leaning against the passenger's-side door, smoking a cigarette. Chitter stepped out of the house, picking at his teeth. He made his way across the yard when he saw John emerge from the woods.

"Dinner?" Chitter asked and followed John inside the barn.

"You're welcome to stick around if you have a taste for it," John said, hanging the rabbit on a hook. Not everybody liked rabbit. It had a gamey taste that took getting used to. "The prospect can stay too," he added.

The prospect walked in behind them, made a face. "I'll pass."

"Do you have what I need?" John reached for the old towel to wipe his hands and face.

"It's in the back of the truck," Chitter said.

He followed him to the pickup.

"You don't look so good," Chitter said. "Are you feeling all right?"

"Yup." He opened the duffel bag and pulled out the .30-06 rifle. "It's clean."

John nodded. "I'm going to need you to round up the guys and take them on a run for the night. Make it some kind of a special event with booze and girls. And make sure everyone is there. I don't want anyone at Sweeney's. Close the place down. Hell, call it a minivacation if you want. The prospect here is going to take my bike with him."

"Seriously?" The prospect smiled.

"Are you sure about that, John?" Chitter asked.

"Yes. And if anyone asks, you tell them I was with you the entire trip. I was there. My bike was there. Tell everybody they saw me. Do you understand?"

"What's going on, John?" Chitter stopped picking his teeth, stared at him.

"I'm taking care of a loose end. That's all you need to know."

"You talked to Hap?"

John turned to face Chitter, the rifle gripped in his hand at his side. "Are you questioning me?" He heard his father's voice coming from his mouth. When had he started sounding so much like his old man? When had he started behaving like him?

Chitter put up both hands. "No. I just think someone should know what the hell is going on, even if it's not me."

"Hap will know."

"Okay," Chitter said. "You're calling the shots." He handed John a flip phone. "It can't be traced if you decide to use it. But whatever you decide, destroy it when you're done."

John took the phone.

Chitter put his hand on John's shoulder. "I'm not questioning you, man. I'm just trying to look out for you."

John covered Chitter's hand with his own. "I know," he said. "Now get the guys out of here. By the time you get back, everything will have been taken care of." He tossed the keys to the prospect. "Don't fuck up my bike."

John was sitting behind the barn watching the leaves burn in the fire pit. He'd eaten some time ago, and the meat lay in his stomach like a rock. His throat was dry. He couldn't spit. The flames rose and fell in flashes of yellow and orange, the black embers falling to the ground by his feet.

He took out the disposable flip phone. Hap picked up on the first ring. In the background, John heard the guys hooting and hollering; then it grew quiet.

Hap must've stepped away from the noise. "What's going on?" he asked.

"Is everybody there?" John asked. "The whole crew?"

"Yes," Hap said. "Everyone but you."

"You tell everyone I'm there too."

"What's this about?"

"I'm cleaning up a loose end. It's best you and the club don't know any more than that."

Hap was silent. Eventually, he said, "Okay. Do what you have to."

John hung up the phone, tossed it into the fire.

CHAPTER THIRTY-SEVEN

Ten-year-old Becca was skipping rope in the driveway not long after she'd watched her father talking with Russell at the edge of the yard. Sheba was chasing the rope, tripping her up.

"Stop it," she said to Sheba and patted the dog's head. "How do you expect me to reach one hundred if you keep biting the rope?"

Her father finished mowing the lawn, parked the John Deere in the garage, and strode to where Becca was petting the dog. He knelt on the ground and grabbed her by the arms, pulled her close so that their faces were inches apart.

"What were you doing in their barn?" he asked. His breath was hot and smelled like cigarettes.

"I wasn't in their barn," she said.

"Don't lie to me, Becca." He squeezed her arms, pinching the skin. "You forget whatever it was you saw. Do you hear me?" He shook her.

Tears stung her eyes. She wanted to tell him that he was hurting her. She wanted to tell him about John and the knife and the dog attacking Sheba, because she wasn't sleeping, because she was scared. "I did see something, Daddy," she whispered. "There was a knife and a blue sweatshirt covered in . . ."

"No." He cut her off. "You're not allowed to tell me."

"But why?"

"Because, that's why. You have to forget all about it, do you hear? You're never to tell anyone. Not me. Not your mother. No one. Ever." He shook her again. "Do you hear?"

She nodded, a sob caught in her throat.

"It never happened," he said, giving her arms a tighter squeeze. "And you're never to talk about it again. Do you understand?"

She nodded.

"Say it. Say you understand you're never to talk about it. You'll forget it ever happened. Say it. Promise me." She heard the fear in his tone, felt it in the grip of his hands on her arms, and it terrified her.

"I promise, Daddy," she said, tears streaming down her face.

He hugged her then. "That's my girl," he said. "It will be our little secret."

She didn't hug him back. Her arms stung and hung at her sides. After another minute, he released her and stood. She looked up at him through watery eyes.

"Now go and wash up," he said and wiped his own cheeks dry. "This never happened."

She did as she was told and went straight to the powder room in the downstairs hall. She washed her face and hands and examined her arms in the mirror. Red welts appeared on her skin where her father had clutched her. He had never raised a hand to her or squeezed her arms so hard, and she was confused and ashamed by what he'd done to her now.

She raced to her bedroom and pulled on a long-sleeve shirt. Sheba followed her, jumped on Becca's bed, and lay down. Becca buried her face in the dog's fur. She would never tell anyone what had happened in the barn with John and the dogs. She'd bury it, force herself to forget all about the bloody knife and the soiled sweatshirt at John's feet.

🦋

Becca stepped into the kitchen to find Jackie hanging up the phone. Romy went straight to her water dish. Jackie kept her back to Becca, as though she were trying to gain some composure before turning around to face her.

In that moment Becca wondered if she'd arrived home too late and whatever had happened had happened in her absence. The last few days, the entire week, living in this house under the same roof with her father, picking at the scars of old wounds had been for nothing. She hadn't accomplished a thing. She should've opened her mouth and talked with him sooner. She should've found a way.

Jackie turned around. Her face was puffy and tired. She hadn't slept more than a few hours the night before, and still she managed a smile.

"I just got off the phone with your mother," she said. "She's going to catch the next flight out."

"Oh." It was all Becca could say. Her mind tried to catch up to the ache inside her heart. "Oh," she said again. She wanted her mother to come. She wanted her here.

"He doesn't have much time left." Jackie was struggling. Her face showed how hard she was trying to hold back her emotions. "You should probably go up and be with him."

"I'm not too late," she said with such relief that she wrapped her arms around Jackie and hugged her. She'd never offered any kind of affection to any of her father's lady friends, but the woman in front of her was so much more. She wondered if her father knew how lucky he was to have not only Becca's mother but also Jackie, two good women in his life.

"You better go," Jackie said. "Spend this time with him." She held Becca's hands. "And if there's anything you have to say, you say it to him now. Don't wait. You may not get a second chance."

"Okay." She turned to go, paused, then turned back around. "How do you know?" she asked. "How do you know it's the end?" She thought of her father's behavior since she'd arrived: one day he was strong and lucid, the next weak and confused. Perhaps the better days had been more of an effort for him than she'd realized, his strong will coming and going in flashes, offering glimpses of the father she'd remembered from childhood.

"Oh, honey," Jackie said. "The signs have been there all along. You should know that. I would imagine it's the same with the animals you treat."

Becca nodded. "In ways, I guess it is. In other ways, it isn't."

Jackie filled the teapot with water and put it on the stove. "When your dad started asking for you to come home, I knew it was close. You see, when a person knows they're dying, they want to be surrounded by their loved ones."

"Did he ever ask for my mother?" She didn't want to hurt Jackie's feelings, but the child inside of Becca wanted to know. No matter what he'd done, she'd always wanted to believe that he'd loved her mother.

"Oh, yes, he asked your mother to come home too."

"I'm sorry. That must've been hard for you."

"No, don't be sorry. I understand. They were married a long time. They share you. And besides, your mother is truly a lovely person. We've talked a lot on the phone in the last few months."

Becca knew they'd talked, but it almost sounded as though Jackie and her mother had become friends.

Jackie continued. "Your mother thought it was best if she stayed away and gave you and your dad some time to be alone together. She wanted the two of you to work things out without her relationship with him interfering. She thinks it interfered enough."

"And she told you all of this?"

"Yes. She wanted me to call her when the time came," she said. "But, Becca, it's *you* he's been asking for all this time. You're the one he wants with him. Go to him and say what you need to say before it's too late."

She nodded or thought she might've nodded. She wasn't sure. She turned to go, each step feeling heavier and heavier as she made her way up the stairs and down the hall. More than anything, she wanted her mother here, but she understood her mother's reasons.

Becca pushed the bedroom door open. Her father's eyes were closed. His breathing was slow. She stood in the doorway watching him. Sometimes there were long pauses between his breaths.

She walked into the room. The smells of antiseptic and sickness were still there, but there was something more, a weight to the air that hadn't been there yesterday. She looked over her shoulder, certain she would see a dark figure of some sort, of death, at the door. It was everywhere, the sense of the end settling into the cracks and crevices, filling the space around her.

She pulled the chair close to the bed and sat. "Dad," she said. She didn't know if he could hear her, but he must have, because after a few seconds, he opened his eyes. He blinked.

"Becca." He said her name as though it had taken a lot of effort.

She slipped her hand into his. His skin was paper thin and cool and bluish in color.

"I need to talk to you," he said, each word coming out thick and slow.

"Take your time. I'm not going anywhere."

His eyebrows furrowed as though he was angry, his expression a ghost of what it had once been. Becca watched his face and waited.

He coughed and tried to swallow.

She picked up the cup of water from the tray on the nightstand and put the bendy straw to his lips. Helping him drink and eat had been so strange, so foreign a few days ago, but today she felt more at ease with the intimacy. It was hard to stay angry with someone who couldn't bring a cup of water to his lips when he was thirsty. Although the anger was still there, it was just that she'd set it aside, no longer giving in to its shape and form.

He didn't even try to sip the water. She put the cup back onto the tray and looked at her hands in her lap.

"Is he a good man?" he asked and coughed. "Jackie told me."

"Oh." She couldn't explain Matt to her father, not without sounding angry or hurt. In ways, her father and Matt were tied together in her mind. So much of her behavior involving Matt had been a reaction to her relationship with her father. When she traced every event, every lie and indiscretion back to its beginning, she was certain how it would end. Maybe she wasn't being fair to either one of them. Maybe she wasn't being fair to herself. And maybe, just maybe, all the lying and cheating they were all guilty of was because they just hadn't found the right one, the right woman or man that was meant for them.

"Is he?" he asked again.

She took her father's hand again, squeezed it gently. "Please, Dad, don't." She wouldn't tell him Matt was more like him than she wanted to admit. She wouldn't hurt him, not now. All she wanted was to let it go. But she couldn't. She couldn't. She had to know. "Why did you do it? Why did you bring that woman here? And in front of me? I was so young. Why were there so many others?" She asked the questions her mother could never ask. Becca asked for both of them.

She waited for him to answer, and when he didn't respond, she wanted to shake him. *Tell me why*, she wanted to shout. She deserved an answer. Her mother deserved an explanation.

"Why weren't we enough?" she asked, pleading to get some kind of response from him.

He struggled to breathe. "I was chief." He choked. "I let it go to my head, thought I could do what I wanted. I was nothing but a selfish fool."

She touched his arm, his shoulder. She didn't know what to say, what she'd expected, but it didn't feel so shattering, knowing the simple truth.

They sat quietly for a long time. His eyes opened and closed as he drifted in and out of sleep. Downstairs, Jackie was banging the cupboards as though she was searching for something. Romy padded up the steps, stopped inside the bedroom doorway. The dog peered into the room. She didn't enter. Instead, she lay down in the hallway, her head resting on top of her paws as though she sensed what was in the air.

Becca wasn't sure how much time had passed, enough time for the sun to begin its descent behind the mountain. The sky turned gray. Shadows stretched across the floor. She'd moved from the edge of the seat some time ago, resting her spine against the hardwood slats on the back of the chair. Her arms dangled over the armrests.

Romy got up and went downstairs. Becca heard the back door open and close. Jackie must've let the dog out for some fresh air or to do her business or both. Now, Jackie was leaning against the doorjamb, arms folded, with a syringe in her hand, the sharp needle pointed away from her body.

"He's resting," Becca said.

"I hate to disturb him, but it's time for his medicine. I don't want to let it go and then he wakes up in pain."

Jackie didn't have to explain herself to Becca. If anything, Becca felt an overwhelming need to explain herself to Jackie. She wasn't a bad daughter, she wanted to say. Sometimes the wounds were too deep. The scars of the past between parent and child weren't always healed. And although her relationship with her father would never be repaired, not completely anyway, she'd found love for him.

She didn't say any of these things to Jackie, though. Instead, she watched as Jackie injected him with morphine. He stirred but didn't wake.

"Parker called. Twice," Jackie said.

Becca nodded.

Jackie continued. "I'm warming up some soup. Why don't you come down in a few minutes and eat?"

"Okay, thanks," she said and watched as Jackie walked out of the room.

Her father's eyes opened the second Jackie had gone. He looked at Becca, and she could see in his gaze he was there, he was present, when earlier he'd drifted in and away.

Her father gripped her hand. His eyes grew wide. "John." He swallowed hard.

The muscles in her neck and back tensed. She nodded, signaling him to continue.

When her father didn't continue, she said, "Tell me."

His eyes closed. His breath came in short bursts.

Her heart thrummed. She put her hands on his shoulders, forcing him to look at her. "Tell me, Dad. I need for you to tell me everything." She felt the pull like a current in the river, forcing her in a direction she had no choice but to go.

He remained silent.

"Tell me." She was aware of the panic in her voice. "I'm not a little kid anymore. I know what I saw. I know why you sent me away."

He blinked several times, trying to stay alert, fighting the morphine pulsing through his veins. He reached for her. His hand covered her mouth, then dropped to the bed. His eyes closed again.

He was telling her to remain quiet. And she hated herself because she was thinking about it. All she had to do was tell Parker she'd made a mistake. She hadn't seen a thing. She could walk away from this place, from John, and forget anything had ever happened.

But what if he killed again? Could she live with herself? She didn't think so. And what about Parker? Was she prepared to forget him too, to walk away from him a second time? It was what she would have to do. She'd never be able to look him in the eyes knowing she was the key witness in his case.

"What should I do, Dad?" she asked, listening to his labored breath before covering her face with her hands.

CHAPTER THIRTY-EIGHT

Becca stayed at her father's bedside, refusing to leave him for even a moment. Twice since the sun had set, she'd used the bathroom, but otherwise she hadn't left the room. She'd skipped dinner and Jackie's soup. Romy had stayed outside the door in the hallway. The dog had been aware of what was happening from her body language. She'd kept her head lowered, a deep sadness in her eyes. Becca had wanted Romy in the bedroom with her so that she could pet and comfort her, so they could comfort each other. But the last thing Becca wanted to do was upset her father by bringing a dog into his room. The truth of it made her sad, the power he held over her still, the leftover childhood fear.

It wasn't until sometime after midnight that she rose and stared out the window at the darkened sky. The night was clear and cool. The stars were plentiful, shimmering and glittering, dancing around the moon. It was almost too beautiful to look at, too happy, a sharp contrast to the sorrow staining the walls of the house.

The small lamp on the nightstand gave off a dim yellow glow that spread across her father's face and chest. Jackie was sitting in a chair on the opposite side of the bed, silent, watching him rest. She'd taken his hand and began massaging his fingers and palm, working her way to his wrist and forearm. All the while, she whispered to him. Becca couldn't make out everything she'd said, but she'd caught some of the words. "We're with you. You're not alone."

It was now close to three o'clock. He opened his eyes. Becca stood and peered at him. "We're here, Dad. We're right here with you." She said the words not knowing if he understood. His eyes were glazed over, and the longer she stared at him, the more she realized he wasn't there. Oh, he was there physically. But whatever had made her father who he was had disappeared. His eyes no longer held any of the emotions he'd once carried, nothing of the life he'd lived.

She sat back down and took his hand, rubbing his fingers and palm the way Jackie had done. His skin was dry and cool, as though his body heat had left him. His nails were blue. "Maybe we should get him another blanket," she said.

"It's normal for his skin to feel cool," Jackie said. "But there's another blanket in the hall closet if it makes you feel better."

Yes, it would make her feel better. She would take any little thing she could to make herself feel better. Becca stood and left the room. Outside the door, she stopped and put her back against the wall, sliding down to the floor next to Romy. The sixty-five-pound dog crawled into Becca's lap, and Becca buried her face in Romy's fur.

Some time had passed, not much time, and Becca stood once again, giving Romy a kiss on the top of her head. Becca pulled a blanket from the hall closet and returned to her father's room. Jackie helped her spread it over him.

They sat in silence. The house was so quiet she could hear the clock in the kitchen downstairs tick off the seconds. On occasion, the old electric heat kicked on, the pipes pinging, the sound much louder than Becca had remembered.

"I told your dad he needed to get a new furnace," Jackie said. "The first time I heard those pipes rattle, I thought someone had lit firecrackers under the bed." She laughed and gazed at his face, seeming to be lost in a memory she'd shared with him.

Becca didn't say anything, and the silence stretched on. They continued massaging his hands and arms, talking to him in whispering voices. He'd stopped drinking more than forty-eight hours ago. It was almost another three hours before his eyes opened wide again. Becca stood over him, touching his shoulder.

"Dad. Can you hear me?"

He looked at her with the same vacant eyes. She would never again see the sternness of his glare, the fear, the twinkle of his charm, the shades of love in his gaze. A deep sadness moved through her, a great sorrow for all the things they were to each other, all the things they could've been, all the things they would never get to be.

"I came home for you," she told him. "I came because I wanted to be here with you."

His eyelids fluttered once, twice, and closed. His skin was dusky. His jaw relaxed, and his mouth hung open as the hollows in his cheeks collapsed. His breaths came in short, shallow spurts with long pauses in between. It was five forty-five in the morning.

Jackie continued rubbing his forearm and bicep and shoulder. Becca lowered herself in the chair, unable to do anything but watch.

"We're here, baby," Jackie said. "You're not alone."

No, Becca thought, they were the ones who were alone. He was gone from them. Maybe Jackie hadn't realized it yet. Maybe she had yet to feel the void, the emptiness in the room.

At six o'clock his breathing stopped, his last breath no different from the one before.

Slowly, Becca rose from the chair and crossed the room to the window. She folded her arms as though she were hugging herself. The top of the sun appeared behind the mountain, lighting the ground with its golden rays. Yellow and orange leaves blew in the breeze and scattered across the yard. Romy entered the room, sat by Becca's side.

Behind her, Jackie crawled into the bed with him. She wrapped her arms around him, rested his head on her shoulder, and quietly sobbed.

Becca left Jackie that way, curled around Becca's father, and walked out of the room with Romy. She dressed in running gear, long black pants and a bright-pink shirt, the color bold and vivid like her father had told her to wear in case there were hunters in the woods. She tied the laces of her sneakers. Then she folded the sheet of paper with the witness's statement into a small square and shoved it into the front pocket of her pants. Romy jumped and pranced at her side, tired of being cooped up in the house, ready for her morning exercise.

Becca stopped in front of the foyer closet and opened the door. She grabbed the small Ruger off the top shelf. Her father had kept it in the coat closet by the door with the Glock he'd carried on the job ever since she'd been a kid. The first thing he'd do after coming home from one of his shifts was to put his weapon on the shelf where she could reach it if she'd wanted.

The Glock he used to carry was no longer there. She imagined he'd had to turn it in when he'd retired. But not the Ruger. The Ruger had been waiting for her. Her father had prepared her for this day when he would no longer be around to protect her. She hadn't understood then that this was his gift to her, a way of showing her how much he'd loved her. *No country girl worth a spit doesn't know how to fire a gun.*

The Ruger felt familiar in her grip, although not as heavy as she remembered. She tucked it into the back waistband of her pants, double-checking it was secure, and threw the back door open.

CHAPTER THIRTY-NINE

John leaned against the oak tree, the same tree Russell had leaned on at the edge of the woods overlooking Clint's yard, the same spot where Russell and Clint had struck a deal.

John had been resting against the tree for the last two hours. It had been dark when he'd arrived, the sky the color of ash, not quite night but not yet morning. His hips and knees ached. He flexed and extended his fingers to get the blood circulating. His joints cracked. His body temperature fluctuated between hot and cold. He gripped the .30-06 rifle in his hand at his side. He'd been awake all night, unable to shut his mind down, turning his options over and then over again, searching for a way out. He'd paced the rooms in his house until his legs had grown tired, and the walls had threatened to confine him. It hadn't been until he'd stepped outside into the night air that he'd started to relax, his muscles unknotting along his spine, his shoulders no longer up around his ears. The night had been cool. He'd lit another fire in the fire pit and spent several hours watching it burn. It hadn't been until dawn approached that he'd picked up the rifle.

Now, while he propped himself up against the oak tree, waiting, he talked to himself. He shouldn't have allowed Becca to see him by the river. It was his fault he was in this position. He'd been sloppy, and he was being forced to clean up the mess. He had no choice. She would talk to her detective friend, if she hadn't already. Without her, the detective had no case.

Or so he believed.

John kept his gaze on Clint's house and the dim yellow light coming from the second-floor window. Behind John the mountain loomed, and the first hint of the sun's rays stroked the ground at his feet. He was here watching, waiting, relying on a gut feeling and his knowledge of her and her routine. He hoped for once his gut was wrong. For the first time in his life, he wanted to be dead wrong.

The back door to the house swung open. Becca's dog raced outside.

John stepped behind the tree, hiding behind it, gripping the rifle with a clammy hand. For a moment, he thought she was just letting her dog out to go to the bathroom. But then she appeared in the doorway. John ducked farther behind the tree, peeked around the trunk. She stepped into the yard wearing tight black pants and a bright-pink shirt.

He recognized her running gear.

Quietly, he slipped away from the oak tree. He would have to be careful and take extra precautions as he moved through the woods so her dog wouldn't smell him and give him away. His adrenaline pumped as he darted soundlessly through the brush, careful of snapping twigs and crunching leaves. When he was a safe distance away, he stepped behind a hemlock tree. Again he waited.

The birds stopped fluttering and chirping in the branches above. The air hummed with silence. John listened.

Not far in the distance, he heard movement, the sound low to the ground, the whipping and crackling of brush and low-lying branches, the sound of an animal moving fast through the woods.

His heart thrummed.

Next, there came the sound of pounding feet striking the ground, the long strides of someone who was running. The stomping was getting closer and closer and closer still.

And then. And then he heard her breathing.

CHAPTER FORTY

Becca was running through the woods, following the same path she'd taken before, the same path she'd always taken when she'd been a child playing in the woods behind her house. Romy raced ahead. Becca tried to keep up. She was breathing hard. Her sneakered feet thumped the ground, alerting anyone and everyone she was there.

"If you're going to play in the woods, it's not enough to wear bright-colored clothing so the hunters can see you," her father had said. "You need to make a lot of noise to scare away the bears."

"What about the wolves?" a nine-year-old Becca had asked.

"It's the same for wolves," he'd said. "They're more scared of you than you are of them."

She hadn't been convinced he'd been right when she'd been a young girl, but she believed what he'd said was true, given her knowledge of animals today. She wished she would've told him this when she'd had the chance. This was the start of many things she wished she'd said to him. It hadn't been easy to find the words to talk with him, but it had been one of the few good memories she'd had of him, these little lessons he'd taught her at a tender age. Of course, it hadn't been until a full year later that she'd stepped into John's barn and her relationship with her father had forever changed.

She raced through the trees, kicking up dirt in her wake, grief and regret like weights around her ankles, threatening to drag her down. Branches whipped by. Red and yellow and orange leaves swirled together in a flash. Her fists pumped at her sides. She was close to the barn. She smelled the fire pit where John burned leaves. Her steps faltered, and her pace slowed. She checked the gun was still secured in her waistband. Romy stopped and circled back, egging her on. She picked up her pace again and ran alongside the stream with a sense she was trying to outrun the last twenty years. But it was too late. Her father was gone. And she was left with the knowledge of what he'd done to protect her. She was left with the awful truth of what she'd seen.

She raced on, ignoring the woods around her. She should've been listening, looking for signs of danger. But the image of her father lying in bed, his eyes dull and empty, kept flashing across her mind, and all she could do was run.

"This way," she called to Romy and veered away from the stream, heading to the small open field and the river. She had to be sure it was the same spot she'd seen John, and only then would she be certain of what she had to do next.

Romy darted across the field, a black-and-brown rocket cutting through the golden grass of autumn. Becca followed behind, using the path made by the dog, passing the tree where the yellow crime scene tape dangled in the breeze. A cramp pinched her side. She was winded, not used to sprinting for such a long distance. She approached the riverbank at a much faster pace than she'd anticipated, having to reach behind her, drag her hand along the ground to keep from falling as she skidded down. She came to a stop at the bottom near the water's edge. She bent over, both hands on top of her thighs, trying to catch her breath. The rapids soared. The noise filled her ears. Romy was drinking from the river where the water had slowed and pooled between two large rocks.

Becca stayed bent over, raising her head slightly to gaze across the river, spying the path she used to run on the Jersey side. There was no way around it. This was the exact spot John had stood the morning before the body had turned up in the river. She remembered it clearly. He'd been wearing a glove, a purple nitrile glove. She hadn't thought much of it at the time. Hunters wore gloves as a safety precaution against disease whenever they'd field dress an animal. And maybe he'd worn the gloves for that reason, but now she knew better. He'd worn the gloves so he wouldn't leave fingerprints behind.

She had to tell Parker everything. She couldn't live with what she knew. It was the right thing to do. *I'm sorry, John.* She wanted there to be another way, but there wasn't.

After a few minutes, her breathing returned to normal and she stood upright, looking in Romy's direction. The dog's ears were alert, her fur in hackles along her spine. Far below the noise of the rapids came a primal sound deep within the dog's throat. Her lips curled, exposing her sharp white canines as she stared at a spot directly over Becca's shoulder.

Fear spread throughout Becca's limbs. She reached for the Ruger, spun around. John was standing at the very top of the riverbank, the barrel of his rifle aimed at her chest. A part of her wasn't surprised to see him. She'd expected him. She'd brought the gun for a reason. Another part, a bigger part, was scared as hell.

Romy took several steps toward the bank, her lips high over her gums, showcasing every inch of her teeth. A low, menacing growl erupted from her throat.

Becca's first thought was for the safety of the animal. "Stay," she hollered.

Romy stopped, although her body language was clear. She would attack on command.

John paid no attention to the dog. The barrel remained pointed at Becca's chest, unwavering.

Becca gripped the gun with both hands. She pulled in a sharp breath. Her arms shook, and the gun jumped around unsteadily. She wanted to send Romy away. None of this was the dog's fault. "Please," she croaked. "Don't hurt my dog."

John didn't move. His eye never left the scope.

She wasn't sure how long she stood aiming the gun at him; long enough for her arms to ache and her legs to stiffen.

He continued pointing the rifle at her, unyielding. But he hadn't pulled the trigger. And neither had she.

She didn't know what made her tell him, but the words came out anyway. "My father is dead," she shouted over the rapids. "He died this morning."

For a moment she wasn't sure if he'd heard her. Then he moved his head away from the scope, the butt of the rifle still against his shoulder, his finger still on the trigger.

Romy growled.

The Ruger was getting heavier, her wrists weaker from trying to hold it steady. She continued. "I know about the deal he made with Russell. I know about everything." She tried to swallow, but she didn't have any spit.

He didn't reply. He only stared.

"I know why you're doing this." Her voice wavered.

He lowered the rifle enough for her to see him clearly. He was covered in sweat, his skin pasty and pale. His face and neck were covered in hair and what was the start of the beard he often grew for the winter months.

"I told Parker I saw you. But I have to tell him everything. *Everything.*" She was pleading, begging for him to understand why she had to turn him in, why she didn't want to. "I can't stay silent. I don't want to keep any more secrets, not from myself and not from him."

Romy continued growling, the river a constant white noise.

"Do what you have to do," she said.

He wiped his eyes.

"Because if you let me walk away, I'm going to tell him what I know." She steadied the gun in her shaky hands, her finger on the trigger.

John swung to his left unexpectedly, raising his rifle in another direction.

She jumped and pointed the gun in the same direction. There was a man standing at the top of the riverbank, an older man, who was also pointing a rifle at her chest. Who was he? Another Scion? He must be. He was wearing the same leather cut. What was he doing here? Why was he aiming his rifle at her?

"Put the gun down, Hap," John said. "This was my mistake. Let me fix it."

"It's your father's mistake," the old man said. "He should've taken her out a long time ago. I didn't agree with the way he'd handled it then. And you can't handle it now."

"You're wrong," John said. "I can. I'm handling it."

The old man held steady, keeping his weapon pointed at Becca. "We're a team, you and I," he said to John. "I was with you both times. I've got just as much at stake here as you do."

Becca swung the gun back and forth between the men. Romy had moved and was now standing by her side. What was happening? She was beginning to understand that there was a lot more going on here than she knew. And whatever it was, it was bigger than what she'd seen.

"You may be right," John said. "That's why you should put the gun down and walk away. Let me take care of this one alone."

The Scion kept his rifle pointed at Becca.

"I'm faster than you, old man," John said. "You'll go down long before you ever pull the trigger."

"So that's it? That's how you want to do this?" the old man asked. "What about your loyalty to me and the club? You ain't been right in the head ever since you lost Beth. Why don't you just let me take care of this, and we'll sit down later and figure it out."

There was a moment when no one spoke. Becca didn't know where to aim her gun. She felt like a small animal trapped between two predators. She was shaking so hard her teeth chattered.

"Are we in agreement here, John?" the old man asked.

"Don't make me hurt you," John said, his voice deep and hoarse, pleading. "You don't want to do this."

"Is that your answer?" the old man asked. "You're taking her side?"

"It's not about taking sides," John said.

"The hell it isn't."

"Just put the gun down."

"You know I can't do that," the old man said, making a small movement of his head, a tiny shift of his shoulder, a signal he was eying up his shot.

Gunfire rang out.

Becca wasn't sure if she pulled the trigger first or who did. The kick of the gun was harder than she expected, jerking her arms up and back. The old man's body hit the ground with a thud before skidding down the embankment and stopping at the river's edge.

The rapids raged behind her. Romy snarled. But everything else had grown quiet. The birds had stopped singing. The squirrels had stopped chattering. The bugs had stopped buzzing. The silence was deafening, or maybe it was the blasting of guns that had muted all other noise in her head. She seemed to be processing the scene in slow motion. Was she shot? She was still standing. She didn't feel any pain. The old man wasn't moving. She didn't know if she'd hit him, whether he'd gone down from one bullet or two.

Romy barked. She sounded distant and far away. It was another minute or two before Becca's head cleared. She looked up the riverbank at John. He had his rifle aimed at her again. She was shaking all over. She pulled in another sharp breath, wondering if it would be her last.

But he lowered the rifle, the barrel pointing at the ground by his feet. He wasn't going to shoot her. She knew this. *She knew.* She took a step toward him. He turned to walk away.

"Wait," she called. Her arms quaked at her sides, the gun in her hand heavy and warm.

He paused and looked back at her, his rifle still aimed at the ground. He stared at her for a long moment.

She couldn't find the words. *I'm sorry, but this doesn't change anything.* But she didn't have to say it. He understood. A deep sadness emanated from him, and she wanted to reach out and touch him, have him hold her and tell her everything was going to be okay. But he turned away from her again, and this time when he walked away, she didn't call him back.

When she could see only the tops of his shoulders, the back of his head, she called out, "There's good in you, John Jackson!"

There's just not enough good.

CHAPTER FORTY-ONE

The sun was high in the sky by the time Becca reached Parker's house and knocked on the front door. Romy panted by her side. They'd walked the couple of miles to Parker's place, following the river downstream. A young couple had been kayaking in the direction of Dead Man's Curve. Fishermen had dotted the shoreline, hoping for a catch. A red-tailed hawk had soared among the cumulus clouds in the blue sky above. She'd seen all of it and none of it. What had she done?

She knocked again, louder this time. There was a good chance he wasn't home. She had no way of knowing his work schedule. When he didn't answer, Becca stumbled across his porch. A couple of jack-o'-lanterns glared at her through their angry eyes and menacing smiles. *Typical Parker.* What he needed was a happy-faced pumpkin. If she ever got through this day, maybe she would carve him one.

She peered in the window. *Be home*, she thought. It was dark inside. She stepped back and tripped over the edge of the rocking chair, banging her shin. She smacked her palm on the wooden door again. *Come on, Parker. Be home.* She didn't know how much longer she could stand. The adrenaline that had surged through her veins, accelerated her heart rate, contracted her muscles when she'd feared for her life, had all but evaporated. She understood the science behind the fight-or-flight syndrome, but she'd never experienced it until now. She was left with the shakes, slight confusion, and an unyielding state of exhaustion.

She raised her hand to pound on the door one more time just as it opened.

"Parker," she said and collapsed in his arms.

"What the hell happened?" he asked and carried her inside. Romy followed them into the living room. Parker put Becca down on the couch.

"I'll explain everything," she said. "But first can Romy and I have a drink of water?" She covered her mouth as she spoke, tasting the bitter acid of stomach bile on her tongue, having forgotten that at one point she'd dropped to her knees, retched into the river. It had been around the same time the gun had slipped from her hand. She'd lost it somewhere on her way there.

Parker returned with a bowl full of water for Romy and a large glass of water for Becca. When she'd finished drinking, he took the glass from her hand and set it on the coffee table. He waited quietly by her side, and for this she was grateful, because she needed time to collect her thoughts. He searched her face.

Romy lay on the floor by the couch. She put her head on her paws, feeling the exhaustion of the morning as much as her human counterpart.

"I need you to be a friend and not a cop," Becca said. "You can do the cop thing later, when I'm finished."

"Okay," he said, drawing out the *o*. "But I have to admit, you're scaring me a little bit here."

"You don't know the half of it," she said and touched her forehead where a headache was starting.

"You don't look so good. Maybe you should lie down." Parker lifted her legs onto the couch. He put an extra pillow behind her head.

"Promise me you'll listen as a friend."

"I will. Please tell me what's going on." His face was open.

She saw the old Parker in front of her, not the cop, and closed her eyes. She started from the beginning, telling him everything she remembered about that day in the barn, the dogs fighting, the blue hooded sweatshirt, the bloody knife in John's hand. She told him about the deal her father had struck with Russell and how John had been following her, how she'd been scared.

She'd been talking nonstop and had to pause to take a breath. There was more she had to tell him, but when she opened her eyes, Parker was wearing his cop face. He paced around the room, running his hand over the top of his head, messing his already messy hair. There was a healthy growth of stubble on his face and neck. His clothes looked slept in, the GONE FISHING T-shirt wrinkled and worn, the same T-shirt he'd been wearing when they'd shared a root beer in his kitchen, the same T-shirt she'd slipped over his head.

She hadn't noticed these things when she'd knocked on his door. But it was a good look on him, rumpled and unkempt, and so different from Matt's constantly polished appearance. It was the first time she'd thought of Matt in the last several hours. She didn't have her cell phone with her, so she had no idea if he'd tried to contact her. It was just as well.

Parker continued pacing, passing by the couch where she was lying, his long legs carrying him across the room in a couple of strides. Romy lifted her head and watched him with interest.

On one of his passes, Becca said, "You promised you'd be a friend."

"I am being a friend, Becca," he said, but there was an edge to his tone. "But you didn't think this was something I needed to know sooner? You didn't think to tell me all of this until now?"

She pulled herself up on shaky arms. "I didn't understand any of it myself until now."

"And your dad?" he asked. "He knew about this guy and what he was guilty of the entire time?"

"He was protecting me."

"Do you know what kind of trouble your dad is in? Do you understand he broke the law?"

"My dad died this morning," she whispered.

Parker stopped pacing. She felt his eyes on her. Neither one spoke for some time. Romy lowered her head back on top of her paws.

"I'm sorry," Parker said. "I didn't know."

She wouldn't look at him. If she did, the tears would start. She wasn't ready to give in to them. She didn't know if she ever would be. Instead, with some effort, she pulled out the folded sheet of paper from the small pocket in the front of her running pants. She handed it to Parker. "I started to put the pieces together when I found this in my dad's lockbox."

He took the sheet of paper from her and looked it over. "Do you have any idea who gave him this statement?"

"No," she said. "I never got around to asking him. But whoever it was described the sweatshirt I saw in the barn. And whoever it was didn't want to be identified."

"It had to be someone from town. No one wants to talk when it concerns the damn Scions."

"I suppose not."

They were silent again, and in the silence, she heard the river flowing behind the house. A flock of geese honked as they made their way south for the winter. A clock ticked, the sound coming from somewhere in the kitchen. Her head felt heavy. She struggled holding it up.

Parker sat on the coffee table in front of her, his forearms resting on the top of his thighs, his eyes full of concern. "Do you understand that you're a key witness in my case? And that I'm going to have to take an official statement from you?"

"I understand, but there's something else you need to know, something that happened this morning." Her tongue was thick, clunky.

Parker continued as though she hadn't spoken. "I can't bury evidence. I can't." He swallowed, his Adam's apple bobbing up and down. "It's my job. I have to do my job. But I promise I'll protect you. I promise I won't let him hurt you."

Outside, an engine rumbled.

CHAPTER FORTY-TWO

Parker jumped up from the coffee table where he'd been sitting, knocked over Becca's empty water glass. Someone had pulled into his driveway.

"Don't move," he said and darted into the bedroom. He walked back into the living room with his Glock in his hand.

Becca stared at him wide-eyed, her body curled against the back of his couch. Becca's dog was on her feet, ears alert. Parker moved toward the window. He pushed the curtain aside with the tip of the barrel, peeked out. He didn't recognize the vehicle parked outside his cabin.

There was a knock at the front door.

He put his finger to his lips, signaling Becca and her dog to stay quiet. Becca whispered to the dog to sit, stay.

Parker eased his way over to the door. "Who is it?" he asked, gripping the gun.

"It's Rick Smith."

He let out a sigh and lowered his weapon, opened the door.

Rick stepped inside, took one look at Parker and the gun, and said, "I gather you were expecting someone else?"

"Something like that," Parker said. "I'm glad you're here."

"That's a first," Rick said and gazed at Becca. He didn't look surprised to find her on Parker's couch.

Becca's dog stood in front of her as though she was guarding her.

"Beautiful dog," Rick said. "Do you mind if I pet him? Is he friendly?"

"She's a girl. Her name is Romy," Becca said.

Rick stuck out his hand. The dog sniffed his fingers and arm. She licked his palm. He knelt on one knee and scratched her chest and back.

"She's a beauty," Rick said. "I knew a couple of guys on the force in the canine unit who had German shepherds. I've always respected what these dogs can do." He continued petting Romy, not making eye contact with Becca when he asked in a casual way, as though it wasn't his intention to pry, although that was exactly what he was doing, "You're Clint Kingsley's daughter, right? I told you I was pretty sure we met before. I never forget a face, and you, my girl, haven't changed since you were little."

Becca glanced at Parker.

"It's okay," he said.

Rick looked back and forth between them.

"He should know," Parker said.

"You mind telling me what's going on?" Rick put his hand on the coffee table for support as he pulled himself up. His joints cracked and popped. He released a little groan, a sign of his years.

Becca's eyes had closed; her head rested against the pillow.

"Follow me," Parker said to Rick, leading him into the kitchen, where he had both river body cases opened and the files spread out in an organized mess.

Rick smiled. "It looks like someone's been working hard," he said. "And by the way, you look like hell."

"You don't know the half of it," Parker said, echoing the exact words Becca had used earlier on him.

He laid the Glock on the counter and cleared some of the papers. The two men sat at the table. Parker told him Becca's version of the facts. While he filled Rick in on the details, he also jotted down notes, connecting the pieces of the puzzle of the cases as he went. There was still some information he didn't have, like who the original witness was that Clint had interviewed and kept hidden.

"I'll be damned," Rick said when Parker had finished. "I really thought Russell was our guy back then. But I was right about Clint protecting someone, and she's sitting right in there." He pointed toward the living room, where Becca and her dog were resting. "It all makes sense now."

"Yeah, except one thing. What was John Jackson's motive?" Parker stood and started pacing, rubbing his hand over the top of his head. "This might sound crazy, and I know this guy is in deep with the Scions, but I think there's more to it than a connection with this group. I think whatever happened, whatever his reason for killing those two men, was personal to this guy. Otherwise, why not just dump the bodies in the river? Why gut them? It seems like a really personal thing to do."

"That, my friend, is what a forensic psychologist is for," Rick said. "I'm more concerned with the physical evidence so we can put this guy away."

Parker stopped pacing. "We lifted a partial print off one of the rounds that was in the clip. But it doesn't look like this guy's prints are in our system. Somehow, I doubt Clint or the other cops in town ever fingerprinted any of these guys." He was already thinking about how he was going to go about getting a search warrant. He doubted any of the judges would be happy to be pulled away from their regular order of business to expedite his request. He would plead if he had to, but even a warrant to search the guy's house, taking him in for questioning, wasn't good enough. What he really needed was to put this guy behind bars as quickly as possible. It was the only way he was going to keep Becca safe.

Rick smiled his biggest smile yet. "Today is your lucky day," he said and pulled a plastic bag from the inside pocket of his jacket.

"What's that?" Parker asked.

Rick dropped the baggie onto the table in front of him. "That is a cup with John Jackson's fingerprints."

Parker picked up the bag and turned it over, looking at the cup and spoon inside. He recognized it as one of the cups the soup lady handed out at the farmers market. "How did you get this?" he asked.

"He threw it in the trash, and I just happened to pick it out."

"How do you know it's his?"

"Oh, it's his. And it's all perfectly legal."

Parker picked up his cell phone from the counter. "Mara, I know you're busy, but I need you to lift some fingerprints for me, ASAP. I think we found our match."

She groaned, pretending to be annoyed, but she wasn't, not really. She lived for this stuff. "Bring it," she said.

"I'm on my way." Parker hung up the phone. "I'm heading out," he said to Rick. "With any luck, I'll have an arrest warrant and this guy in custody in a few hours."

"I'm coming with you," Rick said.

Parker shook his head. "I need you to stay here with Becca. I don't want you to let her out of your sight. Are you armed?"

Rick reached behind him where he kept a snub nose shoved in the waistband of his jeans. "Are you worried our guy might come after her?"

"Yes," Parker said. "That's exactly what I'm worried about."

"He won't come after me," Becca said.

Both men turned to find her standing in the doorway of the kitchen. Her face was drawn, her skin pale. She stared at the papers strewn about, her gaze stopping on the photos of the victims' bodies that Parker had tossed onto the counter. He quickly picked them up and shoved them into a folder. It wasn't something she needed to see.

"He won't hurt me," she said.

Parker exchanged a look with Rick.

"There's something else you need to know," she said. "I tried." She paused. "I tried to tell you earlier." Before either Parker or Rick could reply, she told them about the events of the morning that had led her straight to Parker's place, how there was another body lying at the river's edge.

"I don't know whose bullet hit him, or if both did," she said, shaking. "I dropped my dad's gun on the way here."

Parker was too stunned to move. But Rick had listened and jotted down everything Becca had said. It was only when her shoulders started to shake violently that Parker went to her and held her. He carried her back to the couch.

He smoothed the hair from her forehead as though she were a child. "I've got to call this in," he said. He needed to get his team back out to the clearing and the river. "I promise you, I'm going to get this guy."

She nodded, too exhausted to offer much else.

Rick walked into the living room. He handed Parker the Glock. Parker touched Rick's arm, letting him know he trusted him to stay with her and protect her if necessary.

Rick nodded.

On Parker's way out the door, he heard Becca say again, "He won't hurt me."

CHAPTER FORTY-THREE

John didn't remember how he'd come to be sitting on the stool in the barn or how the traitor's bloody clothes had ended up in a pile at his feet. He wondered where the bloody knife in his hand had come from. And then he heard a voice, a sweet, soft sound coming from outside the barn door, a little girl's voice, Becca's voice. She'd been calling the name Sheba. He turned toward her, seeing her pale face and large gray eyes. And then he heard the dogs, one growling and one cowering. And whatever place he'd gone to, a place where he'd lost track of events and time, he was pulled out of, ripped away, rescued by the little girl with the face of an angel.

"Rubes," he called and yanked on the Doberman's spiked collar, pulling him away from the puppy, commanding him to stay before scooping the little pup into his arms. "Is this your dog?" he asked her.

❦

John walked out of the woods, stopped next to Hap's hog. Hap must've parked it outside of John's barn sometime earlier that morning. He touched the leather seat with his fingers, closed his eyes for a second. He thought about sitting on the bike, putting the rifle to his head, ending this once and for all.

Instead, he left the bike where it was and walked into the barn, setting the rifle down inside the door. He removed the sheath that held the hunting knife from his belt and dropped it onto the workbench. He went to the cabinet and pulled out one of his father's clean white cloths and began wiping down the chopper. He took his time, polishing the chrome, removing all evidence of having ridden the bike in the last few days. While he worked, he mentally checked off a list of the things he had to do, losing himself in the preparation of chores, not allowing his thoughts to venture too far ahead or, more to the point, not allowing his mind to wander back.

When he finished polishing the chopper, he rolled it to the corner of the barn where it had sat after his father had passed. He covered it with the same drop cloths, careful not to let the dust and dirt get in. It was then he thought of his own motorcycle, wishing he'd ridden it one more time before tossing the keys to the prospect. In hindsight, he'd known he'd never see the bike again. Somewhere in his furthest thoughts, he'd known before he'd really known what action he would take, what he'd intended all along, how he wouldn't be able to harm Becca after all. If only he'd come to the realization sooner. He hated himself for putting her through it.

He hated himself for what he'd done to Hap.

John picked up the rifle and slung it on his shoulder as he made his way back to the house. He set it down inside the door, pausing to look around. The place felt strange and wrong, as though he were a trespasser in his own home. The air had a peculiar energy, thick and uninviting. He listened for any sound, but there was nothing but the ghosts he'd been living with, the ones he'd carried for most of his adult life.

He made his way to the living room and picked up one of the few pictures he had of Beth. She'd been sitting on the porch of Sweeney's Bar, her feet propped on the railing, reading a book, the same position he'd found her in when he'd first laid eyes on her. It was one of his favorite pictures of her, the serenity on her face as she gave herself over to the words on the page, the fearlessness of sitting outside a biker bar with something other than a drink or cigarette in her hand. What he liked most about the photo was how natural she'd looked, as opposed to the falseness often found in posed shots; how she'd been captured unaware that the picture had been taken at all. He wasn't sure who had taken the photo, but it was Hap who had given it to him. "Which of these things doesn't belong?" he'd asked John, referring to the book in Beth's hands.

Now, John wondered if he was the one who didn't belong, if he'd ever belonged to the club his father had loved above all else. But in the end, like it or not, it was all John had known.

He set Beth's picture down and removed his leather cut, laid it on the table. He traced the patches with his fingertip, the symbols and colors signifying who and what he was. In one swift movement, he ripped them from the leather, feeling as though he were tearing out pieces of his own heart. He howled, the sound deep, primal, like an animal in pain. He tossed the torn patches next to the jacket.

John picked up the rifle and left the house then, walked outside a free man, wearing only a T-shirt and jeans. The crisp air felt cool on his skin, the sun's rays unable to touch the chill of autumn. He lit a fire in the fire pit and watched the flames flicker, the smoke staining the air black.

All around him the trees sprinkled a rainbow of leaves on the ground, the colors of autumn clear and sharp and beautiful. He took a deep breath of air and held it, storing it, wondered if there would ever come a time when his bones would become at once old and brittle and his mind soft, or if he'd remain forever unchanged. But whatever was waiting for him on the other side, he hoped he'd be able to remember what the mountain air had tasted like, the freshness of morning dew, the earthiness on his tongue, the scent of leaves. He tried to stow it away along with the images of the changing seasons—the new-leaf green of spring, the darker greens of summer, the vibrant colors of autumn, and the stark cold of winter.

How he loved them all.

He continued watching the fire burn. Somewhere behind him patrol cars surrounded his yard, car doors slammed, police officers swarmed his house. He strained to hear beyond the storm of law enforcement, listening hard for the sound of the river, yearning for the rapids to drown the noise in his mind. But it was as if the river itself had refused to grant his last wish, punishing him for what he'd done for having soiled her with his own hands, drowning him in her silence because of it.

He sat with his back against the barn, put the butt of the rifle on the ground between his legs. He thought of Becca again. He thought of her as a child, the one who had stepped into his barn, wide-eyed and trusting, frightened for her little dog's life. And he thought about the woman she'd become, smart and kind and good, the same qualities he'd loved in his late wife, Beth.

But also, he was ashamed to admit, there was a second when she crossed his mind that he felt something close to rage, wanting nothing more than to return to the river with his rifle aimed at her chest, to blame her for all that had happened, to do what Hap had asked him to do.

But the anger was fleeting, disappearing as quickly as it had come. Becca was the one, the only one, who had been innocent in all that had taken place. She had been the one to save him.

He ignored the detective who had started shouting for him to put the gun down, his voice nothing but white noise.

John was a man who lived his life outdoors. And he'd die that same man, on his own terms. He put the barrel under his chin. And pulled the trigger.

CHAPTER FORTY-FOUR

After the sun had set and the last rays had cast shadows across Parker's wooden floor, Rick's phone went off. Becca sat up on the couch where she'd spent that last several hours sleeping, although she couldn't say it had been a restful sleep. In her dreams she'd been running, looking over her shoulder, not knowing who or what was chasing her, but hearing her father calling, hearing the rush of the river rapids.

Rick walked out of the room. Then after a brief conversation, he returned. "That was Parker," he said. "It's over."

She wiped her eyes with the back of her arm. Romy stood at her side.

"Take me home," she said.

Becca stepped through the door of her father's house. She could barely remember having left it that morning; the hours in between stretched and blurred. The house was quiet, but she had the feeling she wasn't alone.

"Jackie," she called and walked into the kitchen. She didn't get an answer.

Romy sat next to her dish. Becca fed her and refilled her water bowl. When she put the bag of dog food back into the lower cabinet, she heard someone walking around upstairs.

Slowly, she made her way up the steps. At the end of the hall, her father's bedroom door stood open. As she approached, her chest tightened, and the pressure of something she'd not yet acknowledged pressed down on her shoulders. She had to force each foot in front of the other, but once she reached his bedroom and peered inside, she found it empty. The bed was stripped of comfort. The imprint on the mattress was the only evidence her father's body had once rested there. The smell of something old and stale lingered. She went to the window and opened it. A gust of fresh air blew the curtains into the room, air that was meant for the lungs of the living. She felt lost, displaced, not knowing where she should go, what she should do next.

A loud thump came from the guest room, as though something heavy had been dropped on the floor. There was the sound of a zipper being opened or closed—which, she couldn't be sure. She walked out of her father's bedroom, leaving the window wide open, and stood inside the doorway of the guest room. Jackie was hunched over a suitcase next to a heaping pile of clothes.

"Hey," she said.

"Hey," Jackie said, pausing for a second. "They came for your dad a couple of hours ago." She continued organizing clothes, putting them into the suitcase as she spoke. "It was getting late, and I didn't know where you were. I hope that's okay. You'll still be able to see him again if you want."

"Okay. Thank you for taking care of it." She leaned against the doorjamb. "I didn't expect to be gone so long."

Jackie waved it off. "Everybody handles these things in their own way. You did what you needed to do under a tough circumstance. I'm not one to judge."

"Thank you." There wasn't anything more she could think to say.

"He wants to be cremated." Jackie shoved a pair of shoes into the case. "I hope you'll respect his wishes."

"Of course." She didn't know what his wishes were, and she was glad at least Jackie had been made aware of them. It was one more thing she'd never talked about with him. She would find over the next several weeks, months, and eventually years, there was so much more she'd missed saying, talking, sharing with her father. Sometimes it would be important things like whether he was proud of her or angry that she'd talked with Parker and the retired detective. Other times, she would think of silly things she'd wanted to ask him, things with no consequence at all.

The questions she would have for him would come to her in time, questions that would forever remain unanswered.

Jackie pulled open the dresser drawers, double-checking all of them were emptied. The closet door was flung open, and most of the clothes were still on hangers. Next to the bed was another suitcase waiting to be filled.

Jackie continued. "Your mom should be here tomorrow," she said. "Her flight was delayed, but I told her there was no need to rush."

"You don't have to leave."

Jacked stopped packing and turned to look at her. She smoothed her frizzy hair. A loose strand fell onto the V-neck sweater she often wore, the one with the plunging neckline. "It's not my home," she said. "We both know if your dad hadn't been sick, I wouldn't be here."

Becca opened her mouth to protest, but she knew that it was true. He wasn't the sort of man who stuck with one woman for long. It was his way.

"Look, I think your dad loved me as much as he could love anyone. And I loved him. I did. Very much. But if it wasn't for the illness . . ." She shrugged. "Well, we both know his track record with women."

"I'm sorry."

"Don't be. I wasn't blind to who he was."

"Then why did you stay? Why didn't you pack up and leave and, I don't know, find someone who would be good to you, who wasn't . . . wasn't . . . you know."

"Dying?"

"Yes."

"Oh, Becca." She sat on the edge of the bed. "There were a lot of reasons. He needed me, for one. He was all alone. There was no one else."

"He wasn't your responsibility," she said. "He was mine."

"No." Jackie shook her head. "Don't do that," she said. "Don't carry that guilt. We both know he was as much to blame as anyone for the troubles between you two." She shoved the suitcase to make room on the bed next to her. "Come here. Sit."

Becca sat.

"I'm not as innocent in all of this as you might think. And I'm certainly not a martyr. You see, I owed your dad in a way."

"What do you mean?" Becca asked.

"Do you know how your dad and I first met?"

Becca shook her head.

"I was a stripper in one of the clubs farther up Route 611." She lifted her breasts. "It was how I ended up with these."

Becca looked at the floor. She wasn't surprised to hear her father had hung out in strip clubs, but it wasn't something she wanted details about either.

"It was how I paid for nursing school," Jackie said. "I'm not ashamed of it." She paused. "Well, maybe I am a little. But anyway, your dad came into the club one night asking some questions. The owner of the place knew your dad. He said he was one of the better cops in the area and said it was okay if I wanted to talk with him. So I did, because, you see, I had danced for the guy your dad was asking about. And your dad, he talked to me like I was a person and not just some stupid girl who took her clothes off for money. Oh, I don't know. He showed me respect, if that makes sense. It's the best way I can explain it. So I told him what I knew, which wasn't much. I found out later that same guy your dad was asking about turned up dead. And it was possible I was the last person to see him alive."

Becca thought about the sheet of paper she'd found in her father's lockbox, the one in his handwriting, the notes he'd taken and buried from an unknown witness. The same sheet of paper she'd given Parker, thinking it was evidence. She looked at Jackie. "You're the one my dad interviewed in the first river body case. You're the one who didn't want to be identified."

She smiled. "I didn't want anyone in the nursing program where I was enrolled at the time to know I was stripping to pay my tuition. And as luck would have it, your dad didn't want me talking to the detectives anyway. So we struck a deal."

"And he buried your statement." *And mine*, Becca thought. "But that doesn't explain how you two ended up together."

"I don't want you to think I was involved with him when he was married to your mom. It was nothing like that," she said, shaking her head. "We kept in touch, a phone call here and there, but no funny business. Like I said, your dad was a respectful man. Or maybe it was because I was still so young. But then one day, we bumped into each other and started talking. By then I was a registered nurse and working in a hospital. He told me he'd been divorced for a few years and that he'd retired. And he was sick."

"So you came to live with him as his nurse?"

"We're talking about your dad here." She laughed. "I did a lot more than play nurse. Your dad was a lively man up until the last year or so."

"Did he ever tell you why he didn't want you to talk with the detectives?" Becca asked.

"No," Jackie said. "And I never asked him either. I figured if he wanted me to know, he would've told me."

"But don't you feel guilty about not telling the detectives what you knew? What if your statement would've helped them in their case?"

"Listen." Jackie held both of Becca's hands. "That guy that turned up dead, the one your dad was asking about, he came into the club that night. I remembered him because the place was empty except for a couple of those motorcycle guys you see around town. They happened to shove a wad of bills into my hand, paying me to give that guy a lap dance. I'm not sure why they did it, but I got the feeling they were messing with him in some way." She shrugged. "So I gave him a lap dance. It was my job. But let me tell you something about that kind of work: you get to know people real quick. And you learn to listen to your instincts. I could sense there was something rotten inside of that one. And that he was a very bad man. The way I figured it, he probably got what he had coming to him."

Becca nodded; if she didn't completely agree with Jackie's decision, at least she understood it.

Jackie released Becca's hands. She stood and smoothed her frizzy hair again before turning back toward her suitcase.

"You don't have to go," Becca said. "You can stay here as long as you like."

"Thank you," Jackie said. "I really appreciate the offer. But I already stayed much longer than I ever intended."

Becca sat at the kitchen table, Romy's head in her lap. She'd just hung up the phone with Matt after telling him she wouldn't be returning to the condo and that she'd be picking up her things. She would be taking Lucky with her, after learning the only reason he'd brought the cat home with him in the first place had been to get to know Becca better. But Matt had promised he'd been taking good care of Lucky in Becca's absence.

"Why are you doing this?" he'd asked. "Why are you leaving me?" He'd begged her to reconsider. She'd said there were things about him she loved, but she wasn't in love with him, not the way she should be. The truth was no matter how many good qualities he had, she couldn't overlook his one big flaw. She couldn't trust him.

"How many women were there, Matt?"

"I don't know, Becca. They were just there, you know. They just threw themselves at me. I swear they meant nothing to me."

"I want to know how many. I have a right to know." She'd told him about Parker then, believing he also had a right to know about what she'd done. He'd been angry.

"There had to be a dozen women," he'd bragged. "Maybe more," he'd said. "Are you satisfied now?"

"Yes," she'd said, shocked to learn there had been so many. In ways, she'd lost her father to other women. And she'd thought she'd lost Parker all those years ago. When she thought about it, which she did at length, the only reason she'd stayed with Matt was because she hadn't wanted to lose him too. But it no longer mattered. Matt had never been right for her, and if she was honest, she'd never been right for him either.

She decided to stay at her father's house until she figured out her next step. The clinic was a short fifteen-minute drive, and she could easily commute. She was eager to get back to work and to the animals she loved.

The upstairs toilet flushed. Her mother was getting ready for the small ceremony they'd planned. George had flown in with her. He stepped into the kitchen, fussing with his tie.

"Let me help you," Becca said. George was a tall man, and she had to stand on her tiptoes to tie a knot around his neck.

"I'm not used to wearing these things," he said about the tie, pulling at his collar. His skin was bronze, and his cheeks were permanently flushed, a trademark of working outdoors in his vineyard.

"You didn't have to get dressed up," Becca said.

Her mother walked into the kitchen wearing a long black skirt and sweater. "But he looks so handsome, doesn't he?" She kissed him on the cheek. She hugged Becca.

"Thanks for coming," Becca said. "Dad would be really glad you're here."

"I'm here for you," her mother said.

They hugged again. And then George hugged them too.

"Shall we do this?" her mother asked.

Becca picked up the urn containing her father's ashes. They walked outside to the backyard. A breeze stirred the trees, scattering yellow and orange leaves across the lawn. Weeds poked through patches of crab-grass. Romy was busy digging away at a groundhog's hole. Her father's yard was a disaster by his standards, but somehow Becca believed he wouldn't mind. His family was here, and as imperfect as they were, they were together.

When the breeze picked up and she believed the wind was strong enough for the job, she opened the urn and let her father go.

🦋

Becca parked her Jeep alongside Parker's cabin. She got out of the car and grabbed the carved pumpkin from the back seat. Romy circled Becca's feet.

"This is not for you," she said to the dog and set the pumpkin down on the porch next to the others. Parker was going to hate the big toothy grin on her jack-o'-lantern.

She'd learned of John's death a few days after leaving Parker's place with Rick Smith. She'd heard it from Parker and then later in the news. She'd been numb at first, not feeling anything at all. But as the days had passed, she'd found herself walking to his barn, searching for him, feeling like a stranger in the woods, by the river, without the weight of his stare resting on her shoulders. What she hadn't told anyone, not her mother or Parker or the therapist she'd started seeing to help with her recent night terrors, a symptom of PTSD, was the emptiness she felt at his absence in her life, the ache for something lost. She'd lived with his presence for so long she didn't know how to live without it. But she was learning.

"Come on," she said to Romy and pulled her jacket collar tight around her neck, feeling the first signs of winter in the early-morning air. Romy followed her down the stairs to the dock, where Parker had finished casting a line. It was the first she'd seen him since she'd shown up at his door after the morning John had pointed his rifle at her. He'd been buried in paperwork, spending much of the last two weeks working. She'd been okay with the distance. She'd been using the time to come to terms with her past mistakes where men were concerned, taking the time to sort herself out.

Parker kept his back to her, concentrating on the river in front of him. He was wearing jeans and a heavy fleece pullover, a knit hat on his head. Romy stuck her nose into a bucket that was on the dock, sniffing the two fish Parker had already caught.

Becca sat in one of the chairs, noticed a thermos and two mugs.

"You were expecting me," she said.

"I was hopeful." He glanced over his shoulder at her.

She picked up the thermos and poured them coffee.

After a few minutes, he put his fishing pole down and sat next to her. Romy lay on the dock between them. "We found the bullet from the Ruger lodged into the trunk of a tree."

"I never hit him?"

Parker shook his head. "He died from a single gunshot wound to the chest. The bullet was fired from John's rifle."

"Okay," she said. She could live with that. She handed him a mug. They sat quietly for a while, listening to the water lap against the shore.

Parker was the first to break the silence. "About Matt."

"It's over," she said. "We broke up."

"Really? That's too bad."

She noticed he didn't bother trying to hide his smile, and this in turn made her smile too. His phone went off. He checked the message, stared at the screen.

"What is it?" she asked.

"I'm getting a partner," he said.

EPILOGUE

Becca stuffed a dog bone inside the front of her coat and zipped up. She grabbed a shovel from the garage and headed to the backyard. The rain overnight had made the ground soft and moist. Digging should be easy despite the chill in the air. The temperatures had been unseasonably warm the last two days, although the weatherman warned winter would return as early as tomorrow.

Romy ran ahead and doubled back, sniffing the ground, following the scent of a rabbit or quite possibly a squirrel. Who knew, really? She trotted to Becca's side, jumping, nudging Becca's coat with her nose where the bone was hidden inside.

"I'm going to have to show you where to dig if we're going to be staying here for a while. You can't be digging up his yard," she said with a smile. She planned to live in her father's house through the winter months at least. Come spring, well, she just didn't know.

Romy ran circles around her until they reached the edge of the woods. Becca spotted the oak tree where she'd spied Russell and her father making their fateful deal, the same tree not far from where she'd buried Sheba's toys. She stood at the base of the trunk, and instead of going right to bury the bone where she'd hidden all of the other dog toys before, she counted twelve steps to her left.

Late last night, she'd woken to the sound of thunder and a bad dream that hadn't been a dream at all but a suppressed memory, the one that had brought her here to this spot. It had all been fuzzy, the edges of her recollection dull and blurry, a feverish consciousness entwined with the kind of fear she hadn't felt since she'd been a kid.

Her therapist had warned her that there might be more memories from her childhood that she'd repressed. She'd tried to prepare Becca for all the ways trauma could have an impact on an individual, especially one who had been so young.

After taking the twelfth step, she stopped. The rock was there, the one she'd carried in dreamland. It had felt so real; her arms had shaken with exertion when she'd sat up in bed. She put the shovel down, gripped the stone with her hands. It wasn't as big as she remembered. Everything seemed so much larger when you were a child. She braced herself with her legs and pushed. She shoved it off to the side inch by inch. When she was satisfied she'd moved it far enough out of the way, she picked up the shovel and started digging. Romy sniffed the pile of dirt that was accumulating, the twigs and leaves and debris.

Becca dug until the blade of the shovel hit what could've been a rock, but it wasn't. It was metal. She dropped to her knees.

🦋

Ten-year-old Becca listened for any noise coming from downstairs. All was quiet. She double-checked her bedroom door was locked. When she thought it was safe, she reached under the bed, wincing from the pain where her father had gripped her arms, leaving them sore and bruised. She pulled out the shirt she'd rolled like a sausage, hiding it in a place where not even her mother would look. Her mother didn't clean underneath the bed—not on a regular basis anyway.

Becca paused, listening again. Not hearing anything, she unrolled the shirt, revealing the knife she'd tucked inside. She'd returned home with it the day the Doberman had attacked Sheba. She hadn't meant to leave with it. She'd only wanted to take it out of John's hand. And then she'd panicked, not knowing what she should do with it, how much trouble she'd be in. So she'd hidden it.

Later, when she'd tried to tell her father, he wouldn't listen, no matter how much she'd begged. *Tell no one, not even me*, he'd made her promise.

The blood had dried on the blade and handle. So much blood.

What was she supposed to do now? This was the stuff of grown-ups, the kind of thing her father should take care of. But he wanted no part of it, no part of her. She rubbed her eye. Sheba jumped onto the bed, sniffed the shirt, the knife. Quivering, she took a small step back. The dog gave Becca an idea.

She wrapped the knife up again and tucked it under her arm. She snuck through the house as best she could with Sheba nipping at her heels. Her mother was in the kitchen. The small TV on the countertop was turned on to a late-afternoon talk show.

Becca slipped into the garage and grabbed her father's shovel. She picked up one of Sheba's old bones that was lying in the driveway, then made her way across the backyard to the edge of the woods. If her mother happened to see Becca, she would assume she was burying one of Sheba's toys, a method to train the dog to dig in one spot rather than all over her father's yard.

She counted twelve steps to the left from the base of an oak tree, not to the right where the dog was expected to dig. She pushed the blade of the shovel into the ground, removing the dirt until enough of it was piled high off to the side and the hole was deep. She looked over her shoulder toward the house. When she was certain no one was watching, she dropped the shirt along with the knife into the hole and quickly covered it. She tossed leaves and sticks on top to make the spot blend into the surrounding area as best she could. It wasn't good enough. Not far from the tree was a large rock. It was too big for her to carry, so she pushed with all her strength, rolling it on top of the packed earth. That was better. Less conspicuous. In time, she'd never notice it at all.

She counted twelve steps to the right of the tree and dug another hole to bury Sheba's bone. As soon as she covered it up, Sheba dug it out.

"Becca," her mother called. "Time for dinner."

"Coming," she answered, trying to make her voice sound normal, not revealing the scared, guilty feeling thrashing her insides.

❦

Becca brushed the dirt away with her hands, the shovel on the ground by her side. Mud was crammed underneath her fingernails, stuck to her palm, cold and wet and numbing.

Her fingers touched on something soggy and rotted and threadbare, scraps of an old shirt that fell apart in her hand. She heard her father's voice telling her how the earth in these parts had a way of hanging on to things, preserving the past, keeping its secrets close.

She removed some more dirt, finding a handle and then the blade, dull and mud caked. She picked it up, turned it over.

The knife that could've changed everything.

ACKNOWLEDGMENTS

A special heartfelt thanks to Karin Wagner, my friend and running partner, for sharing with me a painful time in her life and for helping me understand the stages of grief, of watching a loved one pass from an unrelenting disease like cancer. I hope you found some comfort in talking with me. And to Romy, Karin's German shepherd, making her debut as Becca's sidekick and trusted friend. You're a great dog, Romy.

A big thank-you to my agent, Carly Watters, for always having my back and never giving up on me. To Megha Parekh and the Thomas & Mercer team, thank you for all your hard work and for giving me the opportunity to continue to do what I love. And to Kelli Martin, for understanding the story and characters perfectly and making me dig so much deeper to make the novel shine. Thank you!

To the experts in their fields—Dennis Mullen, retired Pennsylvania State Police homicide investigator, thank you for sitting with me and answering all of my questions. To Lieutenant Joseph Sokolofski, thank you for taking the time to talk with me and keeping me current on investigative practices and procedures. Your expertise has been invaluable. To Michael Ann Beyer, thank you for explaining forensic medicine and what it's like to be present during an autopsy. I assure you any and all errors are mine and mine alone.

Also, thank you to Christa Gordon-Worrell, DVM, for sharing her expertise in the work of veterinarians. Again, any errors here are mine as well.

Sometimes research takes you to places you never thought you'd go. I spent a couple afternoons watching YouTube videos on how to field dress deer and rabbits. I also watched videos on how to load and shoot a .30-06 bolt-action rifle. But it was my nephew, Dalton Marsh, who provided me with the details I needed about the rifle and the field dressing that helped me write some of my favorite scenes. I promise, Dalton, any errors fall on me.

Thank you to the local peeps on the Facebook page "You Know You Grew Up in the Slate Belt If . . ." for answering my questions about the history of the small towns that make up the area.

And of course, a big thank-you to the usual suspects: Tracey Golden, Mindy Strouse Bailey, Tina Mantel, Jenene McGonigal, Kate Weeks.

To Philip and our two daughters, my heart, always. Philip, this one's for you.

ABOUT THE AUTHOR

Photo © 2012 Sally Ullman Photography

Karen Katchur is an award-winning suspense novelist with a bachelor of science in criminal justice and a master's in education. She lives in eastern Pennsylvania with her husband and two children. You can learn more at www.karenkatchur.com.